HER WEREWOLF HERO

WEREWOLF GUARDIAN ROMANCE SERIES

JODI VAUGHN

CHAPTER 1

"There are rules in the world of stripping. Rule number one: don't use your real name." Catty Steele kept her voice and expression neutral, despite the overwhelming urge to shake, scream, and shove the new stripper out the back door before she could make the biggest mistake of her life.

She knew better than anyone that each person made their own choices.

"Not sure I would have chosen Bambi for my stage name. I, personally, would have gone with something a little more creative." The music from within the club vibrated the tubes of lipstick on the various vanity tables, and the air hung heavy with the stifling stench of cigarette smoke.

"Bambi is my real name." Bambi's chipmunk voice matched the look in her doe-like eyes. Good thing making money at a strip club didn't depend on the sound of one's voice. With platinum-blond hair and a body straight out of *Hot Rod* magazine, Bambi would make a lot of money.

"Isn't Catty your real name too?" Bambi's perfectly

plucked brows drew together as she blew a bubble with her gum.

"My real name is Katy." The invisible thread around her heart tightened, filling her with a burning pain. The old familiar ache associated with the reality of what she'd done. How she'd thrown away a normal life and cut ties to her country-clubbish family to work in a strip club in New Orleans. The worst mistake of her life. "I changed it to Catty when I started stripping."

"Ah." Bambi popped her gum and looked down at her costume, a dark green bikini with sequins across the top. She looked back up at Catty and smiled a childlike smile. "I love green. It's my happy color."

Catty wanted to tell her it didn't matter what she liked. It was all coming off in ten minutes in front of some overweight guy with bad breath and grabby hands.

"Rule number two." She held up two fingers. "You can touch the customer, but the customer can't touch you." It was a rule few followed in the darkest corners of the club. She was one of the few, and that was why she avoided the shadows.

"But that's not what Meadow said."

"Don't listen to Meadow." She lowered her voice, letting Bambi know she was serious. Meadow was taking money for blow jobs in the back room. Catty might take her clothes off, but she sure as shit wasn't going to sell her body for all the money in the stripping world.

"Meadow will also tell you that you don't have to pay income tax. Which brings us to rule number three: always pay your taxes. The IRS is a bitch to deal with if you don't."

"Got it." Bambi looked over her shoulder to the far side of the dressing room, where Celine, the club manager, was watching them with an impenetrable glare.

"I don't think Celine likes me. She's already screamed at me twice," Bambi whispered.

"Celine screams at everyone. Don't piss her off and you'll be fine." It was rumored Celine had been a stripper years and years and years ago, but age and nicotine had not been kind to the woman. Being around gorgeous young women didn't help her ego.

Bambi cast an unsure glance across her shoulder to the manager.

"It's not you, Bambi. Celine doesn't like anybody. Do what she says, stay off drugs, and be here on time. She might not be anyone's Aunt Bessie, but she's fair and doesn't tolerate disrespect."

"Five minutes, Bambi." Celine's husky voice cut through the noise of the dressing room. The dancers continued buzzing around the room, changing into the next costume, putting on another layer of lipstick, and checking their boobs in the mirror.

"How do I look?" Bambi propped her hands on her hips and waited expectantly.

"You need a smaller top."

"But this one is my size." She spread her arms and looked down her body.

"That's the problem. You need a smaller size. You need a top that your boobs spill out of. Guys aren't coming in here to see a Miss America pageant. They come here to see boobs. Lots and lots of boobs."

"Bambi! Move your ass!" The tone in Celine's voice had all the girls taking cover at their makeup stations.

"Here." Catty grabbed a tiny black bikini top off a hanger and tossed it at the girl. "Put this on."

"But it won't match."

"Doesn't matter." She shot her a glare.

3

Bambi obediently changed into the smaller bikini top. "It barely covers my nipples."

"That's the point." Catty waved her away. "You need to get going before you piss off Celine."

"Thanks, Catty." Bambi walked toward the stage.

"Another werewolf to the slaughter." Jill eased up beside her and gave her shoulder a nudge. Her light brown hair had been styled into long curls that cascaded down her back. Her makeup, complete with a smoky eye and dark red lipstick that accentuated her full lips, made her look like a model on a runway. She wore a barely there white halter top, bikini bottoms, and tall white boots. She looked like every man's erotic dream.

"Nah. She's not like us. She's human." Catty sighed and sank onto the stool next to her makeup mirror.

Jill sat on a nearby stool, her light brown gaze assessing and cautious. "You okay?"

"I should have encouraged her to leave, to go home and never come back here." She looked in her friend's eyes. "It's dangerous enough for females like us. I can't imagine being a human and working here."

"You know as well as I do she wouldn't have left. If anything, it would make her want to be here even more." Something flashed behind Jill's eyes, something resembling regret.

"I know, I know." No need to make her friend feel bad too. "What do you have?" Her gaze landed on a white gift bag perched in Jill's lap.

"It's a little something for you." Uncertainty flickered in Jill's voice. Catty couldn't decide whether it was excitement or nerves.

"What is it?"

"It's my favorite stilettos." Jill reached in the bag, pulled out the coveted red shoes, and dangled them in front of Catty.

"I can't take those. They're your favorite. Besides, you need them to dance in."

"No, girl. That's the other part of my surprise." Jill put the shoes back in the bag and set it on the floor. She turned and took Catty's hands in hers. "Tonight is my last night."

"You're leaving?" Her heart stuttered and tripped in her chest.

"I've saved enough money for junior college. I start in a few weeks. I'm going to be a nurse." Her eyes and voice brimmed with excitement.

"Wait. What?" Between the white noise buzzing in her ears and the music in the club, maybe she hadn't heard correctly.

"Try not to look so surprised." Jill chuckled.

Catty forced the muscles in her face to cooperate into a smile. "I can't believe you're leaving." She wrestled with the panic growing in her chest. If Jill left, she'd truly be alone. "I had no idea you were even interested in being a nurse. I just thought…"

"That I was content to be a stripper forever?" Jill teased.

"No, I didn't mean it that way, it's…" She was happy for her friend— deep down inside, she truly was. She just didn't want to lose her.

"As you know, I had a pretty rough time. Being strung out half the time didn't help either." Jill lightly fingered the silver cross pendant hanging around her neck.

"So what made you decide to leave?" Catty's heart beat a little faster. She wanted to know the defining moment of choosing a different life.

"I guess I got sick and tired of being sick and tired. Know what I mean?" She lifted her chin and met Catty's gaze.

Catty knew exactly what she meant. These past few months had her entertaining the idea of leaving for good. But she didn't have a solid plan. Where would she go? What would she do?

"It's not too late." Jill leaned in. "You're not that pissed-at-the-world girl anymore, Catty. You need to leave and go live your life."

"I don't know." Fear gnawed at her gut. She couldn't go home. If her parents found out she'd become a stripper, they would be devastated. It was a paralyzing fear that kept her tied to this shit hole.

A tiny shard of hope rose up sharply in her chest. Maybe, just maybe, she could get a do-over, a second chance, and change her life forever. She couldn't go home, but she could make a fresh start somewhere new.

"Girl, I don't even know how you ended up here in the first place," Jill whispered as she looked around. "You're different than us, Catty. You were meant for way better things than this. You don't belong here. You never have."

Catty shifted in her seat. How could she tell her friend she'd gotten into stripping because she wanted to be seen? To be acknowledged? Growing up in a family that was all about high standards and achievements had been like a prison. She'd chosen this career out of her own selfish need for validation.

It all seemed so childish now.

The pain of her brother finding out what she'd done was enough to suffocate her in guilt.

"Leave, Catty." Jill lowered her voice. "You know as well as I do these wolves here are up to some seriously bad shit. Not even the Guardians can help us. Not that they even come in here anymore." She glanced over her shoulder and lowered her voice even more. "I've heard rumors that any dancer seen with a werewolf outside this club will be punished and the wolf killed in front of her. It's not right. If

Big Mike is willing to kill a male Were, what makes you think they won't do the same to you, honey?"

The number of werewolves far outnumbered the humans at the Triple X. To her boss, the humans posed no threat. It was the Weres he watched. She knew Big Mike didn't mind the girls dancing for the werewolves, as long as none of them got involved. But this was the first she'd heard he would kill another male.

Catty blinked back the sting of tears. Getting involved with Big Mike had been the biggest mistake of her life. They were no longer dating, but her gut told her he wouldn't hesitate to hurt her if he was pushed to that point.

"Here, you need this more than me." Jill unhooked her necklace and pressed the cross into Catty's sweaty palm.

Catty let out a shaky laugh and studied the cross gleaming under the lights. "You think God can save me?" She'd been forgotten by God a long time ago.

Jill grinned. "God can save your soul, no doubt about that. But the silver will save your ass."

CHAPTER 2

*L*ucien Sauvage held a two-by-four over his head and nailed it into the skeletal wall. He blinked the sweat out of his eyes and wiped his grimy forehead.

The blistering Arkansas sun was unforgiving, branding everything it touched with fingers of heat.

It was hot. Hot as fuck.

"You need help with your wall?" Jaxon walked over and held out a water bottle. Lucien gritted his teeth, shook his head, and kept hammering.

"I don't need your help, Jaxon." He never did. He preferred doing things on his own.

"It's about time you got your lazy ass out of bed," Lucien added. "The rest of the Guardians have been here since six working. You're two hours late." He didn't keep the irritation out of his voice. The heat combined with Jaxon's interruption made him almost unbearable to be around. Not to mention he was roasting in his leather jacket. Being a were-wolf didn't help matters since his body temperature ran a few degrees hotter than a human's.

"It's not like I'm getting paid to be here. It's for charity."

Jaxon tugged his shirt over his head and tossed it on a stack of lumber.

"You better get used to manual labor, pretty boy. Skylar is hoping once this house gets up and running she can build more like it to help house abused girls." Skylar was the mate to the Guardian Zane. After being abused as a child, Skylar wanted to protect other girls, so she'd started her own charity, Skylar's House.

"And even if you don't have a charitable bone in your body, you should be concerned about the bet you made with Damon and Jayden. If they get their walls up today before us, we're buying their beer." The heat in his body matched the heat in his tone, and it took all his restraint not to punch Jaxon for including him in the stupid bet. Instead, he hooked the hammer in the waist of his jeans and grabbed another two-by-four. The quicker he could get done, the quicker he could leave. He could almost feel his blood thickening with each drop of sweat squeezed through his pores.

"Relax, man. We can still win. You're just letting the heat get to you." Jaxon shielded his eyes with his hand and leaned against the pile of neatly stacked lumber. "It's hot as hell and you're still wearing that damn leather jacket."

"Fuck off, Jaxon." Lucien's words came out fiery and explosive, and to a stranger, it would have been a warning. But Jaxon was no stranger and he certainly didn't heed any warnings.

"Always the Lone Ranger. I don't know how you do it, bro. I bow to your badassness in all your black leather." Jaxon bent at the waist and gave him a mock bow.

"What are you doing, Jaxon? Kissing Lucien's ass?" Barrett Middleton, Pack Master of Arkansas and leader of the Guardians, walked up with a load of lumber balanced on his shoulder. Judging by his tone, he was clearly not amused.

"He's being annoying as hell." Lucien grabbed another

piece of wood and nailed it up. "By the way, Jaxon, badass-ness is not a word, dickhead."

Lucien would love to take his jacket off. He would love to be hauling wood around in nothing but jeans and boots. He would love to be like the rest of the Guardian brothers. But he wasn't like these Guardians. He was different. They all had futures. His had been stolen by someone he'd trusted with his life. He couldn't trust anyone, and without trust he could never truly be part of their brotherhood.

Not now.

Not ever.

"Dickhead isn't a word either. It's slang." Jaxon opened a box of nails and handed it to Lucien.

"Dickhead's a word." Lucien picked up another piece of wood and prayed the werewolf would just leave him alone. He liked alone.

"He's right," Barrett deadpanned.

"No shit?" Jaxon turned and gave Barrett his full attention.

Barrett whipped his phone out of his back pocket and hit a few buttons one-handed. He turned, shielding his phone from the glare of the sun. The lumber swung in Jaxon's direction. Jaxon ducked just in time to avoid getting whacked in the head.

"Watch your wood, man." Jaxon backed up a few feet and scowled.

"Believe me, Jaxon. You're the last person on earth I want touching my wood." Barrett's dry tone pulled a reluctant smile from Lucien.

Barrett looked back at his phone. "Dickhead. Insulting term for people who are stupid or irritating. Synonyms include asshole, bastard, cocksucker, motherfucker."

"Cocksucker's in the dictionary?" Jaxon eyed the phone.

"Dude, does it matter?" Lucien cast a glance at Damon

and Jayden. They were almost finished with their walls. "You're lagging behind."

"Can I see that?" Jaxon grabbed for Barrett's phone, but the Pack Master held it out of his reach.

"Don't even think about it," Barrett warned.

Jaxon was constantly pushing the boundaries with the Pack Master, and Lucien couldn't understand why Jaxon couldn't just keep his head down and work. Life was not one big joke.

"Hey, Damon, did you know cocksucker is in the dictionary?" Jaxon yelled out across the work site as he walked toward the others.

"Yeah. Right under Jayden's picture." Damon hammered a nail into the wood with one hit. Quick as a snake, he drove another nail.

"Hey, Lucien, looks like you're buying the beer tonight." Jayden's smack talk had Lucien bristling. "You want us to send Jaxon back over there or you want us to keep him? We could use some amusement while we win."

"Keep him." Lucien hammered another piece of wood into place. He swiped his hand across his wet forehead. "Maybe he'll distract you guys and I can catch up."

A little past noon, Lucien walked past the line of Harleys to the truck. He grabbed an ice-cold water out of the cooler, leaned against the tailgate, and took a long pull from the bottle. His sharp gaze took in the steady hum around the work site and the acres and acres of sprawling green land surrounding the future home for at-risk girls.

Nostalgia washed over him, reminding him of childhood, of family, of home.

Barrett climbed out of the driver's seat and made his way to the back of the truck.

"It's odd." Lucien straightened and stuck his hands in his

pockets. His carefully guarded thoughts had slipped out as words.

"What's odd?" Barrett grabbed a water and joined him at the tailgate.

"The Pack." He shrugged, trying to loosen the weight that had suddenly settled on his shoulders. "It's more of a family than most people have."

It was more family than he'd ever have.

"True." Barrett, as usual, kept his tone neutral. It was hard to get a read on his Pack Master. Barrett never spoke of his personal life or where he'd come from. It didn't make much difference to Lucien. Barrett had a reputation as one of the most respected and trustworthy Pack Masters of the Southern States. It carried a lot of weight with Lucien.

"Family isn't always blood. Sometimes blood will let you down." Barrett's voice carried an undercurrent of an unspoken secret. A secret only they shared.

"They're not supposed to." Heat flared in the center of Lucien's chest and spread like a trail of gasoline, growing and licking at his heart. He downed the rest of the water, hoping the coolness would quench the anger that had been building beneath the surface for years.

"If you stop expecting shit from people, then they stop disappointing you." Barrett crossed his arms and kept his gaze on the Guardians, assessing the work of his men.

Lucien's breath grew too fast, too hot, too ready to fight. Righteous anger settled over him like an old musty blanket threatening to cut off his breath. "You don't understand. My future was taken from me. My destiny stolen."

Barrett pushed off the truck and stepped in his space. One of Barrett's qualities was never showing emotion. But now, standing in front of Lucien, emotion was written all over him, from his pissed-off expression to his hands curled into fists.

Barrett leaned closer, eyes narrowed, jaw clenched. "No, you don't understand. You're expecting something you won't ever get. It's one thing to cut someone out of your life, but you've not even done that. You keep expecting something from your brother you won't ever get. It's going to destroy you. You have a family here, in this Pack. This is your family, your real family."

"He owes me." He spat the words out and anger boiled in his heart.

"Your bitterness where your brother is concerned will be your Achilles heel if you don't watch it, Lucien. Your wounds will always be there. But if you keep this up, it will scar your soul and then there will be no coming back from it. Be better or be bitter. You can't be both. Make up your fucking mind." Barrett shot him a glare and then walked toward the front of the truck.

Anger pounded in his chest like fists in a bar fight as he watched Barrett get in the truck and drive away. Rage pulsed under the surface of his flesh, and all he wanted to do was shift. He refused. He needed to remain in control. He squeezed his eyes shut and trapped the wolf inside.

"What's up, man?" Braxton slapped him on the back.

Lucien growled and rounded on his fellow Guardian.

"Whoa, bro." Braxton held up his hands in defense. "My bad." His eyebrows drew together. He searched Lucien's face. "Everything okay?"

Braxton, the werewolf with the sleeve tattoos and blue hair, had recently been inducted into the Guardians. He knew from what Braxton had shared that his family life hadn't been pretty. In some aspects, he could relate to the guy.

"Sorry, Braxton." Lucien swallowed back his rage.

"Anything I can do?" Braxton eyed him carefully.

He shook his head. "No. I'm good. Just need to get back to

work." He walked back to the work site and picked up his hammer.

Busy was good.

Busy kept him distracted.

Busy kept the ghosts from his past from resurfacing.

CHAPTER 3

*L*ucien stopped in front of Barrett's office door, knocked, and stepped back to wait. Right after they were finished working at the construction site, he'd gotten a text from Barrett saying he needed to see him. He scanned the hallway for the other Guardians but realized he was alone.

His scalp prickled, and the sensation spread down his torso and settled in his gut.

The door flew open and bounced off the wall.

"Fuck!" Ryker stormed out into the hallway. His narrowed gaze landed on Lucien and he stopped, nostrils flared and teeth bared, looking like a wild animal ready to kill.

Lucien's stomach tightened. He didn't get involved in any of his Pack brothers' business, but he knew Ryker had some beef with Damon after he'd been inducted into the Pack. Afterwards Ryker had made himself scarce, and the Pack never saw him anymore. Until now.

"Ryker." He glared at the Were and didn't bother holding

out his hand in greeting. He'd learned better than to let his guard down around anyone. Even his own Pack.

Keeping his eyes trained on Lucien, Ryker reached for Barrett's door and slammed it shut. The earsplitting sound echoed in the cavernous hall.

Lucien bowed up to the Were, his adrenaline spiking like mountains in his veins. "If you have an issue with me, Ryker, I suggest you speak. Otherwise, I'm due for a meeting with Barrett."

Ryker growled and stepped into his personal space. Lucien's heart jackhammered in his ears as he curled his fingers into fists and prepared to set Ryker straight if he decided to start swinging.

"So he sent for you, did he?" The scorn in his voice echoed the contempt in his eyes.

Ryker's words sent an angry chill straight to Lucien's core.

"If you have a problem with me, then let's settle this right now."

Ryder glared, spit on the floor, and then stormed toward the exit.

"Don't mind Ryker. He's just hungry. Missed lunch. Come in," Barrett's bored voice called out from behind his massive office door.

Lucien looked up and around, searching for a camera before opening the door and stepping inside. He couldn't find one, which meant Barrett either had it cleverly hidden or he had ears like a bat.

He stepped inside the Pack Master's office. Despite the lack of furniture in the room— other than the essentials of a desk, a bookcase, a couple of chairs, and the state seal on the wall— Barrett's presence always seemed to make the office smaller than it was.

"You needed to speak to me?" The tone was more guarded than he liked, but after what Ryker had said, he knew this was no ordinary meeting.

Barrett nodded at the empty chair, and Lucien took a seat.

"I did." Barrett tore his gaze away from the computer screen and opened the folder lying on his desk.

"This is a delicate matter." His hard gaze bore into Lucien's. "What I'm about to tell you is confidential. You aren't allowed to discuss this with any of the other Guardians."

"Understood." The muscles around his gut twisted ever so slightly like someone turning a screw. His eyes tracked Barrett and time slowed as he waited.

"None of the Guardians." Barrett glared.

Something was off. Way off. Usually Zane knew everything that was going on. As Barrett's second-in-command, it made sense for him to be included on the details.

"As you know, I'm not exactly an open book when it comes to the Guardians. Whatever you have to tell me is safe."

"That's part of why you're here and no one else." The muscle in Barrett's cheek worked as he continued to glare. "Some Arkansas Guardians are missing."

"What do you mean, missing?" Every muscle in his body tensed.

"They are being captured." Barrett's gaze narrowed into slits as a muscle continued to work in his cheek. "Something happened today that confirms my suspicions."

He opened his desk drawer and pulled out a metal box. The sharp coppery scent of blood made Lucien's stomach turn. Whatever was inside was not good news.

Barrett flipped open the lid and the overwhelming scent

of blood and flesh flooded the room. Barrett's face twisted in rage as he pulled out something that appeared to be a sheet of leather.

"Fuck me." Lucien stood and fought back the bile rising in the back of his throat. "Is that what I think it is?"

"Flesh." Barrett laid out the large piece of skin across his desk. The signature wings and eyes of the Guardian tattoo stared back at them.

"Whose is it?"

"I'm running DNA tests to confirm, but from the looks of the two scars on the lower back, it's Heimy. Our Guardian in the lower part of Arkansas."

Heimy was a Guardian in his mid-forties who had never settled down and mated. He'd been with the Arkansas Pack since he'd turned eighteen. He always had a quiet fierceness about him that Lucien respected.

"What the fuck happened?"

"Someone skinned his tattoo from his back." Barrett fisted his hands, still stained muddy red from the grotesque flesh.

"You mean someone did this to him? On purpose?" Rage boiled up in his chest and spilled into every vein until his body hummed.

"Yeah. And I don't think he's the last." Barrett growled low and deadly. He turned, drew back his arm and pounded his fist into the wall, shaking the room and leaving a large dent in the cinder block.

"Where's the body?" Lucien forced the words out. The pain Heimy had endured must have been unbearable. Lucien shifted in his seat as his leather jacket slid over his back, reminding him of the pain he'd once suffered.

"Can't find a body." Barrett's low voice hummed with anger.

To kill a Guardian was the severest offense. Punishment involved a slow, tortuous death. To desecrate a Guardian by skinning off his tattoo was unheard of. This went beyond anything Lucien had ever encountered.

"Jesus Christ." Lucien scrubbed his hand over his face.

"Heimy is the second Guardian within a month to go missing." Barrett walked over to the bookcase on the wall. "I suspect whoever did this has the other missing Guardian, Mitchell, too."

"How did you get that tattoo?" Lucien stilled as a shiver ran up his spine.

"It was mailed to me. I had to sign for it at the post office. I thought it was some bullshit paperwork." Barrett pulled out a book and faced him. Rage flashed behind his eyes despite his otherwise calm expression. He was a storm about to blow in. Lucien knew his Pack Master hid his rage pretty well, but he had no doubt the guy wanted blood and he wanted it now.

"This letter was inside." Barrett pulled out a soiled sheet of paper from within the book and pushed the document across the desk.

Lucien unfolded the crinkled parchment paper. His nostrils flared at the scent of blood and dirt.

The hunters have become the hunted.

"What the hell does that mean?" Lucien dropped the letter and shoved the disgusting message back across the desk.

"Someone is targeting the Guardians. To take us out."

"Do you think it's humans?" Unease raised the hair on the back of his neck. The US government knew about their existence and even employed the most lethal werewolves for their special ops teams in the military. But if the general public knew of the werewolves' existence, then there would be an all-out witch hunt for every werewolf alive.

"According to my sources at the government, it's not the

humans." Barrett set his gaze on the Arkansas symbol that decorated his office wall and which promised to protect the Pack. "Feels more like another Pack targeting us."

"And no other Guardians know about this?"

"You and Ryker. For now." Barrett turned.

That would explain Ryker's behavior.

Barrett's expression was grim and unflinching. "That's how I want to keep this thing. No need getting all the other Guardians up in arms. I'm sure as soon as they find out about Heimy, shit's going to go sideways and they're going to want to go vigilante. I can't have that. Not until I have all the facts."

"Why tell me? Why not tell Zane? He's second-in-command."

"Because I have a mission for you, but I want you to think this over before you give me your answer. I'll let you sleep on it tonight."

"I don't need to think about it. I'll do it." Lucien met his gaze.

Barrett shook his head. "You don't understand, Lucien. This is not your typical mission."

"What do you mean?" Lucien frowned.

"The mission is out of state." Barrett crossed his arms and studied Lucien. "I would be sending you down to New Orleans."

Lucien's blood went icy. Louisiana. His home state. "Why Louisiana?"

"I've heard some rumors about a recent lack of Guardians down there. Edward Boudier hasn't mentioned it, and I'm not ready to approach him. As you know, we are not on the best of terms."

Lucien knew Edward Boudier, the Louisiana Pack Master, was still pissed at Barrett for putting the Louisiana Assassins in their place. Tensions were still high between Arkansas and Louisiana.

"Before you answer, take tonight and think about it. You need to know this is not your typical mission. You'd be going alone. No backup." Barrett gave him a hard look. "And you wouldn't be going as a Guardian, so I will not be alerting the Pack Master of Louisiana of your visit. Everything we're doing is breaking the rules."

"I guess it helps I don't have the Guardian tattoo." His back seemed to itch in agreement.

"There is that." Barrett looked away. "If you were caught, having the tatt would be like signing your own death warrant."

Barrett settled on the edge of his desk and crossed his arms. His blue eyes seared into Lucien's. "Your past and what happened to you in Louisiana is the reason I hesitate to even ask you."

"I can do my job without my emotions getting in the way." Lucien clenched his jaw until it ached.

"Maybe. But what happens when you run into someone from your past? Your brother perhaps. What are you going to do when that happens? Will you be clearheaded and emotionally removed enough to remember the bigger picture here, Lucien?"

"I..." He knew what he'd do if he saw his brother. Maybe this mission was fate's gift to him to finally settle the score.

Barrett held up his hand to stop him. Lucien slammed his mouth shut.

"Lucien, this unresolved issue with your brother has not gone away. When you came into this Pack, I saw great potential in your future. I still do. But in order to embrace your future, you've got to let go of your past."

Irritation flickered in his gut like a sore that wouldn't heal.

"I understand better than you might think." Barrett

pushed off the desk and walked around his desk. He continued to stand as he stared down at Lucien.

"Your lack of forgiveness for what your brother did is only punishing yourself. Do you think it keeps him awake at night? Do you think he gives a second thought to what he did?"

The flicker in his gut tightened.

"Or do you think he's gone on with his life?"

"This doesn't define me," he argued.

"Doesn't it? You still won't take your shirt off in front of the other Guardians. It was a hundred degrees today, and you kept your leather coat on. Hell, even Damon was running around shirtless, and you know that asshole is in love with his leather jacket."

Barrett shook his head. "I don't want an answer tonight. I want you to sleep on it. Come back in the morning with your answer."

Lucien got to his feet. He already knew what his answer would be.

"If you decide to go, I'll need you to check out some of the strip clubs in New Orleans. I've had some intel passed along that we might have someone on the inside who might know what's going on. It's a female werewolf. She's from Arkansas, so we might be able to count on her loyalty."

"Anyone I know?" Perfect. A manipulative female who couldn't keep her clothes on.

Barrett gave him an odd look. "Yeah. It's Zane's sister, Katy. She goes by the name Catty now."

"Shit." He ran his hand through his dark hair.

"Shit's right. The last thing I need is Zane going down there to try to find his sister. They're not in a good place. And I need someone levelheaded who's not personally involved with her." He gave Lucien a pointed look. "Now you see why I can't ask Zane to go or even let him catch wind of this."

"Yeah." He nodded and stood, shoving his hands in his jeans pockets.

"Like I said, go get some sleep. Come back tomorrow morning and let me know your answer."

Lucien held his gaze and took a deep breath. "Fine. But you already know what my answer will be. This is my home state now, and this is my Pack." He walked toward the door. "But I'll do what you asked and sleep on it."

Lucien stepped out into the hallway and closed the heavy door behind him.

His heavy footsteps echoed down the hallway, matching the parading thoughts in his head.

His mind wandered as he headed toward his quarters. Some of the Guardians had places of their own, actual homes. But for the single guys who were still unmated, the barracks seemed the logical choice. State-of-the-art gym, indoor pool, hot tub, and rooms rivaling a five-star hotel. It was a pretty sweet hookup and it was free.

He never did see a need to buy a house off the base. It wasn't like he'd ever be mated anyway. Females preferred the whole package, and he was damaged. He'd realized a long time ago that mating was not in the cards for him.

Bitterness crept up his chest and wrapped around his heart. Damon had Ava, Braxton had Kate, Jayden had Haley, and Zane had Skylar. It seemed like within the past year so many of the Guardians had partnered off and mated. Hell, Jayden was taking it a step further and marrying his female as well. He wanted to make sure Haley was his in both were-wolf law and the human law.

Not him. His destiny had been stolen by his brother in Louisiana years ago.

He fought back a cruel smile as his heart pounded.

He would finally have his chance, his opportunity to find his brother and make him suffer as he'd once made Lucien suffer.

Finally, after all these years of waiting, he would get his chance to settle the score.

And he'd take his payment in blood.

CHAPTER 4

*C*atty opened the door to her cramped studio apartment and smiled when the familiar scent of jasmine candles greeted her.

When she'd first moved in, she'd noticed a stench whenever it rained. The landlord continued to give her excuses with no solutions, so in the end she'd bought as many jasmine-scented candles as she could afford to drown out the mildew smell.

She dropped her bag on the floor and shuffled into the kitchen for a hot cup of tea.

She rolled her shoulders and reached her arms over her head, stretching out the tight muscles in her back. She lifted the hem of her T-shirt and sniffed.

She normally reeked of cigarette smoke and liquor, but with the Louisiana heat at an all-time high, the overpowering smell of body odor clung to her clothes.

She stifled a gag and walked to the window and threw it open.

It wasn't just the stench of the club that turned her stomach. Working as a stripper made her want to vomit too.

She was ashamed to admit stripping hadn't always had that effect on her.

In the beginning, she'd liked the way men looked at her with lust and adoration when she stepped on stage. In the beginning, it had filled a void in her chest that hadn't been filled in a very long time. In the beginning, stripping had been fun.

When Big Mike, the owner of the Triple X, had taken an interest in her, she'd been flattered and had thought he truly cared about her. He'd showered her with pretty words and pretty flowers. They'd quickly developed a sexual relationship, and she'd thought it was the real deal. But as time passed and she witnessed how he couldn't stay faithful, she'd realized she didn't mean anything to him.

So she'd broken it off but continued to work in the club because she couldn't find another job. His attention had quickly turned to the newest stripper who came into the club looking for a job.

She learned the lust and adoration men felt toward her never turned to love. The men wanted her body and what she could give them. She was a fantasy.

She'd contemplated returning home to Jonesboro, Arkansas to her parents' house, but she never followed through. She'd listened to Big Mike when he told her she was worthless and that her own parents would disown her after she'd shamed the family by taking her clothes off.

She'd believed him.

And in the end, she stayed.

Her fingers brushed the cool metal of the cross.

Jill. Before she'd left the club, Jill had given her one last hug and whispered in her ear.

"Don't be ashamed of your story, Catty. Your mistakes will inspire others. Sometimes you have to just let go and take that first leap of faith."

A thick heaviness settled over her heart.

Jill would go on, reach her dreams, and make a difference with her life. She'd probably find a mate, settle down, and have a family.

Unlike Catty.

Peeling off her clothes, she walked toward the bathroom. The tea would have to wait.

She needed to get the stench of the strip club off her body and out of her soul.

* * *

"I ACCEPT THIS MISSION. What do you need me to do?" Lucien had made it to Barrett's office before the sun was even up.

"This is completely under the radar. If the other Guardians ask where you are, I'm telling them you're on a road trip on the Pig Trail." Barrett took a sip of his coffee and met Lucien's gaze.

"But we're already short-staffed. They're not going to believe you." Lucien had heard chatter among the Guardians about having to pull overtime. They weren't going to like it if he was suddenly gone on vacation.

"They won't dare question me." Barrett reached in the desk drawer and pulled out a cheap throw-away cell phone. He tossed it to Lucien, who caught it. "Use this if you need to report in. Leave your personal cell phone behind."

Adrenaline spiked his veins. He studied the floor as something stirred in his gut.

"I know it's always bothered you, Lucien. That the ink wouldn't take over your…"

"Charred flesh?" His lips stretched into a sarcastic smirk while his eyes hardened.

"I was going to say 'scar.'" Barrett narrowed his eyes and sat back in his chair. "As I mentioned yesterday, the fact that you don't carry the Guardian tattoo is one of the reasons I'm sending you. You'll discover that what you consider a weakness is your biggest strength on this mission. You don't need anything that will identify you as a Guardian."

His heart gave an angry squeeze and pumped hot blood through his veins.

Every time the Guardians were initiated, it was Barrett who took them to Jonesboro to get their Guardian ink. When it had been his turn, Barrett had made the show of taking Lucien to the Moon Goddess despite knowing the tattoo wouldn't take.

His first thought had been that Barrett was doing this to embarrass him, to shame him because of his deformity.

Barrett had told the tattoo artist, Matt, he was going to do Lucien's tatt himself.

Once they were alone in the tattoo shop, Barrett turned to him. He said he knew Lucien's back wouldn't take the ink. He told him his heart and dedication to being a Guardian meant more than just some fucking ink.

He'd locked the door and turned on the TV in the corner. They'd spent hours playing video games, neither saying anything other than the occasional curse word when they managed to get killed in the game. Hours later, they headed back home to Little Rock.

"Remember this, Lucien." Barrett's voice broke his train of thought. "You watch your ass like never before. If someone in New Orleans even thinks for one second you're a Guardian, you make damn fucking sure you change their mind. Do whatever it takes. You're going to be alone on this trip, and I need you to make sure you get your ass back here in one piece. We clear?"

"Crystal." He wouldn't get caught. He had a lot of work to do, including finding his brother.

Barrett narrowed his eyes and then looked away. "There's more."

"What?"

"I didn't tell you everything yesterday." Barrett put his elbows on the desk and leaned in. "There was a list in that package. With the names of all the Arkansas Guardians. They'd crossed off Heimy's name. And they put a star by Mitchell's name."

"So they are hunting us."

"So it would seem." Barrett's eyes hardened. "Your name was missing from the list."

A mixture of emotions— part relief, part offense— rumbled around his chest.

"That's why you're sending me. I'm invisible." Hatred for his brother grew.

Silence stretched between them.

"This isn't an easy assignment, Lucien," Barret said.

"That's why you gave it to me. To make sure it's handled correctly." He stood and stuck out his hand. Barrett gave him a tight shake. "I won't let you down."

"I never thought you would."

* * *

JAXON WATCHED from the shadows as Lucien entered Barrett's office. Usually when there was a meeting, they were all included.

Not today.

Lucien had joined the Guardians not soon after he had. He felt like Lucien had held himself back, kept himself from really being part of the Pack. He suspected it had to do with whatever fucked-up past the werewolf continued to drag along with him.

29

Jaxon knew what it was like to watch someone haunted by their past until it swallowed them up like a giant crater.

Shit was cancerous. Ate away at your soul until you were a walking zombie.

He didn't want that for Lucien.

He glanced at his watch, then bent his neck from side to side to side, stretching out the stiffness in his muscles.

He contemplated, for a brief second, knocking on Barrett's door. But he knew better than to bother his Pack Master when he had a meeting behind closed doors. Barrett would rip Jaxon a new one and make him enjoy the trip to the ER.

If Lucien needed to talk, then he knew where to find him.

* * *

"HOME SWEET HOME," Lucien mumbled as he pulled into the busy city of New Orleans a little after four.

The heat from the engine of his Harley rose up and mingled with the heat from the asphalt. Sweat beaded and rolled down his head to his T-shirt, where it was quickly soaked up in the cotton material. The streets were lined with motorcycles, and he knew the dangerous pull of New Orleans had made them gravitate to the city.

The light switched to green and he revved his engine, heading in the direction of Bourbon Street. The plan was to scour the city before heading over to his hotel. Barrett had made arrangements for a low-rent room because he'd look out of place in a high-end hotel.

He needed to keep a low profile and gather information, then find his brother and take his revenge.

The smells of Cajun food and Hurricanes saturated the thick air as he passed by rows and rows of restaurants.

He knew the aroma wouldn't last. The second he got near

Bourbon Street, he would be faced with the familiar scent of vomit and urine from last night's partiers.

He turned the corner onto the notorious street. The stench hit him and he grimaced. With his heightened sense of smell, it was overpowering as the odor baked in the summer heat. He wondered how humans could even stomach walking down the street.

New Orleans. Home to the all-night bender and never-ending street-pissing contest.

"And they think animals are nasty," he grumbled and pulled into a parking lot. Killing the engine, he set the kick-stand and eased off the Harley.

He slid his assessing gaze across his surroundings. People moved at a slow pace, wandering, drinking, and laughing. They seemed immune to the heat.

The temperature bore down on him, like a demon from the sky, as it tried its best to bake him alive.

His lips curled into a slight smile as he imagined Jaxon standing beside him bitching about him wearing his leather jacket in this Southern heat. Jaxon wouldn't hesitate to rip off his T-shirt and walk around bare-chested in the city for all the females to admire.

The sounds of car horns, the heartbeat of jazz, and the rumble of laughter reminded him of an old familiar friend. It'd been a while since he last visited New Orleans, but suddenly he found himself back in the flow of things.

New Orleans. Attractive and inviting, and once it got you liquored up and addicted to the sounds of the street, you had to make a choice. Stay or leave.

Unfortunately, he'd never had a choice. It was taken from him, along with his destiny.

Now he had a chance to make things right.

Now he had the chance to settle a score.

CHAPTER 5

"*F*inally. Food." Barrett eased into the chair at the head of the dining room table. His stomach growled, reminding him he hadn't eaten all day. Between attempting to gather intel on why his Guardians were being targeted and getting a positive DNA for Heimy on the tattoo, he hadn't had the time or the appetite for food.

"Where's Lucien? I made a coconut cake for him, his favorite." Granny frowned as she looked around the room while the Arkansas werewolves took their seats around her table.

"Said he was taking off for a while." Jaxon's sharp tone had Barrett cutting his eyes at him. "Said that he was heading to the Pig Trail."

"Pig Tail? I haven't heard of it." Granny pursed her lips and looked at her grandson, Jayden. "What's the Pig Tail? Is it a strip club for large women? I don't think Lucien needs to be at some strip club."

"Jesus, Granny. It's called the Pig Trail. Not Pig Tail." Jayden scrubbed his hand across his face.

Damon snorted.

"Jayden, watch your language." Granny's eyes almost disappeared behind the wrinkles in her frown.

Barrett sat back in in his seat at the head of the dining room table and watched the interaction with slight interest. He knew his Guardians wouldn't have the balls to ask him where Lucien was. But there was one werewolf who wouldn't hesitate.

"Barrett." Granny turned her hawk-eyed gaze on him. "Where's Lucien?"

And she never disappointed.

"Where he said he was. Riding the Pig Trail." He forked a large piece of roast beef onto his plate. Eating Sunday dinner at Granny's house had become a tradition for their group. Since Granny had moved to Arkansas from Louisiana, the Guardians had kind of adopted her as their matron figure. Or mascot. He couldn't decide which.

"Why are you making Lucien a cake? Why does he get a cake?" Jayden mumbled as he spooned a healthy helping of mashed potatoes onto his plate.

Haley, his mate, slapped Jayden's hand when he dug in his spoon for another helping. "Save some for someone else, Jayden,"

"Yeah, Jayden. Quit being a pig." Damon's tone smacked of sarcasm.

"No, really, Granny. Why did you make Lucien a cake and not me? I'm your grandson." Jayden's brows drew together and he stabbed a piece of meat onto his fork.

"It's not your birthday. When it's your birthday, I'll make your favorite cake too. Or trifle. You do love my chocolate trifle." Granny patted his hand before passing a large bowl of green beans to him.

Damon snorted and whispered something to Jayden that sounded like "pussy."

Barrett shoveled a forkful of buttery mashed potatoes

into his mouth, grateful he was left out of this conversation. The less he said, the better.

"It's Lucien's birthday?" Jaxon's head jerked up. He looked around the table. "I didn't know that."

"I don't think he wanted anyone to know. I had to drag it out of him while I was in line at the grocery store. That boy is more tight-lipped than you, Barrett." She pointed her fork at him.

"Lucky bastard," Barrett mumbled and then shoved more potatoes in his mouth.

Guilt ached in his stomach. Maybe he shouldn't have sent Lucien on such a dangerous mission since it was his birthday. Who was he kidding? If he hadn't sent Lucien, then a lot of them might not see their next birthday.

He'd had no choice. It had to be done.

"That's probably why he wanted to go ride the Pig Trail. To celebrate his birthday." Damon shrugged.

"Hey, we should go." Ava, Damon's mate and all-around troublemaker, brightened and elbowed Damon in the side. "We should ride the Pig Trail."

Damon gave a lustful look at Ava. "How about I ride you instead?"

"Damon! No sex talk at the table." Granny pursed her lips and then held up a finger. "Unless it involves my new line of vibrating panties."

Just like that, his appetite was gone. Barrett threw his fork down and pushed away from the table.

* * *

Catty woke to the rhythmic, hypnotic strains of jazz drifting up from under her window, played by a lone saxophonist.

While tourists and some New Orleans residents might

find this a lovely way to wake up, she did not. Every time she heard the sounds of saxophone music, it made her stomach twist into knots. For her, it meant another night of working in the club.

The light outside had faded to a light purple, soon to slip into inky darkness of night. Soon the energy of the city would change, become something darker, something stronger.

Turning over, she grabbed her phone.

Eight fifteen.

She blinked, remembering what day it was. Tonight was her night off.

She lay back and stared up at the ceiling. Her mind wandered to her friend.

Jill was leaving, getting out, starting over.

It was something Catty had longed to do but hadn't dared voice, too afraid if she spoke it out loud it would disappear like wisp of smoke. Like a wish on a birthday cake, those hopes had to be kept silent until they grew into reality.

Her phone shrilled to life.

She grabbed it off the night stand composed of a stack of secondhand books.

"Hello?"

"We had one of the girls not make her shift, and we're going to need you to come in and work." Celine's raspy voice made her heart sink.

"It's my night off. I haven't had a night off for two weeks now." Her stomach twisted. She'd planned on treating herself to dinner at Muriel's Jackson Square, her favorite restaurant.

"The club needs you." Celine's brusque tone was sharp and unrelenting.

She caught the meaning behind Celine's words. If Big Mike found out she didn't show up for work, he might take it out on her with his fists.

He'd never laid a hand on her, but she'd seen some of the girls after they'd refused to come in for a shift. They'd been short one night and Mary had had the night off. She'd made plans with some friends who were in town. When she said she couldn't cover the shift, Big Mike had done a number on her. It had taken her two weeks to heal from the bruises on her face.

She shuddered and cleared her throat. "I just woke up, so it will be a while before I'm ready."

"Good girl. Make sure you look extra nice tonight. There's a urology conference in town tonight, so we are expecting a big crowd."

She flung the phone across the bed and stared at the piece of plastic. She contemplated tossing it against the wall and breaking it into a million pieces so she couldn't be reached. But it wouldn't matter if she had a phone or not. Big Mike would find her.

She kicked off the thin sheet wrapped around her legs and climbed out of bed. The weathered hardwood floors were cool to the bottom of her feet as she padded to the tiny bathroom. She turned the water on. Quickly shedding her T-shirt and panties, she stepped into the shower under the spray of tepid water.

She longed for a day when she could have a steaming hot shower. Her studio was old and the water only got warm. But at least she had running water. If tepid water was all she had, she would take it. Hell, she'd take a freezing cold bath in the middle of an Alaskan river if she needed to.

One day, maybe one day she wouldn't have to have water to wash away the sins on her soul.

Maybe one day she'd be white as snow.

* * *

"ANOTHER ONE?" The pretty blonde bartender nodded at his empty beer bottle and gave him a sultry grin.

"Sure," Lucien said.

She went about the business of popping the top off another bottle and sliding it toward him. He didn't miss the invitation in her eyes, but he wasn't interested. He was here on business. Not to get laid.

"You new in town?" She rested her arms on the counter of the bar and leaned forward, pressing her large breasts up over the top of her skintight shirt.

"Passing through." He took a drink of his beer. The icy liquid cooled his dry throat but did little to cool the rest of his body.

"Passing through alone?" Her eyebrow shot up as she ran her tongue across her lips.

"Yes." He kept his tone cool and averted his gaze, hoping she would get the hint.

"Well, if you need anything, come see me. I'm working all week." She grinned and straightened as a waitress approached and gave her a drink order to fill.

"Know of any adult entertainment that might pique my interests?" Barrett didn't know the name of the strip club where Catty worked, so he hoped the bartender could give him a place to start.

"Yeah, there's the Triple X Club down the street," the waitress interrupted, ignoring the dirty looks the bartender was shooting her. "Strippers mainly, but if you want to pay for a little more I've heard the girls are willing. But it's a rough club." She looked him up and down and shook her head. "But I get the feeling you are used to rough hangouts."

He chuckled as he caught the scent of wolf on the waitress.

The bartender narrowed her eyes at the waitress before heading down the bar to fill her orders.

"Thanks," he mumbled before pulling out a couple of twenties.

"For the strip club info or blocking Lisa?" She nodded at the bartender before looking back at him.

"For both. Name's Lucien."

"I'm Helen."

She leaned close. "Be careful, wolf. When I say the club is rough, I meant rough for other werewolves. I've never seen you before, so I'm assuming you're not from here." She lowered her voice. "There's been rumors about a lot of illegal stuff going on in the club. If you're looking for a piece of tail, then go down to the next bar over. It should be easy for you to get laid with the bad biker vibe you're giving off."

"I'm a big boy. I think I can handle myself." Did the illegal shit involve missing Guardians?

"Then you need to be even more careful. New Orleans is not what it used to be." She cast a worried glance around. "It would be wise to stay away from humans as well. No matter how hot they are." She nodded at the bartender.

"I'm not interested in her."

"Yeah well, here in the Big Easy, women have a hard time with the word no." She straightened as the bartender set a couple of Hurricanes down on her tray. "See ya around." She whisked the tray up and skirted the nearest table as she made her way toward her customers in the corner.

It was his cue to leave. He'd gotten a lead. He didn't need to stick around anymore to give the bartender any hope she was getting into his bed tonight.

He hated to break it to her, but there had yet to be a woman who could lure him in with just one look.

It would take much more than a hot body and a pretty face. It would take an angel.

CHAPTER 6

"*I*'ll give you a hundred dollars for a blow job."

The greasy, fat human waved a couple of damp twenties under her nose as if that would tempt her.

Catty grimaced as the revolting stench of body odor rolled off the bills.

"Sorry. I'm not that kind of girl." She finished her dance move on the stage and stood, ready to get the hell out of the way in case the man couldn't take no for an answer. He was human but could still overpower her since she was forbidden to shift.

"Stupid bitch," the man muttered. He turned to the next stripper, who saw him waving the cash like a flag. Luckily, the man's attention was diverted and Catty eased her way into the dressing room.

Smoke and cheap whiskey saturated the air, making her curl her nose in disgust. If hell was real, it looked and smelled like a strip club with all its aromas.

A skirmish broke out over at the bar involving two guys and a waitress. She held her breath and quickened her steps.

She knew the rules. Don't make eye contact. Don't get involved. Don't be visible.

Once she stepped backstage, she let out a deep breath.

"Help a girl out, Catty," Meadow whimpered as she gave Catty her back. "Zip me, please?"

"I don't know why you bother putting anything on." The boobs were cut out, exposing her entire breast. Shaking her head, Catty tugged the zipper up.

"Part of the fantasy. Thanks, doll," Meadow smiled. A cigarette rested between her yellowed teeth. Working in the club had aged her to the point she looked more like forty than the twenty-nine she claimed.

"Sure thing." Catty made her way to an empty dressing station and sat. She kicked off her platform heels and rubbed her aching arches.

"You're up next, Catty," Celine called out as she passed by.

"But I just finished."

Celine stopped in her tracks, turned, and narrowed her gaze on her. "Yeah, well, you're up again. We're short tonight, and the crowd is heavier than we expected." Celine flicked her lighter and lit her cigarette. She inhaled a few puffs before tugging it out of her mouth.

"I thought I was covering the girl who couldn't come in. We shouldn't be short." She didn't have time to change. Not that it mattered. Men didn't come to the strip club to check out her outfits.

"Well, another girl called out sick with pinkeye. The last thing we need is for all the girls to catch it. Heard it's been going around." Celine took another long drag and blew out a cloud of smoke. "Now get your ass back out there."

"Fine." She stifled a smartass reply and turned back to the mirror. She studied her heavily made-up face and grabbed her lipstick. She applied another layer of the bubblegum pink to her lips.

Satisfied by her obedience, Celine turned her attention to Kimber. Kimber said she was twenty-one, but she barely looked sixteen. Catty figured her to be closer to eighteen and even that was stretching it.

Kimber teetered on her platform heels and stumbled into Aston.

"Watch it, bitch," Aston spat out as she shoved Kimber off her.

"Sorry." Kimber giggled and tried to regain her balance. Catty knew right away it wasn't the heels making the girl unsteady. It was drugs.

Celine grabbed Kimber by the arm and dragged her in the direction of her office. Catty knew what was coming next. Kimber was either going to be fired or put on probation.

While Celine ran a tight ship when it came to the girls, she was only the manager. If Big Mike were here, Catty felt sure Kimber wouldn't have faced much of a consequence. She might even be encouraged to do drugs before going on stage to lower her inhibitions.

Catty shivered and turned her attention back to her mirror.

This wasn't the life she envisioned for herself. As she stared into the haunted eyes of the girl she once knew, a tiny sliver of hope flashed through her eyes.

She knew what she had to do.

She was going to get out or she was going die trying.

* * *

LUCIEN SHOULDERED his way through the crowd into the Triple X strip club, growling at anyone who didn't move. Thick smoke and cheap whiskey made his stomach clench. He wondered how female werewolves could stand working in such an environment.

Every table in the club was already taken. Groups of men ranging from college age to middle age to older men sat taking their pleasure as the strippers danced for their dinner.

Lucien grimaced as his gaze drifted over the room. He didn't have a clue what Catty looked like. Half the girls looked way too young to be taking off their clothes, and the other half looked way too old. It was hard to tell which strippers were werewolves and who was human since the stench of the place masked the scents.

The music suddenly changed to a slower beat as a new stripper stepped on stage. Long legs and a slender body with curves in all the right places almost made Lucien a little sad this girl had chosen this lifestyle when she could have had any guy she wanted. Her long blonde hair hung in waves over her shoulders, curtaining the features of her face.

Her face was hidden from view by the pole as she leaned her head back and slid down the pole. She wore denim cutoffs, which showed off her nice ass, and a red gingham bra that barely covered her nipples. With the red cowboy boots, it was clear she was the X-rated version of the farmer's daughter.

His heart beat a little faster in his chest.

He shoved away from the bar and slid into an empty seat near the stage. There was something about the way she moved that compelled him to get closer.

He couldn't tear his gaze away as she slipped her hand down her breasts and unhooked her bra. Her pert breasts burst free as she bared herself to the male audience.

He shifted in his seat as his dick hardened. Embarrassed and angry at the way his body was reacting, he looked away. He flagged down a passing waitress and ordered a beer, hoping the alcohol would cool his lust.

He tipped her generously when she returned quickly with

an ice-cold beer. Taking a long pull on his drink, he cut his eyes to the girl on stage.

The stripper didn't try to get to close to the customers, nor did she ignore them. She seemed to do a careful dance of knowing who to get close to and who to stay away from. She'd pay more attention to the safe older gentlemen and limit her interaction with the aggressive younger guys.

She was probably a gold digger looking for a sugar daddy to take her out of this lifestyle. Like that stripper turned Hollywood actress.

He continued to study her, and when she made her way to him, his heart sped up. He looked away, not wanting to draw her attention to himself.

She knelt down before him and arched her back, thrusting her breasts upward. She came up on her knees and hooked her thumbs on the side of her denim shorts. With a quick tug, the shorts came off, revealing a tiny red G-string. His body tightened and pulsed as unwanted lust shot through him.

He should look away. He knew he should look away. But he was helplessly trapped under her spell, unable to tear his gaze away from her.

He wanted to see her face, see if the sinful body had the face of an angel.

His hand went for his wallet. His heart pounded and he suddenly wanted to leave, escape outside where he could gain control over himself. He knew the stripper had him where she wanted, but his body was bent on a course of its own. If she had asked him for his soul, he would have signed the papers over to her that night.

Glancing down, he pulled out a couple of twenties. His fingers itched as he leaned forward, ready to hand them to her. She moved closer to the edge of the stage, and he caught a glimpse of her face.

JODI VAUGHN

"Thanks, sugar." She grinned and hooked her thumb in the side of her G-string, presenting a slender hip for him to stick his bills in.

He caught her wolf scent and froze.

She gave him a sexy grin, her white teeth gleaming in the darkened room. He studied her eyes and he immediately knew. He'd seen her eyes before.

"You gonna stick it in? Don't be shy. I won't bite." She leaned closer and traced her finger down his chin.

An invisible electric current sparked between them. It knocked the breath out of him, and from her widened eyes, he knew she felt it too.

Her smile slid off her face, and she eased away. He grabbed her wrist, and panic darted through her eyes.

"Let go of me." Her chest was rising and falling fast, like that of a cornered animal. Her gaze darted around the room, looking for help to escape his grasp.

"I can't do that, Catty Steele." He tightened his hold so she knew he was not someone to play with.

She jerked her gaze back to him. Her face went white and her bottom lip quivered. Fear poured off her.

He'd gotten her attention. Good.

"Who are you?" Her voice cracked as she tried and failed to keep her expression neutral.

"I need to talk to you. It's important." He couldn't talk with her here. Too many eyes. "Meet me at Jackson Square."

"I can't. I have to work all night. Besides, I don't even know who you are." She narrowed her gaze and tried to compose herself.

"If you care about your family, you need to meet me. Tomorrow morning. Jackson Square. Six thirty." He leaned in right as a strong hand landed on his shoulder. "Think of your family."

"All right, asshole. Time to go. No touching the merchandise." One of two burly security guards pulled him by the shoulder while the other grabbed him under the arm, ready to restrain him if he didn't comply.

He itched to tell these two humans that if he got good and pissed, neither one would be able to restrain him. But he wasn't going to blow his cover that easily. He had only just arrived in the city and had a long way to go to uncover who was behind kidnapping the Guardians. Not to mention that he needed to find his brother.

He reined in his anger and didn't fight them.

Sadness darted in her eyes as they led him away. Opening the door, they shoved him outside, slamming the door behind him. The repulsive scent of piss and vomit in the alley greeted him in the dark humid night. His stomach hitched.

So that was Catty. Zane's sister. He'd recognized her when he'd seen her eyes. They were the same odd color as Zane's.

He hadn't expected to find her so fast. She was gorgeous, and with a body like a supermodel, she probably made a lot of money stripping. But she didn't fit in with the rest of the girls. The other girls were flirty, didn't mind touching the customers, and didn't mind getting touched either.

It didn't make sense. Catty didn't come from a broken home, nor did she come from poverty. How the hell did she end up in a strip club? Was it drugs? A broken heart? Something more sinister?

It didn't matter why she was there. What mattered was finding out what she knew about the missing Guardians. And if he was lucky, she might have some information on where his brother was.

He wasn't sure whether she would even show up for their meeting.

What he did know was Catty Steele was a beautiful woman with haunted eyes and a family she didn't seem to know anymore.

The latter, he could relate to.

CHAPTER 7

"*F*uck, fuck, fuck." Catty hurried to the dressing room.

"Did he hurt you, Catty?" Celine wrapped her bony fingers around Catty's arm and halted her escape. The woman might be old, but she had a grip like a vise.

"I'm fine, I'm fine." She forced her mouth into a semblance of a smile and tried to shrug out of Celine's iron-clad grip.

Celine narrowed her eyes into snakelike slits and released her hold. "Don't sound fine. Don't look fine either. You look like you've seen a ghost."

No ghost, but she did catch a glimpse of her past.

"I'm okay. Really." Her voice cracked, betraying her despite the heavy smile she held in place.

"You're not on your game tonight, girl." Celine let go of her arm and pulled out another cigarette she kept tucked behind her ear. Sticking the slender stick in her mouth, she lit up and took a long pull.

Catty squinted as the woman blew a long stream of gray smoke in her direction. She fought the urge to fan the smoke.

She didn't need to give the woman another reason not to like her.

Celine didn't like anyone, but once you got on her bad side, she made life a living hell.

"Look at you, dark circles under your eyes and hands shaking like a leaf. I knew you needed a night off." She took another long drag, angled her head away from Catty, and blew out a stream of smoke.

So why did you call me in?

Celine's eyes softened, and for once she gave Catty a look of pity.

It was the closest thing to a smile she'd ever received.

"The boss can't make money when all the pussy looks like they've been beat to shit." Celine rubbed her brow with her thumb while she clasped the cigarette between two fingers.

"I need to get ready for my next dance." Catty clenched her jaw.

Celine leaned into her personal space. "Your eyes are looking mighty red. Bet you're getting pinkeye." She uttered a curse. "Work until midnight. Then you're off. You've got the next three days off. I need you rested and in good shape when you get back." Celine ran her astute gaze up and down her like she was assessing a side of beef.

"Thanks." It wasn't an olive branch, but she'd take what she could get from the old bat.

She dodged the other strippers as she made her way back to her seat in front of the vanity table. The first time she'd sat at the little table with the mirror lined with large white bulbs, she'd pretended she was a famous model getting ready to walk down the runway.

She'd held onto the delusion until a few months in, when she kept getting her ass smacked or her boob grabbed by drunk patrons.

Reality set in the night she was approached in the parking

lot and offered twenty bucks for a blow job. She was nothing more than a piece of pretty ass for men to look at.

She'd been a fool to believe she was valued.

To them, she was a means to an end. Not even a person.

And now, having someone here in New Orleans who knew her family was another issue. While Arkansas and Louisiana weren't far apart, wolves tended to stick within the boundaries of their state. When she'd first left Arkansas for NOLA, she'd worried her family would find her. But after a while it became clear they had no interest in looking for her. It should have made her relax, but all it did was create a fissure in her heart.

Now a stranger in black leather showed up and wanted to talk to her. *And who the hell wears leather in the middle of summer in New Orleans?*

If she didn't show, he could track her down.

Unease snaked up her body as she stared at her reflection. She should have left this morning. She should have taken what little money she had, bought a bus ticket, and gotten the hell out of this cursed place. But she couldn't. She had to have a plan and money before she made another impatient move. She wasn't going to make the same mistake of running off somewhere with no money, no idea how to support herself, and no place to live.

Those days were over. She needed a plan before she left.

Fear tightened its fingers around her heart.

And now it might be too late.

* * *

LUCIEN STARED up at the ceiling from his cheap-ass hotel bed as sweat pooled underneath his body. The rough sheets scraped against his soaking wet back with every rhythmic breath he took.

"It's hot as balls," he murmured and wiped his forehead with the sheet. He'd been gazing up at the ceiling since he'd gotten back from the strip club, trying to come up with a reason why Catty Steele was still on his mind.

Every fucking time he closed his eyes, he saw her. Not just her face either. Hell no. He saw everything. From the skimpy G-string to the boots and bra she'd stripped off in front of him.

The thought of her had him hard in three seconds.

The fact that a perfect stranger could do that to his body had him white-knuckling the sheets while his breath turned to a pant.

"She's only a woman. Nothing special." He moaned and swiped his hand across his sweaty brow. The air conditioning in the room was out, and the ceiling fan was going the speed of a turtle.

Something about Catty sent his instincts on high alert.

With Catty, he knew he needed to be wary. He needed to be watchful. He needed to be on his guard.

"Fuck it." He threw back the sweaty sheet wrapped around his legs and sat up. The aged wooden floor on the bottom of his feet did nothing to cool his body.

What he wouldn't give for a five-star hotel.

He stood and stalked toward the window. Opening it, he stuck his head out. A sticky slap of humidly hit him in the face like a wet rag. Even after the sun went down, there was no cooling off in the Crescent City.

The smells of asphalt and Cajun food and the occasional putrid whiff of someone losing their dinner after too many drinks hit him like a wall.

He rested his hands on the top of the windowsill and stared down into the city that did not sleep. Neon lights from bars and glow sticks around the necks of tourists lit up the street while music blared from nearby clubs, street musicians, and passing cars. It was almost three o'clock in the morning, and there was still a steady traffic of people looking for their next adventure.

He remembered a time when he'd actually enjoyed visiting New Orleans, back when he was a kid.

His family had been in Louisiana for years and was highly thought of. His father, Robert, had inherited his wealth through the family shipping business and the railroads. He was always out of town on business while his mother had stayed at home and raised their two sons. She was the Martha Stewart of werewolves. She kept a perfect house with maids and a chef. And like clockwork, every three years she would have the house completely redecorated.

When she wasn't decorating, running a charity, or hosting parties, she was busy chasing after Lucien and his brother who were always hell-bent on doing whatever they wanted and always getting into trouble.

But that was a long time ago.

A time before his world had gone upside down and his family had been destroyed.

Now all New Orleans was to him was a reminder of pain and devastating loss.

He rolled his shoulders to alleviate the tightening in his flesh that started at his shoulder blades and traveled down to his waist.

He growled, pushed off the window, and headed for the bathroom. He'd shower and get ready to meet with Catty, if she didn't bail.

As he crossed the room, his reflection caught his eye.

He stopped and turned on the lamp. The light illuminated the room in an eerie play of dark shadows and shapes. He turned his back to the mirror.

He narrowed his eyes as he gazed upon the scarred flesh that had been burned so many years ago by one of his own blood. His deformity had caused him such great pain and loss. The mottled skin seemed to tighten as he took in the length of his scarred back.

The pain of being burned had faded, but the hatred against his brother still burned bright.

No one had ever seen him naked. Not even the other Guardians. He would wait to work out until the gym on the base was empty, and even then he'd dress in a long-sleeved tee.

His secret had almost been discovered by Jaxon.

Jaxon had stumbled in one time after working a forty-eight-hour shift and discovered him lifting weights.

Lucien had soaked his shirt when Jaxon had slapped him on the back. The asshole had apparently been too damn exhausted to notice the unevenness of his flesh. After cracking a few jokes, Jaxon had headed back to his room.

It was something Lucien kept to himself. He couldn't trust his secret with the other Guardians. He'd be an outcast. He'd experienced it with his own family.

He wasn't about to experience it with his Pack.

He'd learned the only person he could trust was himself.

CHAPTER 8

"*C*offee and beignets, please." Catty gave her order to the waitress at Café du Monde. The restaurant was already buzzing with the voices of customers ordering the sugary doughnuts and chicory coffee. People didn't visit New Orleans without at least one trip to Café du Monde.

She didn't usually treat herself to the city's renowned delicacies, but with her meeting with the stranger in only a few hours, it might be her last day alive. So she was going to enjoy her last meal.

There was something lethal about the Were's eyes, the way he carried himself. Fear had paraded down her spine when he'd grabbed her, but when he'd started talking about her family, that's when shit had gotten real.

Her family knew where she was. They knew what she was doing. She couldn't imagine her father allowing her to come home, not with the amount of shit she'd landed in. She was covered in it.

She studied the plate of beignets and the cup of black coffee in front of her. She stirred an ample amount of creamer and sugar into her coffee to mask the bite of chicory until the coffee was the color of caramel.

She took a sip of the hot brew. "Ah, that's good."

She bit into the confectionary sweet and sat back in her chair, watching the city come alive around her.

The majority of the shop owners had not opened for business, and traffic was sparse. The morning had a soft gray glow that covered the sidewalks in a dreamlike state. If she were a tourist visiting the city, she would be enjoying herself. But she wasn't. She was a captive.

Her stomach clenched and she dropped the half-eaten beignet on the plate, her appetite gone. In a little while she'd be meeting the werewolf in Jackson Square. She wasn't sure what he had to tell her, but she knew it had to be bad. Like a phone-call-in-the-middle-of-the-night bad.

Maybe her dad was sick? Or her mom? Maybe something had happened to Zane?

She wiped the sugar off her fingers with a napkin and thought about her big brother.

She'd been a pain in his ass when she was a kid. She knew because he'd told her plenty of times. She'd always gotten the feeling Zane was more tenderhearted than he let on, that he put on a tough facade because her dad expected it.

Her lips tugged into a smile as she thought about the times she'd sneak into his bedroom when it would storm outside.

She'd always hated thunderstorms. She wasn't scared of the thunder. No, she was afraid of the lightning. It would flash at the right time on the right shadow and she would start imagining her dolls coming to life and trying to climb into her bed to hurt her. She would pad quietly over to Zane's room and crack open the door. She'd done it so many times he wouldn't say anything, just wave her in with his hand and pull back the cover. They'd sleep back to back until the early morning, and then she'd head back to her bed before her parents would wake up.

She'd had a picture-perfect life growing up. She'd lived in an affluent neighborhood and made friends easily enough. But she didn't really find her best friend until the day she met Skylar.

Skylar was beautiful with bright red hair and big, curious eyes. She'd seen her out on in her front yard in front of her trailer. Catty had cried and screamed to play with the little red-haired girl until her mother had finally relented and turned the car around. Even at young age, Catty had known how to get her way.

That moment had led to Skylar coming over to her house about every day.

Skylar had a totally different personality from hers. Skylar liked to color-coordinate her Barbies' clothes, making sure everything matched, while Catty preferred them to look dramatic, mixing colors to make them stand out. Skylar would put away the toys when they were finished playing, while Catty didn't want to waste time doing something so menial. She always had another game to play, another adventure to explore in the backyard, or another way to irritate Zane. She didn't like to wait or she might miss out on something.

At the time she didn't realize Skylar was different in other ways too. While Catty was a gray wolf, Skylar was a red wolf. Red wolves were mortal enemies of the gray wolves.

Race didn't matter to her. Skylar was her friend no matter what.

Although her friend had never spoken about her home life, she knew it wasn't ideal. Not by any means.

"I thought I said Jackson Square." The deep masculine voice made her jump in her chair.

"You said six thirty. It's only six." She pressed her hand

against her chest as her heart *thump-thump-thump*ed against her palm.

"No time like the present." He grabbed her elbow and brought her to her feet. "Let's go."

"Don't touch me." She didn't keep her anger out of her voice. She snatched her arm out of his grip and gathered up what was left of her breakfast to toss it into a nearby trash can.

He shadowed her every step, the heat of his body almost suffocating.

She turned and glared. "Haven't you ever heard of personal space?"

"Making sure you don't run." His tone was hard and flat and unapologetic, making him an easy wolf to hate.

"Where would I go?" The words left a bitter taste in her mouth and hit all too close to home. She curled her fingers into tight fists, her hands thrumming with each pulse of blood. "It's not like I could outrun you."

"Let's go." He motioned with his hand toward the direction of Jackson Square.

She hurried across the crosswalk before the light turned green. She didn't need to glance over her shoulder to see whether he was following. She could feel him.

At this early-morning hour, few people were hanging around. Artists hadn't even started setting up their highly coveted places around the square.

"Here is fine," he growled.

He stopped behind the shadows of the shrubbery and trees in an attempt to hide his large frame and crossed his arms over his massive chest.

He was large, larger than the majority of the Weres she'd been around, with large broad shoulders that moved with the agility of a large lethal safari cat.

He wore dark jeans, black biker boots, and a white T-shirt

stretched within an inch of its life. She wasn't sure if he was trying to show off his muscled body or if the department store didn't make a shirt in his size. With his size, it was probably hard to find clothes that fit.

He still had on the same damn black leather jacket she'd seen him in last night. A bead of sweat curled at his temple, and she knew he had to be sweltering. If not now, he would be once the sun was high in the sky. She wanted to tell him he didn't need the coat for intimidation. He was intimidating without it.

She met his gaze and shifted her weight, digging the toe of her tennis shoe in the dewy grass and staining the white canvas green.

His dark blue eyes, almost a cerulean color, bore into hers. His face was handsome enough, but the glare he was giving her tempered her thoughts on his physical appearance.

His raven-colored hair brushed the tops of his shoulders. A rogue breeze ruffled his locks, sending his male scent directly to her personal space.

Her body tensed, and something stirred deep in her belly. Shivers raced through her system, and she wasn't sure whether it was from fear or attraction. He smelled like no wolf she'd ever come across.

Right then, she knew she was screwed.

* * *

"Avocado flavor. Can you believe it?" Jaxon held up a woman's green thong and waved it under Barrett's nose. "I thought they only made candy-flavored thongs."

"You would know." Barrett gritted his teeth and shoved the lingerie out from his line of sight. It was bad enough he was trying to keep everyone in the dark as to where Lucien was, but now Granny had invaded the barracks, armed to the teeth with edible undergarments.

"They make all kinds of flavors, not just candy," Granny stressed to the group of interested Weres. "There's chicken and waffle, taco and refried beans, and don't forget bacon. If you can put it on a potato chip, then they can put it on a thong."

The slight headache that had started at his temple when he'd seen the old lady barging in was now building up to a migraine. She'd said she was dropping off some snacks for his Guardians.

He hadn't realized she was dropping off thongs.

"Bacon's pretty good," Jayden growled with a red thong hanging out of the corner of his mouth. His canine worked the garment like a dog working a barbeque rib.

"Hey, pair it up with this avocado and see how that tastes." Jaxon tossed the green thong and Jayden caught it one-handed. Jayden stacked the underwear together and began to go to town on them.

"What did I do for karma to put me in this hell?" Barrett mumbled to himself. He had a lot of shit to worry about besides standing around all day watching Jayden slobber over a pair of panties. "Why would you even bring those here?" He shot the old woman a look.

"Because I ordered the jelly bean assortment of thongs and bras." Granny pursed her lips. "Those idiots at the factory messed up and sent me the football fantasy ensemble." Her eyebrows furrowed to the point they almost got lost between her wrinkles. "And my ladies don't want a bunch of underwear that smells like a Super Bowl party."

"I don't know. These things are pretty damn good." Jayden eyes glazed over as he finished off the crotch.

"That's what you think until you see the reviews. There have been more accidents with this package of thongs than you can shake a stick at." Granny propped her hands on her skinny hips.

"What do you mean?" Jaxon stopped chewing, dropped the underwear, and gave Granny his full attention.

"There are reports coming in by the droves that men are going wild with lust. Once they start eating, they can't stop. Why, one woman in Mississippi got her big toe bit off by her husband who wouldn't wait for her to pull her undies up. He smelled bacon and went in for the kill."

Barrett felt a bit nauseated.

"What did the woman do?" Jayden asked as he reached for another pair out of the taco-flavored box.

"Apparently it wasn't the first extremity she'd lost. Lost her pinky finger when she was helping her husband set traps for nutria rats."

"Damn, she got her finger caught in a trap?" Barrett winced.

"Not exactly. When she went back to check the traps there was a live nutria rat. That sucker latched onto her pinky finger and snapped it right off. Like biting into a candy bar."

"Damn." Jayden cringed but reached for another set of underwear, obviously intrigued by Granny's storytelling.

"Now she's trying to sue the company for an unsafe product and for being traumatized. Said her husband couldn't help himself, he was attracted to her drawers like a bee to honey."

"Sweet Jesus," Barrett mumbled and scrubbed his hand down his face.

Jaxon snorted.

"Granny, please," Jayden implored.

"I think she's trying to make a quick buck. Any woman who goes trapping nutria rats with her husband knew what she was getting into when she purchased those bacon-flavored drawers." Granny glared.

"So why did you bring them here?" Barrett rubbed the bridge of his nose. His headache was now approaching hurricane strength and he wouldn't be surprised if he blew an aneurysm. On the bright side, if it did happen, he wouldn't have to listen to Granny and her bacon-flavored thongs, and he would be put out of his misery.

"The company doesn't want me to send them back. Said they're not going to make them anymore. Too much bad publicity. So you lucky boys get them." She picked up a cardboard box, opened it, and spilled the contents out onto the table. Colorful thongs— green, pink and red— decorated the table like a strip club on Mardi Gras.

"Try this. It's the waffle-and-chicken flavor." Granny held it out to him with a smile. "You look like a waffle-and-chicken kind of guy."

"I'm not." He scowled, hoping to scare the old woman into quiet submission.

"Taco?" She offered him a red thong.

"No!" He shook his head and struggled to keep his voice calm. "Look, you can't keep this stuff in here. I'm not running an adult store." Besides, he had bigger fish to fry, like trying to keep his Guardians from getting skinned alive.

"I think Lucien would like the waffle." Jaxon picked through the thongs spread out on the table. "Speaking of which, how much longer is he going to be gone?" He met Barrett's steady gaze.

"As long as it takes." He narrowed his eyes, daring Jaxon to push the issue. Silence stretched between them, and Jaxon finally shrugged and went back to eating.

"In the meantime, you boys eat up!" Granny clapped her hands and smiled.

CHAPTER 9

"*L*et's get this over with. I'm not going back to Jonesboro." Catty lifted her chin and pointed her finger in his chest, despite the pounding of her heart. She wasn't going to let some stranger roll into town and start dictating to her, no matter how big he was.

"What are you talking about?" His brows drew together and he scratched his unshaven cheek.

"I know my parents sent you to find me." The desperate words seemed to echo and bounce off the shrubbery as she fought and failed to keep her voice confident. "You can forget it. I'm not going back."

"Your family didn't send me." His tone, slow and deliberate, landed like a punch to her chest.

Her heart felt like it weighed a thousand pounds, and any moment she expected it would break out of her chest and land on the grass with a thud.

"They didn't?" She cleared her throat and mentally shook herself. What had she been thinking? Why would they want her back if they knew what she was?

She could feel the heat rising in her face but forced herself to maintain eye contact.

"No, they didn't send me." He looked around and then narrowed his eyes at her.

"Then what do you want from me?" He might be hot as hell, but she knew better than to trust a handsome face. He was up to something.

"I need some information. There is something going on with the Arkansas Guardians. Some are missing."

"So?" She snorted. "Maybe they got tired of doing what they were told and decided to leave." She understood all too well the desire to follow her own rules and not live under the command of anyone else.

"Catty, don't play with me. A girl like you working in a strip club that has more werewolves than humans has bound to have heard or seen something." He leaned in closer. His anger, his frustration, and his scent snaked around her like a vine. He was pissed, really pissed, but she couldn't help herself. Without thinking, she leaned in slightly to get a better sniff.

"What are you doing?"

She took a quick step back and shook her head. *Sniffing you up* didn't seem to sound right in her head, so she decided to shift the focus.

"Look, I have no idea what you're talking about. I've not heard anything about any Guardians. I'm not the kind of girl a Guardian would hang with." She smirked. "You must have gotten some bad intel."

"I don't get bad intel." His eyes blazed.

Her heart went into overdrive and a bead of sweat rolled down her temple only to be swallowed up by her T-shirt. Freaking Louisiana heat. She probably resembled a drowned rat.

"Look, buddy." She pushed her finger into his chest. He

didn't budge. "I don't know anything about missing Guardians. Louisiana isn't exactly swimming with Guardians since Edward Boudier has been running the state."

"Edward Boudier? The Pack Master?" He blinked.

"One and the same." She shrugged. "He seems to think the state is fine without Guardians and has been firing them right and left. Maybe that's what your Pack Master is doing too."

* * *

LUCIEN KNEW Edward Boudier had been an asshole to Barrett ever since the Louisiana Assassins had crossed into Arkansas without letting Barrett know. The whole thing was bad business to start with. Lucien had been surprised Barrett hadn't come down harder on Boudier.

But now with Heimy skinned and Mitchell missing, the Louisiana Pack Master would take a harder stance on illegal activity within the state. He would want *more* Guardians.

Unless Barrett hadn't told Edward about the missing Guardians.

"You're telling me civilian werewolves are okay with everything like it stands, with having fewer Guardians?" His eyes bore into hers. She'd better be honest with him. He wasn't here to play games.

"Civilians don't get a say." She cocked her head and crossed her arms.

The wind changed. Her scent— soft, sultry, sexy— washed over him. His mind blurred and he couldn't control his body as his gaze dropped to her full mouth. His dick tightened behind his jeans. In that moment, time slowed and noise ceased. From the curve of her lips to the glint in her eye, he was trapped in the spell of her scent, unable to focus on anything but her.

What did her body taste like? What did she sound like when she came? What did she look like in the afterglow of an orgasm?

Shocked, he stepped back and sucked in a deep breath, dislodging the surprising erotic thoughts that had come out of nowhere.

Women didn't affect him. Not like she had. When he was horny, he paid for ass. It was a lot less complicated and the women never asked why he kept his jacket on during sex. Many thought it was a turn-on.

As he stared down into Catty's blue-gray eyes, his heart thudded in his chest. He glanced up at the approaching sunrise and blamed his reaction on the heat of the city.

Surely it had nothing to do with her.

"Everyone has a say. It's the duty of the Pack Master of every state to protect its Weres."

A shadow of sadness crossed her eyes before a mask of indifference slipped carefully into place. A hardness etched into her pretty features, and he knew she wasn't going to give him any more information today.

"I guess I won't take up any more of your time." He stepped back and propped his hands on his hips.

Her lashes fluttered for a second. She held her breath as if he were waiting to trick her.

He wasn't. It wasn't his style.

"Good. I've got things to do." She lifted her chin and turned on her heel.

He watched the sway of her hips as she walked away. Even in cutoff denim shorts and a baggy shirt, the girl had a body that had the early-morning male crowd stopping what they were doing and turning to watch her.

A nearby artist stopped setting up his artwork and watched Catty with lustful eyes. Lucien let out a growl before he could remember himself. The man caught the look in Lucien's face. His smile faded and he quickly got back to work.

He watched until she turned the corner. He would give her a few seconds before following. He knew how to tail someone without getting made.

Keeping to the shadows was how he'd survived the city before. It was how he planned on surviving it again.

* * *

WITH HER HEART in her throat, Catty made it halfway down the alley before she glanced over her shoulder. She fully expected the large wolf to be following her. The empty alley sent a smidge of disappointment settling across her gut.

She shook her head. No, she wasn't going to be disappointed. She was relieved.

Fisting her hands at her side, she continued walking. The soft tap of the rubber of her tennis shoes against the pavers echoed quietly between the two buildings. The rising sun and the shadows of the alley did nothing to shield her from the heat of the day. The humidity would reach its fingers through every nook and cranny of the Crescent City and not leave any living thing untouched.

She plucked her sweaty shirt away from her stomach and cursed the heat.

Reaching into her back pocket, she fished out a ponytail holder. She secured her sweaty hair with the tiny scrap of elastic. A heated breeze skimmed the back of her naked neck and a loose drop of sweat rolled down from her hair.

She swiped her hand across her forehead and glanced both ways down the street. After a car rolled past, she hurried across and then took another left toward the run-down part of town.

This wasn't a part of town she would ever brave alone at

night, but right now, with the sun coming up over the horizon, she felt safe enough to travel and not worry about getting mugged.

This was a high-crime area, especially after dark. Though drug houses were abundant in the neighborhood, so were the elderly people. Those were the people who'd lived there all their lives and couldn't afford to move out. Their neighborhood had been taken over by the drug dealers, and the elderly were stuck.

She stopped when she came to Mrs. Willis's house. The shotgun-style house, painted a vivid yellow many years ago, had seen better days. After weathering storms like Hurricane Katrina, the house was more the color of a coffee-stained tablecloth than a bright friendly yellow. A peeling white picket fence and the small gate hanging off-center were more evidence of how the house had fallen into disrepair.

Every now and then, Catty would squeeze her eyes and imagine the house in its glory days, when it looked like a picturesque portrait of the typical American dream. It was a blessing in disguise that Mrs. Willis had gone blind a few years ago from glaucoma. She would hate to know what her house looked like now.

She shoved open the damaged gate and walked down the uneven brick walk to the front door. The porch was small and empty with an old white rocking chair. In the spring, Catty had come by and hung some purple petunias from the porch. Mrs. Willis had commented on the smell and assured Catty they must be pretty. To some, it might seem like a waste of money since Mrs. Willis would never see the flowers, but it was worth it to see the old woman smile.

She rapped briskly on the wooden door. "Mrs. Willis, it's Catty."

She glanced over at the neighbor's unkempt yard. The grass was in desperate need of mowing and the bushes against the house looked like they hadn't been trimmed in over a year. An old Lincoln sedan sat in the yard with its naked wheels up on cinder blocks.

The other houses on the street were not much better. Mrs. Willis would cringe if she could see the forsaken state the neighborhood had fallen into.

She'd tried to get Mrs. Willis to move, but the old lady was stubborn. She said it had been her home for eighty years and she wasn't about to move. She said the way she was going to leave her home was in a pine box.

The door creaked open, revealing Mrs. Willis dressed in a simple yellow cotton dress and a gray apron.

"Catty, dear." The excitement in Mrs. Willis's voice touched something deep inside her and made her homesick. "I didn't expect you today. Come in, come in."

"It's my day off and I thought I would come for a visit." She gave the woman a hug, inhaling the comforting scent of drugstore perfume.

"I'm glad you came. I'm not sure if I have any cookies for tea, but you're welcome to look." Mrs. Willis placed her hand at the base of her throat and frowned. Being brought up in the South, she thrived on being a good hostess, even after her eyesight failed her.

"I ate some beignets and I couldn't possibly eat another thing," she declined politely as she stepped inside. The high ceiling fan stirred up enough breeze, sending a welcome relief from the heat.

She glanced around, noticing the dust on the end table beside the couch.

"I hope I didn't disturb you. I didn't mean to drop in on you like this." *But I needed someplace safe away from Lucien's probing eyes.*

The way he looked at her had her feeling a certain way about the male. She didn't want to put a name to the emotion. He might be hot, but he was dangerous. And she was done with dangerous werewolves. She wanted someone safe.

Right now a relationship would have to wait. Her love life was officially on the back burner.

"You know I always love to see you, dear." Mrs. Willis tapped the floor with her cane as she shuffled into the living room. "Shelly came and cleaned yesterday. It wasn't her normal day, but she said she needed some extra money for school clothes so I let her."

Catty gritted her teeth. Shelly was Mrs. Willis's grand-daughter. She'd met her a few times. She'd come over once while Catty was visiting and asked her grandmother for money. With dark hair and blue eyes, Shelly was attractive and knew how to dress to accentuate her body. She didn't have any tattoos or piercings and seemed nice enough. But there was something about the girl Catty didn't trust.

When she found out Shelly was cleaning Mrs. Willis's house for money, she'd made a point of checking out the furniture and floors when she came over. While the floors had been swept and stuff picked up, it was evident no deep cleaning had been done. Nothing had been dusted, the toilets hadn't been cleaned, and the rugs had not been vacuumed. She didn't want to worry Mrs. Willis with her suspicions of a lazy girl, so she kept her mouth shut.

"Is she still liking school?" She tried to keep her tone casual as Mrs. Willis shuffled over in the direction of her rocking chair. Catty gently laid her hand on the woman's arm to escort her.

"She's doing fine. She says her classes are going well." Mrs. Willis eased into the rocker that had been in her family for generations. And although it squeaked like a mouse, she said she loved it and had no reason to get another.

"You're up mighty early. Did you have to work last night?" Mrs. Willis asked.

Catty worried her lip with her teeth at the mention of her job. She'd lied to Mrs. Willis when she'd asked what she did for a living. She knew what the woman's reaction would have been if she found out she was a stripper. So instead she'd told her she worked at a convenience store.

"I do worry about you working so late at night. Crime gets bad in the city at night when people think God ain't watching. But believe me, God is always watching."

Catty's stomach twisted. That was what she was afraid of.

"I was in the neighborhood and thought I would pop in and see if you needed me to do anything for you."

"How sweet of you. You know, Shelly can run errands for me, but lately she's been in a hurry when she drops by. There's no time for a proper visit." She shook her head and rested her cane against her knee.

"I'm sure she's just busy." Busy with what, she wasn't real sure.

"How about I fix you a cup of tea?" Catty stood before she could be waved off.

"You're so sweet, dear. Thank you."

She walked into the kitchen and frowned when she saw the state of the cabinets. They were all open and the dishes inside disturbed. Not the way Mrs. Willis usually liked her tidy kitchen.

She quickly filled the kettle with water and placed it on the stove. She turned on the heat and then turned her attention back to the cabinets. She went to the first one and straightened the dishes as quietly as possible.

"Are you finding everything okay, Catty?"

"Yes, ma'am. Getting your pretty china," she lied.

After straightening the set of plates, she closed the cabinet and moved to the next one. Immediately she spied the blue and white china pattern. The intricate pattern was no knockoff, and she knew the set must have been in Mrs. Willis's family for years. It had to be valuable. Catty was always worried someone would break in and steal it and hurt Mrs. Willis in the process.

The kettle whistled as she finished setting the cabinets to rights. She set two cups and saucers on the counter and found the tea canister and pulled out two tea bags.

She poured the hot water over the bags and watched as the water turned light brown. She opened the cabinet to pull out the silver tray.

It wasn't there. Maybe it had gotten moved when Shelly cleaned.

She found a wooden tray instead and set the cups down. She grabbed some lemon cookies she found in the pantry and placed them on the tray as well.

"Here we go." Catty smiled as she set the tray down on the coffee table.

She passed a cup and saucer to Mrs. Willis before taking her seat on the couch and placing her saucer and tea cup on her lap.

"Ah, cookies too. You're such a dear, Catty. Your mother must be so proud to have such a lady like you."

She flinched. Her mother would be anything but proud.

"So tell me what really brings you here today." Mrs. Willis took a sip of her tea as a smile settled around her wrinkled lips. "I may not see well, but I know when a girl is having some man problems. You, my dear girl, are having some man problems. Wanna tell me his name?"

CHAPTER 10

"*S*on of a bitch." Barrett threw the package across the room and curled his fingers into tightly coiled fists. His heart pounded as rage swelled in his gut.

He knew without opening it what the box held. The coppery scent of blood permeated the room and sent anger raging through his veins.

His gaze searched the room before landing on the stained piece of paper sitting on his desk. It had been taped to the outside of the package that had been delivered via the FedEx man, who'd left in a hurry after Barrett gave him a *fuck off* look. The delivery man had been human and he had no idea of the horrific contents the box held.

He glanced down at the barely legible scrawl.

"Your wolves will pay for your arrogance, Barrett. Make no mistake about that. I will skin each Guardian until there are none left."

The inside of the box held a hand. He could only guess it was Heimy's.

His mind raced as he tried to think who would be behind such a horrendous act. He knew as Pack Master he certainly pissed off a lot of Weres, but there was nothing that demanded this type of retribution.

A heavy knock landed on the door. Before he could tell whoever it was to go to hell, the door swung open and Jaxon stepped through.

Jaxon must have caught the look on Barrett's face because he stopped short. His brows knit together and his nostrils flared as he caught the faint scent of blood.

"Did someone die in here?"

"Not yet," Barrett snarled.

Jaxon held up his hands and his eyes narrowed. "Does this have anything to do with Lucien?"

"Maybe."

"If he needs help, then send me." Jaxon lifted his chin as if preparing for Barrett's wrath.

"He doesn't need help. He's fine on his own." Barrett turned back to the Pack Master seal that covered the wall. Serve and protect. That was what the Guardians did. They laid down their life for their civilian Weres. So who was going to lay down their life for the Guardians?

The whole thing made him mad as hell.

"I know you sent him on a mission and he wouldn't say shit to me about where he was going. But if he's in trouble, then tell me so I can help him."

Barrett rounded on the younger Were and snatched him up by the collar of his T-shirt. Hauling him off the ground, he held him at eye level.

"Don't try to tell me how to do my job, Jaxon. You forget your place." Adrenaline cascaded through his body. His muscles twitched, aching to punch something until it bled.

"Easy, man," Jaxon said calmly.

He had to hand it to Jaxon. He didn't try to act like a pussy when he was in his cross hairs. Nor did he beg.

Barrett blinked, released his grip, and stepped back. His

gut twisted with regret. He'd never laid a hand on any of his Guardians, ever.

"My bad, boss." Jaxon nodded his head but didn't back up. "I shouldn't have overstepped my boundaries." He ran his hand through his hair. "It's not that I don't trust you. I'm worried about Lucien."

"I know." Barrett's hardened gaze landed on the package. He was worried about his Guardian too. But Jaxon didn't need to know that.

"I'll let you know when I need you, Jaxon."

Jaxon nodded and looked as if he was about to say something else and then thought better of it. Without another word, the Were slipped out the door.

Barrett had to handle this correctly, had to keep things quiet. He wasn't going to let one more of his men get hurt because he'd managed to piss off some psycho.

His gut told him there were no easy decisions in this matter. He was betting everything on Lucien.

If Lucien came up with nothing, then they were all as good as dead.

* * *

LUCIEN WAITED in the obscure shadows of a ramshackle house. He couldn't imagine why Catty would be in this part of town unless she was up to something. Maybe she had a drug habit he hadn't picked up on.

His brows knit together as he recalled both their meetings. He shook his head. She wasn't on drugs. She didn't have the usual signs of being a druggie, nor did he smell it on her.

Her scent.

He closed his eyes and inhaled a breath. She smelled hot and sweet, like a breeze coming off the ocean in the middle of a scorching summer.

Her scent was as unique as her sassy mouth. Who would have thought she'd be as strong-willed as Zane?

He let out a little chuckle as he tried to image what life had been like for her growing up. And what had happened to make her end up here?

He'd seen the fear in her eyes when she'd thought her parents had sent him to find her. And the flash of disappointment that had followed when he said her parents hadn't sent him.

Catty had a wall up. A boundary she kept up between her and the men she danced for. He'd seen it at the club, how she'd placed her mask of sexuality on, and he'd seen it when it slipped.

She didn't belong there in the bowels of hell.

He caught a whiff of marijuana. He jerked his head in the direction of the smoke, and his gaze met a pockmarked-faced druggie.

"You looking to party?" The guy nodded at his joint before glancing nervously over his shoulder.

Lucien doubted the cops would even dare venture into this crack-infested neighborhood.

"No." He growled and looked back at the house.

"I got some harder stuff if you want, man." The guy shoved his hand into his baggy jeans pocket and pulled out a bag of crack. His hand shook as he held it out.

"Take a hint and fuck off." He bowed up and took a step toward the guy.

The guy's eyes widened and he got the message. He shoved his bag of drugs back in his pocket and took off at a run down the street.

"Fucking asshole." Lucien kept his gaze locked on the guy until he disappeared down the alley.

"What did you expect in this neighborhood?" Catty asked.

"I could ask you the same question. You don't strike me as

the druggie type." He turned and faced Catty. She'd managed to sneak up on him. Not good. Not good at all.

"I'm not." She glared and crossed her arms over her amazing chest. "And you already knew. Don't lie. I know you can't smell drugs on me."

"Why are you hanging around this neighborhood? Don't you know what guys like that do to girls who look like you?" He nearly growled the words as another tweeker walked by and openly eyed Catty.

"I'm here checking on a friend." She narrowed her pretty gaze, and he thought for a second flames would spark out of her eyes.

He stepped closer.

"Oh yeah? Who is this friend?" He fisted his hands at his sides to keep from grabbing her by the arms. Her insolence grated on him in ways he couldn't describe. He was here for a reason, a mission. And he sure as hell didn't have time for her frivolous games.

"Well, if you must know..." She smiled. "My friend's name is Go Fuck Yourself." She gave him the bird, turned on her heel, and marched down the sidewalk.

The blood pounded between his ears like an ocean wave matching the beat of his heart. Who the hell did she think she was talking to?

Shoving off the side of the house, he went after her.

Grabbing her elbow with his hand, he spun her around. "No wonder your family hasn't come looking for you."

Her confidence slid off her face, and for a moment he saw a hurt little girl.

His stomach lurched and twisted. It was a dick thing to say. He shouldn't have even gone there. He'd wanted to hurt her, to see a real reaction. But even he hadn't wanted that reaction.

He released his hold and softened his voice.

"Look, I'm sorry. I shouldn't have said it." He ran his hand through his hair.

She shrugged and adjusted the mask of indifference she wore so well. "Even if you didn't say it, you would still be thinking it. So it's the same. You think because I'm a stripper I must be a whore and use drugs. To you I'm a nobody. A nobody who has no family."

"That's not fair. And it's not what I…" He studied the tip of his boot and shoved his hands in his pockets. His chest ached, and he shifted his weight.

"Stop." She held up her hand. "Just stop. It doesn't matter." She glanced at the house she'd been visiting and nodded. "If you want to know what I was doing here, then look for yourself."

He looked up and the front door opened. A petite elderly woman stepped out onto the porch. She had large dark sunglasses and a cane. Lucien knew immediately the woman was blind.

"Is she a relative?" He really felt like a dick. He was no better than his brother. Instead of violence, Lucien hurt with his words.

Her face softened. "No. Just someone who was kind to me when I first moved here. I met her in the grocery store one day. Her caretaker was high and trying to steal her money at the cash register and I caught her. Since then I've looked after her. She doesn't get many visitors, so I go check on her." She shrugged.

"You help her." He squeezed his eyes shut and scrubbed his hand down his face.

"Yeah, well, maybe I do it to even out my karma." She smirked and walked away. "You know, to cancel out my sins."

He forced his feet to move and caught up with her. "I'm sorry. I didn't mean what I said earlier. I don't know you, so I can't judge you."

She said nothing.

She was going to make this hard on him. If he wanted information, he was going to have to eat crow.

He sucked in a deep breath and blew it out. "My karma isn't looking positive right now. What do you suggest?" He met her gaze.

The corners of her lips twitched, threatening to break out into a smile. "Perhaps keeping your nose out of my business. That would be a great start."

"I wish I could." He couldn't. He needed to find the missing Guardians and then find his brother. "Catty, there are things I've been sent here to find out. I think you might know something about what I'm looking for."

She stopped and stepped into his space. There it was again. The hot tingling sensation that arced between them even though they were not touching. It was hot enough without having her standing so close, but good god, she seemed to make their space explode like a volcano.

She cocked her head and stared up at him, a hardness to her eyes.

"Honey, I'm sure there are a lot of females who would do anything you want. But I really don't know what you're talking about. Maybe that's why I'm still alive. I try to stay invisible." She shook her head and stepped back. "Sorry, I'm not your girl."

"I think you are." He dug out his wallet and pulled out some money.

"If you want me to tell you a lie so you can pay me some money, then go right ahead." She pressed her full lips into a line of thinly veiled rage.

"How much?"

"For what? Look, I told you I don't have any information." Her eyes narrowed.

"How much for a night?"

Her eyes widened as her mouth dropped. Clamping down her mouth, she curled her hands into fists at her side. "Look asshole, I'm not a whore."

"I didn't say you were." He looked around as a couple of guys passing by eyed Catty with interest. "And you need to keep your voice down," he hissed.

A guy stopped in front of them and nodded at Catty. "If you ain't gonna take her, I will." He reached in his pocket and pulled out a twenty-dollar bill. "How much for a blow job, sweetheart?"

Liquid anger filled Lucien's vision as the guy grabbed Catty's arm. He swung at the guy, landing a hard blow to his face and knocking him on the ground.

"Don't you fucking touch her." He snatched the guy off the ground by the collar of his stained T-shirt. The man's eyes rolled back in his head and his head lolled to the side. Lucien punched him in the face again for good measure.

"Lucien, behind you!" Catty screamed.

He let go of the guy, who crumpled to the ground. Pain ripped through his shoulder. He spun around. A guy held up a knife covered in his blood. The guy had cut Lucien's arm.

Adrenaline pumped through his cells and spilled over. Rage replaced pain. Revenge replaced control.

He looked up from the wound in his arm and met the guy's gaze and smiled.

"Jesus, man. What kind of shit are you on not to feel that?" The guy backed up and stumbled over his own feet as he tried to get away.

"Lucien, we need to go." Catty tugged on his arm.

He dragged his gaze from the asshole who'd stabbed him to the one lying on the ground. They were quickly drawing a crowd as thugs came out of the houses like cockroaches.

"We need to go," Catty stated.

He glanced around. He might be a werewolf, but there

were thirty humans who were either drunk or high and they were all carrying guns. Even if he could take them, there was a high chance of Catty getting hurt. He couldn't chance it. He needed to get her out of here.

"Come on." He grabbed her hand and hurried down the nearest alley.

CHAPTER 11

"*L*ucien." Catty snatched her hand out of his and stopped.

"What?" He turned and glared.

"Your T-shirt and jacket are soaked with blood." She reached out and touched his back. She held up her blood-stained fingers. "You can't tell it's blood on your jacket, but you are leaving a blood trail with every step you take."

He sucked in a hissing breath as the burning pain begin to register in his cells.

"Someone will call the cops when they see all this blood. We need to get this bandaged up. Now." She met his gaze.

He looked up the street toward his hotel. "My hotel is five blocks from here."

She shook her head. "No, it's too far. My place is closer." Sighing, she grabbed his hand. "Come on, this way." She made a left and kept to the inside of the sidewalk. People were beginning to stir and he did notice some stares from some people they passed, but they didn't say a word.

By the time they made it to her apartment, his shoulder was pounding like a bitch. He couldn't tell if the wetness on his shirt was blood or sweat, but he guessed it was a little of both.

She hurried through the front door of the building. The outside didn't seem like much, old brick with vines growing along the side. Once he stepped inside the darkened foyer, the décor didn't get much better.

"The stairs will be quicker."

He didn't argue.

They stepped out onto the third floor. The dated wallpaper and dim lighting illuminated the dark, dingy floors. A long time ago the complex was probably stylish and beautiful, but time and lack of upkeep had eaten away at her beauty and dulled her shine. The building was sitting on the edge of the dangerous part of the city, and unless the city council decided to rejuvenate this part of town, it was going to continue to decline into disrepair.

She dug in her pocket for her key and unlocked the door. She motioned him inside with her hand.

He stepped in and was surrounded by the soft scent of jasmine. His gaze swept the small space and landed on the candles sitting on the bedside table. The wooden floors creaked under his feet as he walked farther into the small space. It was a loft-style living area with a bed in the middle of the area where a living room should have been.

"Sit down and let me look at your shoulder." She nodded toward her bed.

"It's fine. Give me some bandages and I'll do it myself." No way was he letting her touch him. She'd probably cut his throat first chance she got.

"Are you always this rude?"

"I'm not rude." He was honest. There was a big difference.

"Sit." She nodded to the bed. He reluctantly complied. The mattress squeaked under his weight. The ache in arm matched the pain in his shoulder.

He glanced across the studio, taking in her place. It was a studio apartment with wood floors and brick walls. The bedroom and living room were in the same space, and off to the right was a small kitchen separated by a curtain. A door off the living room led into a small bathroom.

There were splashes of her personality scattered around the room, which made the small dark space feel less cramped.

A small writing table, which doubled as a makeup table, sat alongside the wall. Scattered tubes of lipstick and eye shadow were strewn across it along with a laptop computer.

Her bed had no headboard but was decorated with a ton of pillows in every shade of pink. The comforter matched the pillows.

He noticed a silky tank top and matching bottoms near his boot. Ignoring the searing pain in his shoulder, he bent and picked up the pink material.

He inhaled. She'd slept in this last night. Her scent was all over it.

He slammed his eyes shut as his body stirred with lust and hardened to a point of pain. His hand clutched the bed covering as he fought to get images of Catty's scantily clad body out of his mind.

"Here, take this."

His eyes popped open. She shoved a glass half full of amber-colored liquid into his hand. A sharp whiff told him it was Jack Daniels. He hated Jack Daniels.

"It will help with the pain." She gave him a hard look.

The adrenaline was leaving his body, and the pain was increasing with every breath. He tossed the glass back and downed the whiskey. He grimaced as the liquid slid down his throat, burning all the way.

"Not a fan of whiskey?"

"I prefer beer."

"I don't like it either," she admitted. "One of my girl-friends left it here the last time she came over. Some guy gave it to her at the club." She knelt on the bed and set her bandaging supplies beside her. "Take your jacket off."

He eyed her for a moment and then reluctantly slid the leather jacket off his shoulders and laid the leather across his lap.

"This cut isn't so deep." She wrapped the white gauze around the wound on his arm and taped it down. When she was done, she grabbed the hem of his shirt.

He wrapped his fingers around her wrist. "The shirt stays on."

"But how can I stop the bleeding on your shoulder with your shirt still on?"

"Here." He ripped the sleeve of his T-shirt and shoved it up over his bicep.

She shook her head but didn't say anything. Perhaps she'd thought better of trying to argue with him.

"This one's deeper. If you were human, you would need stiches."

"Good thing I'm a werewolf then."

"Yeah, good thing," she murmured. Her hair brushed the top of his bicep as she worked. His body warmed and tight-ened. Her scent was all around him, trapping him with invis-ible fingers— trapping him and refusing to let him go.

"So is your friend a stripper too?" He nodded toward the bottle of whiskey.

"She is. You got a problem with strippers?" She held the bandage over his wound and craned her neck over his shoulder to meet his eyes.

Her scent and the heat from her body felt like lightning from a summer storm. He sucked in a breath, and he could swear he could taste her on his lips.

"No, I don't." He gritted his teeth. She was way too close for his liking. "You take things the wrong way."

Her mouth parted and it took all his strength not to move those final three inches closer and press his lips against hers. When he forced his gaze up to her eyes, he realized she'd caught him looking at her mouth.

"Don't even think about it." She glared.

"Think about what?" He swallowed.

"Don't think about kissing me." She shot him a look like she could kill. "Kissing you is the last thing I need to be doing."

He reacted on instinct before his mind could process what he was doing.

He cupped his hand around the back of her neck and closed the distance between them. His mouth covered hers, hard and unflinching.

He swept his tongue inside her mouth, tasting her spicy sweetness. He growled as he deepened the kiss. He wanted to taste her fully so he could get her out of his mind once and for all.

She pressed her hand against his chest and broke the kiss.

"Apparently, you don't listen," she said breathlessly. "I said, don't kiss me." She shoved away and walked into the kitchen.

What had he done? Body on fire and trembling with lust, he stood and made his way to the window. He needed to look at anything but her.

He wished he regretted what he'd done. But he didn't. He wished he had gotten her out of his system. He hadn't. He wished he didn't want to kiss her again. But he did.

He braced his arm above the window and studied the floor.

He'd lost control.

A vision of his brother echoed in his head, leaving a bitter taste in his mouth. If he didn't gain control over his actions, he was going to slip into that same fucking abyss and become what he detested the most.

His brother.

He was nothing like his brother.

He took a deep breath, held it, and counted to ten before he blew it out. He glanced at the traffic below as cars and motorcycles moving at a snail's pace down the street. Unhurried with no one to see and nothing to do. It was the vibe he got from New Orleans.

Unlike him. He, on the other hand, had places to go and people to find. He had a mission and it sure as fuck didn't include trying to get Zane's sister into bed.

"Fuck me." He cradled the wound in his shoulder as the pain returned full force. As a werewolf, he would heal soon enough. It didn't ache any worse than the ache behind his zipper.

"I think we established I wasn't interested." Her voice trickled over him and he turned.

Gone was the anger he'd seen in her eyes. In its place was the stalwart, confident barrier she seemed to carry with her like heavy armor.

"I apologize. I shouldn't have kissed you." He forced the words out despite the urge to take her into his arms and kiss her again.

She narrowed her eyes and cocked her head. "I almost believe you."

His head snapped up. "I always respect women. I've never forced a woman to do something she didn't want to do. I'm not that guy."

"I said, I almost believe you. Why did you think you could take what's not yours?" She walked toward him until they were toe to toe and far, far too close.

His body raged with lust as her scent became overwhelming. He took a step back to regain his composure.

She took a step forward.

He angled his body away from the window so his back wouldn't hit the wall. And when she took another step into his personal space, the backs of his legs hit the bed.

Smirking, she stepped closer and shoved his chest.

He had no choice but to sit. As his body landed on the bed, he felt his resolve slipping.

"Tell me something, Lucien." She straddled his legs and sat on his lap. "Tell me, what makes a male think they have the right to a woman's body?"

Her sweet ass pressed into his jean-clad legs. His dick hardened and throbbed. He fisted his hands in the comforter to keep from touching her.

"They don't. A male worth anything respects a woman."

"Hmmmm." She scooted closer until her sweet spot was resting right over his erection.

He gritted his teeth and growled.

She smirked and pressed her hands to his chest, knocking him back onto the bed. With her advantage over him, she hovered over his stomach and leaned down. Her warm breath hit his cheek as she leaned to his ear.

"Is it because some males think just because some girls take their clothes off for a living they are whores?" Anger flashed behind her eyes.

"No."

She ran her finger down his chest. When she reached the top of his jeans, she dipped her finger inside, touching the flesh of his stomach.

"If that's true, then why are you hard?" She smirked.

"Getting hard over a beautiful woman is a natural reaction."

"You think I'm beautiful?" She held his gaze.

"You know you are." The hated words grated his throat as sweat popped out over his skin.

"And if I were to do this, would you still stop if I said no?" She leaned back and reached for the bottom of her shirt. Slowly, ever so fucking slowly, she lifted it over her head, revealing a black bra and a smooth expanse of flat stomach.

He tried to swallow but his mouth was like sandpaper.

"Catty, you are messing with fire."

"No, Lucien, you are." Her smirk changed into something hard. "I've known men like you. Males who think just because a girl takes her clothes off for money that it includes sex too. That we are asking for it." There was a hard edge to her voice, hard enough to cut through steel.

"I never said that." The blood pulsed in his ears.

"But back there you offered me money."

"I offered you money for your time. Not sex."

"So if I took this off"— she ran her fingertip under the strap of her bra— "you wouldn't take it as a sign I want you to fuck me."

"Catty, stop it," Lucien warned.

"Why? Unable to control your urges around a naked woman, Lucien?" She smirked and reached around her back to unhook her bra.

He grabbed her hand. "Cut it out, Catty."

"Why? Isn't this what you want?" She leaned down and playfully nipped his ear.

He grabbed her waist and twisted his body, putting hers underneath his.

Fear flitted through her eyes before she fixed her face into the same confident cold mask she usually wore.

"I don't hurt women. You don't fucking know me, so stop lumping me in with every other asshole who's ever hurt you. You are the one who started this bullshit about me thinking you were a whore because you are a stripper. It's frankly none of my business, to be quite honest. Stop being a brat and grow the fuck up." He scrambled off the bed, grabbed his jacket off the floor, and headed for the front door.

"Lucien, wait."

"Why?" He didn't turn to look at her. Her assumptions about him had him more pissed off than turned on.

He heard the soft falling of clothes over her body. When he turned, she was dressed and standing behind him with her hands in her jeans pockets. Her cheeks were stained red and she studied the floor.

"I'm sorry I offended you." She lifted her eyes to him.

He said nothing. The uncomfortable weight in his chest made him look away. "I'm not here for fun. I'm here to try to help your brother. And your games aren't helping anything." He turned and grabbed the doorknob.

"Lucien, wait. Is Zane in trouble?" She grabbed his arm.

"The Guardians are all in trouble."

She blinked and paled a bit. "So he's a Guardian now."

"Yeah, why? Do you have something against Guardians?" He fired back.

"No, of course not. I didn't know. That's all." She swallowed before she spoke. "You can't go yet. I haven't bandaged your shoulder."

"I'm fine. The bleeding's stopped." He opened the door and made his exit.

He stepped out onto the street, the heat of the day bearing down on him like a wet quilt. He glanced down at his arm. His body was already showing signs of healing. He caught the wide-eyed stares from passersby who openly stared at his bloodied shirt. He shot them a glare and they quickly averted their eyes to the ground and hastened their steps.

He needed to get away from her, to calm down, to think. Whatever had happened between them couldn't happen again. Not ever again.

CHAPTER 12

Catty stayed anchored to the spot, her joints and muscles refusing to move. When the door slammed behind Lucien, her gut hardened and twisted with painful regret.

She'd been a bitch to him, a tease. She was trying to force his hand, get him to show his true colors. She knew he was hiding something, something he wasn't telling her. God knew she couldn't trust people's words. But she could trust their actions.

She'd practically thrown herself at him. Something she'd never done before. He'd turned her down. Something no male had done before.

Although it had been a test, he'd not been impressed with her one redeeming quality. Her body.

She wanted to go after him, to apologize, to explain herself and tell him she didn't normally act this way. But it was risky. Especially now that he'd spilled the reason he was here. To help the Guardians.

She placed a hand over her nauseated stomach. Too many troubles were coming at her at a speed she couldn't control.

Zane was a Guardian and in trouble. He was her brother and if she could help him out, then she would.

If the wolves at the strip club caught wind of her hanging out with Lucien, who had ties to the Arkansas Guardians, there would be hell to pay. Louisiana werewolves hated Guardians. They didn't like anyone in their business, and Guardians had the power to keep them in line. Especially Big Mike. If he found out she'd been trying to help the Guardians, her boss would want her blood.

I have to help. Even if it will cost me somewhere down the line.

* * *

BARRETT SLOWED his speed on his Harley Davidson Breakout as he approached the solitary driveway of the dusty rural road. He knew by the time he reached his destination the black denim finish on his bike was going to be covered in a film of dust.

He'd ridden his bike like hell was on his heels down the lonesome highway in the dead of night. He needed to get away from his Pack, his obligations, and his helplessness.

He needed to find some answers.

The hot night air stuck to his T-shirt, making his flesh drip with sweat like drops of rain. He'd grown up in humidity and heat in his home state of South Carolina. He could handle whatever Arkansas threw his way.

He slowed his bike as his headlight fell upon the five-foot iron fence surrounding the isolated cemetery only a few knew about.

He was meeting someone. Someone who might have some answers or could at least point him in the right direction.

Another package had come in that afternoon after all the Guardians had headed out for dinner. This time when he opened the small box, it was something more than a tattoo.

It was Heimy's middle finger.

Apparently the assholes had cut off one hand and now were cutting off the fingers of the other hand one by one. There was no way the werewolf would still be alive after all that. Barrett knew the captors were playing with him, making sure to let him know how much his Guardian had suffered before he drew his last breath.

Barrett had sworn to protect his werewolves, and he meant it.

He'd failed Heimy, but he sure as hell wasn't going to fail anyone else.

He killed the engine and slid off his bike. He made his way into the cemetery and looked around. He glanced at the time on his phone.

He was early.

He spotted a large headstone in the shape of a tree trunk and walked over. Sticking his hands in his pockets, he rested against the stone. Humans were weird, wanting the biggest headstone and showing off long after they were dead. Didn't they realize no one remembered you after you died? Not even if you put up the biggest monument of yourself. The only thing people remembered was what you did for them. Good or bad.

A few minutes later, soft footsteps had him turning his attention in their direction.

"I was beginning to wonder if you would show up." Barrett pushed off the headstone and met the gaze of Jack Welbourn, Pack Master of Mississippi.

"I always keep my promises, although your request for a meeting was on short notice." The large figure stepped into a stream of moonlight and smiled. Jack was dressed in a black business suit and loafers.

"That's no way to travel on a Harley, Jack." Barrett nodded at his clothing.

"There wasn't time to bring my Harley." Jack arched his thick brow. "I had to take my private plane so I wouldn't be late for this meeting. You know it takes a few hours to travel from Mississippi."

"Did you land in Little Rock?"

"Nah. I like to keep this under the radar. So I landed about a mile from here. Small landing strip through the woods." He nodded over his shoulder. "I keep a map of all the air strips throughout the Southern states. Never know when you might need an emergency landing."

Barrett knew the real reason. Jack wouldn't want to be seen with Barrett, especially since finding out what had been happening to his Guardians. It might put his Mississippi Guardians in danger.

"I'm in a tight spot, Jack." He rubbed his hand down his face and met the Pack Master's gaze.

"So I hear." The Mississippi Pack Master knit his brows together as he walked down the little deer path that wound its way from the cemetery into the thick woods. Barrett fell into step beside him.

Jack Welbourn was twenty years older than Barrett. When Barrett had assumed the seat of Pack Master in Arkansas, Jack was also one of the ones to welcome him without having anything to say about his age. Jack was hard but fair, something Barrett strived to be with his own state.

"I have to say I've never heard of our Guardians being hunted before."

"You've not had any Guardians come up missing?" Barrett cut his eyes at him.

"No. All of mine are accounted for." Concern etched into the granite of his tone and the hard expression on his face.

"Forgive me for asking, but have they all been accounted

for while on their missions in Arkansas?" He hated to ask, but he had to know.

Jack halted in his steps. His gaze tightened on Barrett. "Are you insinuating my werewolves have been hunting other Guardians?" His tone deepened. The older Pack Master might have some years on Barrett, but the old fucker was still a wall of muscle.

"Like I said. Forgive me." Barrett looked away and ran his hands through his hair, his muscles twitching, needing to release this built-up hostility that was slowly poisoning his body. "But I've got Guardians missing and packages arriving with their fucking extremities in them." His gut tightened in disgust.

Jack nodded and relaxed. "Your anger is understandable. If it were my men, I'd want someone's dick on a stick too." He shook his head. "I've asked around as much as I can without giving away too much. No one in Mississippi has heard anything. Hell, I've even put more Guardians around the state border to increase security."

"Fuck." Barrett curled his fingers in a fist and slammed it into the oak tree. The tree groaned and splintered, leaving the interior exposed.

"I know this is hard, but you've got to keep your head straight. Your dad wouldn't want you acting like this."

"My father is dead. It doesn't matter what he thinks of me anymore."

Jack laid a gentle hand on his shoulder. "Barrett…"

He shrugged him off. He didn't want to talk about his father. He had too many important issues to deal with to go down memory lane. "Look, is there anyone else, anyone in your state, who might have a lead on what's going on with this?"

Jack frowned and looked away.

"You know someone."

"Some people shouldn't be relied upon for any kind of help, Barrett. Once you go asking, they're always going to want a favor. You don't want your soul indebted to the devil." He planted his feet in a wide stance and glared at him. The intensity was not lost on Barrett. What Jack didn't realize was that Barrett was willing to risk it all.

"If it means stopping whoever is hurting my Guardians, I'll gladly sell body and soul to the devil."

Jack glanced at the ground and then back up. "You might be singing a different tune after you meet that bitch."

* * *

"Wow, this place hasn't looked this good in… who am I kidding, this place has never looked this good." Catty stuck the cleaning product back in the cabinet and glanced around her apartment, seeing whether she'd forgotten to clean something.

Nervous energy still pulsed in her veins despite cleaning her apartment from end to end. Her muscles ached from scrubbing the floor, but her mind was as restless as a cat in a paper sack. She might pick up from time to time but clean? She never cleaned.

But today she'd needed something to take her mind off Lucien and the way he had looked at her before walking out the door.

She sat down in front of the window, heart heavy and regret tugging at her gut. She looked down at the busy street. Night was falling across the city, lulling its victims into debauchery for a dime.

When Lucien had mentioned Zane, shame had washed over her like a waterfall. Was her brother okay? And what trouble was he in? What trouble were the Guardians in? Now she'd never know since Lucien had stormed out.

"What were you thinking, Catty?" She laid her head against the window and screwed her eyes tight.

No wonder her life was so messed up. She always acted without thinking and then she had to face the consequences.

Even as a stripper she wasn't facing her consequences. She was hiding.

She was tired of hiding. She wanted something more. She wanted some direction in her life, some purpose.

Sighing, she stood and headed over to her laptop. She powered up her computer and sat down at her small desk.

Making decisions on the spur of the moment wasn't working in her favor. She needed a plan with clear direction.

It was one reason she'd left home. She didn't have a purpose or a plan there. She couldn't live up to her family's perfect image.

She wasn't smart like Zane or cultured like her mom. She wasn't determined like her father. She'd felt like a wild child, a gypsy. People always asked her what she wanted to do when she grew up, and she honestly couldn't answer them. The only time she did answer was when Skylar asked her.

Skylar had wanted to build things, to help people. It seemed so noble and so unlike anything Catty had ever wanted. But when Skylar kept asking her, Catty blurted out she didn't care what she did as long as she was seen.

Catty had held her breath, waiting for Skylar to judge and make fun of her. But Skylar never did.

Catty stared at the search bar and typed in *How to find your perfect job*. She hit the enter key.

She scrolled down the search list until she came to a test designed to tell her what job she would best be suited for. She grabbed a quick cup of tea and settled in to answer the questions.

No matter what it turned out to be, she was going to

follow it. From here on out, she was sticking to a plan for her life.

* * *

LUCIEN BENT his head under the spray of water. The hot water had long since turned cold, but he was reluctant to get out. He needed the icy chill to help get Catty out of his mind.

Turning the water off, he grabbed a towel and rubbed it across his long dark hair before tossing it on the floor. He crawled into the middle of the bed and lay on his back, letting the cool air drift over his naked body.

He'd called and given Barrett an update about Catty. He'd told him to stay on the girl to see if she'd trip up and reveal something.

Lucien was no closer to finding anything out about the Guardians than he had been when he'd gotten there. He hadn't seen a trace of his brother either. After leaving Catty's apartment he'd hit a few bars and asked some questions, but no one seemed to know the whereabouts of his brother.

He didn't trust Catty, not after the stunt she'd pulled. If she did know who was behind taking the Guardians, she wasn't talking. She might be in deep and too afraid to say anything. If she discovered he was a Guardian, it could be his ass on the line.

A quick rap at the door had his muscles tensing and him on his feet in seconds. He grabbed a clean pair of jeans and pulled them over his hips. He grabbed his .9 mm off the dresser and eased to the door to look through the peephole.

"What do you want?" he growled.

"I have an envelope for you, sir." The young man on the other side of the door had to be no more than twenty. Small build, dark greasy hair, and, judging by the stench of fear pouring out of him, most definitely human.

He stuck his gun in the back of his jeans and opened the door.

The guy took one look at Lucien and his eyes grew round and white.

"Well?" Lucien held out his hand.

The human blinked, seemed to remember why he was there, and shoved an envelope in Lucien's hand.

"You're dismissed," Lucien barked when the guy didn't move.

The human almost tripped over himself as he ran down the hallway.

Lucien shook his head and shut the door. He wasn't usually abrupt with people, but he wasn't shopping in the patience department today.

He sat on the edge of the bed and opened the envelope. He pulled out a piece of paper with a message scrawled in Barrett's familiar handwriting.

I'm arranging a meeting for you with the Witch. Be in Yazoo City, Mississippi at midnight tomorrow night. Go to the city's cemetery to the witch's grave. She's got information regarding the missing Guardians.

"Yazoo City?" Growing up in Louisiana, he'd heard the name bandied about a few times, mostly to do with urban legends and such. Being an urban legend himself, he didn't really remember the stories about the witch. Now he wished he'd listened better.

His stomach rumbled in the empty room, reminding him of the late hour. He grabbed his leather jacket off the back of the chair. His gaze settled across the slash in the leather. Ruined.

He'd had to get another jacket as soon as he got finished with this mission.

It was part of him, part of who he was now. He wasn't about to let anyone see his vulnerability.

CHAPTER 13

"*A*nother Mojito." Catty sighed and shoved her glass toward the bartender. She'd planned on staying in on her night off, but she was going stir crazy. So she'd gone out, hoping drinking would distract her. She needed to relax.

"What's wrong, sweetheart? Someone break your heart?" A man slid onto the barstool next to her and leaned in. He was in his late thirties, nicely dressed with blond hair and blue eyes. If it hadn't been for the predatory smile on his human face she would have thought him handsome.

"Not exactly." There were some who didn't believe she had a heart. There was a good chance one of those people was Lucien.

"Is he bothering you?" Lucien's deep voice had her stomach turning to Jell-O as her heart climbed into her throat.

She turned.

He stood there wearing the leather jacket and a pissed-off expression.

"Nobody's bothering anyone." She bounced her foot

against the rung of the stool and tried to keep her voice even, strong, and calm. Her words sounded odd in her ears.

Looking past her, Lucien grabbed her drink and dumped it out on the floor.

"Hey, why did you do that?" Her mouth dropped and she crossed her arms.

"We were just having a conversation, buddy." The guy smirked and rested his elbows on the bar. He gave Catty another smile that made her skin crawl.

"Actually, we're not having a conversation and I'm not interested in starting one."

"Now, wait a minute. You've got some nerve acting all high and mighty while dressing like some two-cent hooker." The man stood.

Her mouth dropped. "Look, asshole…"

"First you're going to apologize," Lucien growled at the guy. "And then you're going to call your mom and tell her what you said and how much of a dick you were tonight."

"Let me tell you something—" The man's deceptive smile slipped and revealed a snarl that made Catty cringe.

"I'm not finished." Lucien stepped into the man's personal space, their chests touching. The human might be big, but Lucien was bigger. "You're never going to come into this bar again and harass another woman. And you're sure as hell not going to try to drug another woman."

"Drug? What you mean?" She tried to stand, to make her legs move, but the signal wasn't getting to her brain. Her body felt weightless, like she was floating on a white puffy cloud.

"I saw him slip something in your drink." Lucien's tone dripped with venom, the kind that could kill in seconds.

"I'm calling the cops." The bartender grabbed a phone behind the bar and punched in some numbers. "I don't put up with that shit in my bar."

"No need. I am an undercover cop." Lucien answered. "I'll take care of this."

Catty frowned. Undercover cop. She hadn't pegged him for that.

"Fine, fine," the man stuttered, his face going pale. "I'm sorry for what I said. I didn't mean any harm. I'll just go."

"You're not going anywhere. You still need to call your mother." Lucien held out his hand. "Give me your phone."

"What?" He rubbed his palms down his pants leg and jerked his gaze around the room.

"Your phone. Now. Or I'm going to punch you in the throat. You can't talk to your mom when your throat is collapsed."

The guy blinked and dug around in his trouser pocket. He fished out his phone and handed it to Lucien.

"Your password."

"What?"

"What is your password?"

"BigDick."

"An asshole and a liar." Lucien snorted.

Catty squeezed her eyes tight, trying to clear her muddled head. Whatever he had put her drink must be strong. The bartender shoved a glass of water at her and told her to drink. She complied but kept her gaze locked on Lucien.

His jet-black hair fell across his forehead and scraped his shoulders as his breathing increased with each heavy breath. His lips were stretched across his white teeth in a sneer and his hands were fisted at his sides. He looked like he was ready to kill in his black leather jacket.

The drugs must have affected her brain because she was starting to imagine herself naked and in his arms. He was hot, for sure, but he had a calm, deadly demeanor, like he could snap at the flip of a switch.

He was the last guy she needed to be getting all hot and

bothered about. If Big Mike caught wind she was hanging out with a werewolf outside the club, then her life would be in danger.

She watched the scene play out in a blur of activity.

The guy put the phone up to his ear. The next few minutes consisted of him confessing to his mom what he'd done and trying to apologize. Lucien then took the phone out of the man's hand and began telling the guy's mom he would make sure he got the help he needed.

He hung up and shoved the phone in the man's chest. "You will leave and never harm another woman again. If you do, I will find out about it. I have eyes everywhere. You can't hide from me. Are we clear?"

The guy slipped a finger beneath his collar and tugged. Sweat popped up across his upper lip and forehead, and his chin quivered. He nodded several times before he backed away and finally fled out the front door.

"Are you all right?" Lucien stepped between her legs and leaned in close, his warm breath tickling her cheeks.

"Mmmm." Her stomach tingled and she closed her eyes. His scent was washing over her like a tidal wave of sexy alpha male.

"Catty?" The unmistakable tone of concern was stamped into his voice. She opened her eyes to find him staring intently at her. He cupped her face, his eyes scanning her face.

Mentally she was telling him to leave, to step away and stop touching her. But she couldn't seem to make herself say the words.

"Lucien." His name rolled out of her mouth like a moan.

"Come on." He tugged her to her feet. Her legs buckled.

He swept her up in his arms before she could fall. She wrapped her arms around him and tucked her face into the crook of his neck.

Big mistake. Her stomach warmed, sending delicious tendrils of lust through her body.

"Ugh," she moaned.

"We're leaving," he whispered against her cheek, his voice deep and urgent.

He hurried down the sidewalk, taking long strides as he put distance between them and the bar. She opened her eyes and looked over his shoulder. He was not headed toward her apartment. She should have questioned him, but right now she really didn't care where they were going.

"I'm taking you to my hotel."

"Are you a mind reader?" she murmured against his neck, her lips scraping across his flesh. His hotel was the only place she wanted to be right now.

"If I were a mind reader I wouldn't still be trying to get information out of you, now would I?" He groused.

"Or maybe you'd realize I don't have any information." She let her head loll back against his shoulder.

"Maybe," he said softly. "Or maybe you're just a tough nut to crack."

"Are you saying you want to crack me?" She lifted her head and smiled.

He stopped in his tracks, his heart beating rapidly against her body, and looked down at her.

When he started walking, she laid her head back down and closed her eyes. "You sure don't trust people, do ya?"

He adjusted his grip. "I have too many reasons not to trust people." His fingers brushed the side of her breast. Pleasure shot through her body straight to her core. Her breathing turned to a pant as she buried her face in his neck.

She opened her eyes long enough to see plenty of women on the sidewalk openly eyeing Lucien. Apparently he either didn't notice or didn't care because he ignored them all.

He stopped at the hotel and opened the door. He walked through the corridor and stepped into the empty elevator.

Her heart tumbled in her chest. She wasn't sure what was going to happen once they stepped inside his room, but she certainly didn't want to give him the wrong idea about her for a second time.

"Lucien, I can walk."

"Not going to happen."

Her heart heated and tumbled.

The elevator dinged and he stepped off with his arms full of her.

He stopped and unlocked the door. Once inside, he kicked the door shut with his boot.

He carefully laid her on the bed and knelt in front of her.

She blinked slowly and met his gaze.

"Are you having blurred vision?"

"No." She held his gaze.

"Is your heart racing?"

"Yes."

He frowned. "Are you having difficulty breathing?"

"Yes." With him so close, how could she breathe easy?

He pressed his hand to her forehead. "You're burning up."

"You have no idea." She clutched at the comforter to keep from grabbing at him and ripping his clothes off.

"Lucien, stop." She pulled his hand from her head and pressed it to her chest. "It's not because of the drug or whatever that asshole gave me that I feel this way." She'd only had a drink before Lucien interrupted them.

"Then what is it?"

"It's you."

CHAPTER 14

"*W*hat do you mean?" Lucien's fingers tingled, aching to reach out and touch her. Had he heard her correctly? What was she saying? He needed total clarity before assuming anything.

"Apparently I'm really rusty when it comes to seduction." She buried her face between her hands.

"Catty." Her name on his lips sent excitement thrumming through his veins. Was she playing with him again? Setting him up for another fall?

"I want you, Lucien. As much as I know me and you are a bad idea, I can't help but still want you." She pressed the palm of her hand to his chest. His heart thudded with a vengeance.

"I know you feel it too." She cocked her head, daring him to deny it. "I can smell your arousal."

He'd wanted her the second he had walked into the bar and seen that guy flirting with her. He'd tried to deny it, to bury it deep, but it wasn't going away.

"You were drugged. You don't know what you're saying." He wrapped his fingers around her tiny wrist.

"The drug wore off the second you picked me up. The

second I smelled your scent, my body started reacting to you. Trust me, it's not the drug. I felt this way when you touched me in the club."

"I don't play games, Catty."

"Neither do I."

He arched his brow.

"Okay, then I'll do all the work. I'm not too proud to admit my attraction. Even if you can't bring yourself to say it." She pressed both hands to his chest and shoved.

He sat back on the floor, his legs stretched out in front of him. He watched, hypnotized by the way she stood and slowly moved toward him. The sway of her hips and the smell of her scent had his body aching for her. He was stuck in a dream and he couldn't move.

Her fingers tugged her shirt up over her head. She held the garment between her fingers and let it drop to the floor. Her eyes never left his as she reached for the button on her cut-off jean shorts. She shoved the shorts down over her slender hips and stepped out of them.

His heart beat faster, loud and angry and insistent.

She stood before him in matching black panties and bra, her curves and secrets barely covered. His dick hardened as his gaze drank her in like ice-cold water on a scorching summer day.

"Catty, be careful what you unleash. Once we start, I might not be a gentleman and stop." His eyes narrowed and his nostrils flared when her feminine scent hit him.

"Good. I don't much like gentlemen." She knelt on the floor by his feet and began taking off his biker boots. After ridding him of his socks, she crawled up between his legs and fumbled with the button on his jeans and then unzipped him.

"Jesus, Catty." His heart thundered in his head.

"Let me, Lucien." She looked up at him beneath her long dark lashes.

He sucked in a harsh breath at her beauty.

She hooked her fingers in his belt loops and tugged. His erection tented his boxers as she pulled his jeans off his legs.

"You should probably get rid of the jacket. You won't need it." She purred and straddled his hips.

His muscles tensed and flexed as he took his leather jacket off and let it fall on the floor.

She reached for his shirt. He grabbed her hands and panic surged through his chest.

She frowned and released his shirt.

He was more than his scars. He wasn't going to let something from his past still control him.

Fuck it.

He tugged his shirt over his head. Her eyes widened in appreciation as she took in the numerous tatts adorning his arms and chest. He couldn't get ink on his back, but it didn't stop him from inking what flesh he could.

Her lips parted as she ran her hand down his chest, trailing down his abs until her fingertips brushed the elastic waistband of his boxers.

"Nice ink," she murmured as her hand dipped inside his underwear.

His dick twitched against the soft graze of her fingertips.

Looking up into his face, she wrapped her fingers around the base of his shaft and squeezed.

He growled at the delicious pleasure. Cupping her face, he pulled her near.

"Are you sure?" He searched her blue-gray eyes for any hesitation.

"I've been sure since you were in my room." She smiled shyly before pressing her lips against his.

He growled as he dipped his tongue into her sweet mouth, tasting her, claiming her in this one moment. She moaned against his lips.

She laced her fingers around his neck and clung to him, pressing her slender body against him. His heart thundered in his chest and desire licked through every cell of his body, igniting intense desires he didn't know he possessed.

"More." She rocked against his erection and pressed him back into the floor. She broke the kiss and reached between their bodies, taking him in her hand and stroking him until he was pumping himself against her palm.

He grabbed her hand. "Slow down. Ladies first." He grinned up at her as he found her bra and unhooked it. Her bra slid down her arms and she tossed it behind her. His mouth watered as he pulled her down. He captured a pretty pink nipple in his mouth and sucked.

"Oh, god, that feels good." She cupped his head to her breasts.

He licked and sucked at her breast until she was writhing on top of him.

"I need you inside me, now," she said, her voice hoarse, her breath in a rushed pant.

"Like I said, ladies first." He gave her nipple a final lick and then hooked his thumbs on either side of her panties and tugged. The lace panties ripped and he tossed the shreds to the floor.

She smiled and rubbed her wetness against him.

"Not yet," he growled and grabbed her hips.

He nudged her up past his chest until her thighs were on either side of his face.

"Oh," she cried out as he licked her between her legs in one slow movement.

She trembled underneath him as he tightened his hold on her hips. He kissed and tasted of her sweetness and she rubbed herself against his mouth. Fuck, he could do this all damn day and never get tired of her taste, of how she felt, of the erotic sounds she made.

His hands trailed up over her ribcage to her beautiful breasts. He brushed his thumb over the hardened pink nipples and she moaned. Reaching behind her, she grabbed his dick and squeezed. He growled against her pink folds and jerked against her hand. He gently rolled her nipples between his fingertips and she tensed.

"Lucien," she cried out as her head fell back. Her body trembled as she rode out her orgasm in an uninhibited, wild display of pleasure.

When her body relaxed, he gently rolled them to the side. He removed his underwear and kissed his way up her body.

* * *

"I'VE NEVER COME SO HARD in my life," she murmured. She was still humming from the orgasm he'd given her, and she didn't know if she had the strength to move.

"That was just a warm-up. I'm nowhere near done." He grinned and kissed the tender spot at her neck.

Her stomach warmed all over again at his smile and his touch. She wrapped her arms around his neck and pulled him closer for a kiss. Her palms slid down over his shoulders, memorizing the deep lines of his defined muscles and raw strength.

She couldn't stop touching him. She wanted to discover every area of his body and then start all over again.

He kissed her hard and deep. She arched against him. Her fingers trailed down his hard abdomen and then to his ribcage. She needed more.

She slid her hands around to his back, and he jerked away. He grabbed her hands, restraining her. His wide eyes were unsure.

"What's wrong?" She looked up at him, her body aching for him.

"Don't touch my back," he said softly and then looked away for a brief second.

She knew better than to ask. She'd seen that haunted look before when she looked at her own reflection.

"It's okay, Lucien. I'm not going to hurt you." She pressed a gentle kiss to his muscular chest, against the pounding of his heart. He shivered at the intimate gesture. "I just want to be with you."

He released her hands and pressed his fingers to her lips. She parted her lips, sucking the digits one by one inside her mouth. By the time she was done, desire streaked through his gaze.

He was aroused, as much as she was. He just didn't trust her. He was like a caged animal.

There was only one thing to do with a frightened animal.

She had to go slow.

CHAPTER 15

"*I* won't touch you. But I want you to touch me." The words glided passed her lips, hovering and hanging in the thick air between them.

She'd never done this before. She didn't know if she could do this now. All she knew was she wanted Lucien any way she could have him.

She lifted her gaze to his, refusing to look away. His eyes flickered and flashed with lust, turning her stomach to ache and need and desire.

"How many times have you done this with a male? Let yourself be vulnerable?"

"Never. I've never done this before." She eased back on the floor, her gaze locked on his. Her face flushed and her chest fluttering, she slid her hands across her flat stomach up her ribcage. His eyes tracked her movements and his breathing grew ragged.

She tamped down the shyness tightening her chest.

She shouldn't be embarrassed. She took her clothes off for a living. Why was she getting all nervous?

She stopped at her breasts and ran her thumbs across her

nipples. Pleasure streaked through the sensitive flesh, and a moan escaped her lips.

He growled, low and lustful, and his nostrils flared.

Confidence seeped into her chest, drowning out insecurity. She would give herself to him, open, exposed and completely at his mercy.

She rested her arms above her head and looked up at him. "Lucien."

"Mine. Tonight you are mine." He let out a low growl and covered her body with his. Resting his weight on his elbows, he hovered above her as he reached down to position himself at her wet entrance.

She bit her lip, trying to resist the overwhelming need to wrap her arms and legs around him.

"Please, Lucien. I want you in me now." She arched toward him.

"Easy, love," he whispered against her cheek before covering her mouth in a blistering kiss.

He thrust into her, stretching and filling her. He was big and she hadn't been with a male in a while. The brief sting of pain was soon replaced with a sweet streak of pleasure.

"Oh, god." She moaned. She lifted her hips, trying to rub against him.

"Fuck, Catty. Am I hurting you?" He groaned against her neck. "You're really tight."

"It's been a while." She wrapped her legs around his, trapping him inside her body. "Don't you dare think about stopping. Not now."

"I want this. I want you." He kissed her. She opened her mouth under his, tasting his hot mouth and memorizing his scent.

He began a slow, methodical movement in and out of her body, the rhythm so delicious she almost forgot to breathe.

She'd never had two orgasms so close together, but Lucien was about to change that.

He pistoned his hips faster, sliding in and out of her wet heat.

He grabbed her hands, laced his fingers through hers, and stretched them over her head.

She tightened her grip and held his gaze as he moved in and out, setting every inch of her skin on fire.

Her body tightened. She was close, the pleasure pressing in on her.

"Lucien." She tightened around his shaft and came hard.

He bent his head and sucked her nipple in his mouth as he pumped hard and fast. Pleasure arced through her system.

He held her tight until she rode out her orgasm and then gathered her in his strong arms. He growled, buried his face in her neck, and bit down. He bucked against her, spilling his seed deep inside.

When he was finished, he collapsed on her, their bodies slick with sweat, their breathing laced with pleasure.

She slipped her hand down his sides.

He stiffened.

"It's okay. I wasn't going to touch your back. I just want to touch your ass." She grabbed his butt and kissed the side of his neck.

He laughed as he lifted himself off her.

"You're not like most women, Catty."

"Damn straight I'm not." She nipped his shoulder.

He cradled her against his chest. She closed her eyes, savoring the feel of him all around her.

"Lucien?"

"Yeah?" he murmured as his fingers made small caressing circles on her back. She snuggled in deeper.

"What happened to your back?"

He stilled, and she could feel the invisible barriers edging their way between them.

"I don't judge people. You don't have to be afraid to trust me, Lucien." She hugged him tighter.

"I'm not afraid," he said stiffly.

"You can't see my scars. But I carry them around every day of my life." She squeezed her eyes shut and grimaced. "I can't go home. Not after what I've done."

"What do you mean?" He lifted her chin with his finger.

She opened her eyes and met his serious stare. "How can I shame my family by going home? If I go home, they will find out I've been stripping in New Orleans. It's not something I can hide." She shook her head. "I wish I'd never left Arkansas. Now I can't ever go back."

"You can always go back." His fingertips brushed her cheek.

"My father is a well-respected Were. I know the choices I've made have consequences. Right now, they don't know where I am or what I've become. They are free from the shame of having me as a daughter, or a sister." She glanced away and sat up.

"You don't know your family at all." Easing up to a sitting position, he placed his hands on either side of her and looked down into her eyes.

"Believe me, I know my family."

"So do I."

She blinked in surprise. "You know my father?"

"Yes. And your mother. But I know Zane better."

"It would kill him to find out what I've been doing. I think it would hurt him the most. Guardians have a reputation to protect, you know." She swallowed hard and looked away. She couldn't take the pity in his eyes.

"And I think Zane would understand. He knows everyone makes mistakes."

"You don't understand. I made the decision to strip. Not out of desperation but for the attention. To be seen." Her stomach twisted and she fought back the urge to throw up. "But I was so wrong. When I'm up on stage taking my clothes off, those men don't see me, they don't love me, they don't even lust after me. They want to possess me. To take something and use it and then throw it away."

"He's still your brother. He still loves you."

"You must not know him well. Zane is as straight-laced as they come. There is no room for messing up." She drew her legs up to her chin and dropped her head. "Even if I went back home, there wouldn't be any forgiveness. Not for me."

He scooped her up in his arms and settled her into his naked lap. "You are too hard on yourself."

"No, I'm realistic." She laid her head on his shoulder and snuggled into his warmth. Despite the heat of the night, she felt cold to her marrow.

"People change. Zane might have been a hardass once, but he's been through some stuff and he's… changed."

She jerked her head up. "What stuff? Is he okay?"

He grinned. "He's fine. He has Skylar to take care of him."

"Skylar? They are together? But she's a red wolf." She'd known Skylar had been crushing on her brother when she was younger, but Zane had never really paid any attention to her friend.

He cocked his head. "Yeah, Skylar. You have a problem with them being together?"

"No, of course not. I didn't mean it like it sounded. Skylar was my best friend. I figured Zane would mate with someone of his equal…" She bit her lip and groaned. "I didn't mean that. God, I sound like an idiot." She rested her head on his shoulder and wished she could stop talking.

He laughed.

She looked up. "I think it's great Zane and Skylar are

together. She deserves someone who will treat her like a queen."

"And what about you?"

"No male is going to want to mate with me. So it's not something I think about." She swallowed the bitterness in her mouth.

"Is that what you want? To be mated?"

She stared at him for a long moment, putting her thoughts into words.

"I want a do-over, to escape and build a new future. Maybe find out what I'm good at." She shook her head. "More than anything, I want a different life."

"Why not start over at home?"

She sighed. "Because I can't. That door is closed. Growing up, it was always about Zane. He was the golden child. The superstar of the family. He could do no wrong." She idly ran her fingers through his dark hair as she talked. "Hell, even Skylar got more attention than me."

"Wasn't Skylar's home situation bad? Like abusive?"

If he knew this much about Skylar, then he was closer to Zane than he was letting on.

"I think her dad neglected her a lot. I'm not sure. She didn't talk about it. He always gave me the creeps though."

"No doubt." He held her closer. "Are you curious to know how your parents reacted to Skylar when Zane mated with her?"

"No. I don't need to know."

"But…"

"But nothing." She shook her head. "Look, they may have accepted her into the family fold, but with me it's different. I'm held to a different standard." She looked away. "Always have been."

Silence stretched between them. She wanted to get up and leave before anything else was said about her past.

"I was burned." His voice sliced through the silence.

"What?" She jerked her head back at him.

"You asked what happened to my back. I was burned when I was younger." He glanced away. She knew how hard it was to share his past.

"Oh my god, Lucien." She touched his cheek. "That must have been horrific for you."

"It wasn't exactly a picnic." He snorted.

Her heart broke for him. "What happened?"

"You and I are more alike than you think." He gave her a thoughtful look. "We were both born into families of high ranking. I'm from Louisiana."

"Really?"

"My family, the Sauvages, came here from France many generations ago. My great-grandparents became wealthy when they started their own shipping company. Soon they were one of the wealthiest families in New Orleans."

"I had no idea. I thought you were just a hot biker."

His expression softened, and he grinned before leaning in to kiss her. Her body heated at his touch. As much as she wanted him again, she also wanted to hear his story.

"So what happened?"

"I was eighteen and I wanted to be a Guardian. My brother tried to gain acceptance into the Louisiana Pack but didn't make it. When he found out I had applied, he got angry. Angrier than I'd ever seen him. It was winter and there was a bonfire in our backyard. I had some friends over and we were drinking beer and we got into a fight." Lucien's eyes glazed over as if he were seeing it play out in front of him. "My brother ended up knocking me back into the fire."

"But why didn't it heal?" Werewolves had properties in their blood that made them heal at an incredible rate.

"Because after I was pulled out of the fire by my friends,

my brother threw salt at my back. He wanted to scar me for life so they wouldn't accept me into the Guardians."

"What an asshole." Catty's gut twisted in anger. She wrapped her arms around his neck and held him tight, wanting to take away his pain. "Did he say why he did that?"

"He didn't have to. He was jealous. If he couldn't get into the Guardians then he sure as hell didn't want me to get it. He left that night. After a while I moved out of the state of Louisiana and into Arkansas."

He lifted her off his lap. He stood and pulled her up with him. "I've never showed anyone my back before." He released her hands and backed up. He swiped his hand across his forehead and then lifted his unsure gaze to hers.

He turned, revealing his back to her.

Her breath caught in her throat as she took in the discolored, mottled flesh that once was smooth flesh. She stepped closer and placed her palm on in the middle of the scarred expanse.

He hissed.

She jerked her hand back. "Did I hurt you?"

"No." He shook his head and then looked at the floor. "It's just… No one has ever touched my back before. Not even my mother."

Her heart cracked like glass for all he'd endured. Anger, sadness, revenge all poured out at once through the tiny fissures. She stepped closer, wrapped her arms around him and pressed her lips to his angry flesh.

"I'm so sorry."

"Don't pity me. I've never done well with pity." His hardness in his voice made her flinch.

"I don't pity you, Lucien. I'm sorry for all the pain it caused you. I'm sorry your brother did this to you."

He grabbed her arms and tightened them around his waist. She smiled and laid her head against his uneven skin.

She swallowed back the angry tears bubbling up in her eyes. She knew how he felt.

He felt less than worthy.

She felt the same.

"So since we are sharing, there is something you need to know about me." She cleared her throat.

"What's that?" He turned.

"Apparently even if I got out of stripping, my options for jobs are quite limited. I got really excited and motivated to take one of those online quizzes to see what my purpose was in life."

"And?"

"I got personal snuggler." She shook her head. It sounded even more stupid when she said it out loud. "It's where you hold people so they can go to sleep."

"That's a thing?"

"In Japan it's a thing." She cringed and looked away.

"And you took this seriously?" A slow smile crept onto his face.

"Yes! It's how you find out your calling, your destiny in life!" She looked at him with wide eyes.

"Well, did you take it again?"

"Yes, two more times. The second time it said funeral director."

He barked out a laugh.

"It's not funny, Lucien." Her heart pounded in her chest. She should have kept it to herself.

"It's a stupid test. It doesn't mean anything."

"Says the guy who's never taken it." She narrowed her eyes.

"I've taken it. It told me I should be a male model."

"Ha! See! It's accurate." She dropped her head. "The last test gave me the most ridiculous answer of all."

"More ridiculous than a funeral director?"

"Yes." She sighed. "A lawyer."

"What's so ridiculous about that? It makes perfect sense to me. You would be carrying on your family's legacy." He nudged her chin up with his finger. "Plus you're stubborn and like to argue."

"You have to be smart to be a lawyer." She shook her head. "I don't think it's up my alley."

"I think you don't give yourself enough credit. We need good lawyers, smart people who care about others. I've seen how you look after those who can't look after themselves. Like Mrs. Willis."

His faith in her tugged at her heart.

He pulled her into his muscular chest. The city streetlight beamed across his sinfully handsome face. His heavy lidded gaze seared her. The energy shifted. His erection pressed into her stomach. Her body warmed and then melted as he covered her mouth with his.

"I want you again," he murmured against her lips and he picked her up in his massive arms.

"Good. I want you to have me," she said breathlessly.

He carried her to the bed and carefully laid her down. Time and noise fell away until they were the only two people that existed. He moved between her legs, kissing and touching her with slow deliberation.

She'd never felt more loved and cherished even if it was for a moment.

In life, she knew a moment was all she was guaranteed.

CHAPTER 16

*L*ucien squinted as the blinding morning sun filtered through the lace curtains. He rolled over to his side and pulled Catty into his arms.

"We don't have time for another round." She laughed and she tried to wiggle away.

"There's always time for another round." He buried his face in the crook of her neck.

His hand went between her legs and stopped.

He frowned. "Why are you already dressed?" He inhaled her scent at her neck. "And showered?"

"Because it's almost eight o'clock and I need coffee." She rolled over and kissed him on the mouth. "Besides, you said something last night about some meeting today. I thought you needed to be up early."

He sat up in bed and glanced at the clock on the bedside table. "Shit."

"Relax, I'm sure you've got plenty of time." She tugged on her shoes and glanced over at him.

"I've got to be in Mississippi tonight." He grabbed his

phone and pulled up his map and confirmed how long the trip would take on a Harley.

He relaxed when he saw he had plenty of time to make it.

"Where in Mississippi?" She grabbed the brush off her night stand and ran it through her blond hair. The silky blond strands glistened like gold in the morning sun. He itched to reach out and run his fingers through her hair. The way it had felt against this chest as she slept was one of the most intimate moments he'd ever shared with a woman.

"Yazoo City." He put his feet on the floor and tugged her toward him.

She froze. "Please tell me you're not going there to see her." Her pupils dilated and her lips parted.

"Who?"

"The witch."

"How did you know who I was going to see?" An uneasy feeling crept up his spine.

"Because there's no reason for any werewolf to go to Yazoo City unless you're looking for trouble. She is nothing but trouble." She shook her head.

"Do you know her?"

"Unfortunately." Her beautiful eyes narrowed into hardened slits and she pressed her lips into a thin white line.

"If I asked you not to go, would you listen to me?" She shot him a glare.

"No." He couldn't help but grin. "Sorry, baby, but I'm on a job here."

She frowned. "Am I part of the job?"

"The job is the reason I came looking for you. But what's going on between us is not part of the job." He swallowed and pulled her into his arms. Guilt stung his gut like bees. He hadn't been totally honest with her. He hadn't told her what he was.

He hated lying to her when she'd bared herself to him in so many ways.

"So how do you know her?" He pulled into his lap.

"Keeping her hands to herself when it comes to someone else's boyfriend is not a skill she possesses."

Jealousy spiraled down in his stomach. "Boyfriend? How long ago was this?"

She snorted. "It's been a few years. So you can stop looking at me like that."

"What happened?"

"I saw her in a bar one night when I was out with my boyfriend. We were dancing and she kept trying to cut in. He kept turning her down. It didn't matter to her. He went to grab us some beers. When he didn't come back, I went looking for him. I found him banging her in the alley out back. He had this weird unfocused look in his eyes, like he was seeing right through me. I didn't realize at the time, but she had cast a seduction spell on him."

"I'm sorry." He really wasn't. He was glad she wasn't still dating the douchebag.

"I think a guy who is weak enough to cheat doesn't need a spell. He probably would have done it eventually. Better that I found out when I did so I didn't waste any more time with him." She shrugged. "Needless to say, the witch and I are not going to be BFFs anytime soon." She narrowed her eyes at him. "And it's also why I'm coming with you."

"You don't trust me?" He arched his eyebrow. His chest filled with warmth. It felt good to have someone feel protective over him. Even if it was for the moment.

"I don't trust her." She stood and pulled out of his reach. She shoved her thumb in the direction of the bathroom. "Now hurry up and shower. We're going to need to stop by my place so I can change into jeans and my biker boots."

* * *

IT HAD BEEN a while since Catty had been on the back of a Harley. With the wind in her hair and her arms around Lucien's waist, she couldn't stop smiling as they sped down the highway. It was an escape from reality she desperately craved.

"Doing okay?" Lucien yelled over the wind and the roar of the engine.

"Never better." She smiled as she laid her head on his warm leather-clad shoulder and tightened her grip. She'd tried to convince him to take the heavy jacket off, but he insisted on wearing it.

They rode for hours, only stopping a couple of times to get gas. He tried to get her to eat something, but the heat sapped her appetite. She was too eager to get back on the Harley and get to their destination.

Would Lucien be drawn to the witch? Would she seduce him like she'd done so many men in the past? Or would Lucien be able to stand strong and resist her under his own power?

She inhaled deeply and pushed away her negative thoughts. Lucien was different.

He had to be. He'd been nothing but honest with her, and she'd seen how hard it had been for him.

Whatever reason he was looking into the dirty dealings in New Orleans made her think he had been hired from within the Arkansas Pack. Maybe he was running intel for the Pack. Maybe it was personal. She wasn't sure.

She was sure he wasn't a Guardian. The Guardians always had their back tatted up with their insignia. Guardians were lethal and were the peacekeepers among the civilian were-wolf population. She couldn't imagine Zane being a

Guardian. They were the muscle for the Pack Master, and her brother was always more of the brains kind of guy.

But people change. She knew better than anyone. She wanted to change for the better.

At least Lucien wasn't a Guardian.

If anyone at the club caught wind she was hanging with a Guardian then it would mean her life. She knew Lucien would never put her in danger.

* * *

LUCIEN SLOWED his speed once he hit the city limits of Yazoo City, Mississippi.

It was well after dark and the streets were illuminated by streetlights and headlights of traffic. He made a turn and continued down the steep hill that led into the heart of the city. Keeping his speed well under the limit, he continued his trek through the historic little town.

Streets were lined with oak trees, Victorian homes, and sidewalks. For an outsider passing through, it looked enough like a normal small town. But he wasn't fooled. His senses went on high alert and he could feel some odd paranormal energy flowing through the town that seemed to get stronger the closer he got to his destination. It felt like a curse hanging over the small town.

When he reached the entrance to the Glenwood Cemetery, he parked and killed the engine.

Setting the kickstand, he slid off the bike and then lifted Catty off.

"I can do it myself."

"I know. I just like touching you." He held her close and gave her a quick kiss before taking a quick glance around.

"The gate is locked." He frowned.

"Yeah, I figured it would be. The witch's grave has been

vandalized so many times that they started locking it at night."

"How did you know?"

"I Googled it." She shrugged.

"Climb on my back and I'll scale the fence."

"I can climb, Lucien."

"I don't care. If you slip and fall on the fence, it will impale you. I'm not taking the chance." He pointed to his back. "Get on."

She sighed heavily and climbed on his back.

His body immediately warmed when she pressed her lips against his neck. "Just so you know, don't look her in the eyes."

"Why? Is she Medusa?"

"The only thing she's interested in turning into stone is your dick. Just make sure it doesn't happen." The icy tone in her voice and the glare she shot him made him realize how much she hated the witch.

He smiled. "I like your jealousy. It's turning me on."

"As long it's not her turning you on." She climbed on his back and wrapped her arms around his neck.

He jumped, scaled the fence, and landed on the other side. She slid off his back.

Lucien took the opportunity to assess his surroundings. The cemetery was empty and he could see there was no one else around. But the distinctive sound of seventies music drifted around them.

"What the hell is that godawful sound?" He flinched and looked around, trying to determine where the sound was coming from.

"Oh yeah. I forgot to tell you. Our witch prefers listening to ABBA." Catty cocked her head and stilled. "Sounds like she's listening to 'Dancing Queen.'"

"Fuck me. This is going to be torture." He hated any

music that wasn't rock. He especially hated seventies music.

He took Catty's hand in his and led her farther into the rows and rows of graves and headstones.

Some of the graves were illuminated by solar lights loved ones had placed near the headstones. Others had flowers, both artificial and real, sitting around the graves. Few security lights were within the cemetery, making some areas well-lit and others surrounded by darkness.

Catty looked up from her cell phone. "According to my map, her grave is over there, not far from the fountain and near the funny-looking headstone."

They found the identifying markers, and the closer they got the louder the music was.

There was headstone broken and lying on the ground with large chains around it. Some of the links in the chains were missing.

"I'm guessing the chains are supposed to keep her here," he said.

"Which is why they are broken." A sultry feminine voice came from a nearby tree.

A woman dressed in a white sundress stepped out from the shadows.

The nearby security light illuminated her flaming red hair which flowed in waves across her slender shoulders. Her eyes, a startling shade of electric green, held a hint of amusement as she studied them both with interest.

She looked to be in her mid-twenties, and she was a far cry from the image of an old hag Lucien had imagined.

"I was expecting you to be alone." She smiled as her gaze roamed down the length of his body and settled on his crotch. He shifted under the scrutiny of her vulgar stare.

"Hello, Ella," Catty said.

"I'm sorry. Do we know each other?" The witch turned her attention to Catty and glared.

"Yeah. You fucked my boyfriend in the alley in New Orleans." Catty's dry tone held a deadly edge.

"That doesn't narrow it down at all, honey." Ella smiled sweetly.

"I'm not surprised." Catty snarled.

Ella lunged for her. Catty let out a feral growl, ready for a fight. Lucien stepped in between the two women.

"I was told you have some information for me. About some of the missing Guardians." He glared at the witch.

The smile dropped off her face "I think you heard wrong." The tone in her voice was too sure, too forced, too ready to change the subject. She snapped her fingers, and the music changed to a different song by ABBA.

Lucien closed the distance between him and the witch.

"Listen, don't waste my time. I'm here because I was told you could help me."

She arched her perfectly plucked brow and gave a chuckle. "I don't give information away for free. That's not how I play." She sat on a nearby headstone and spread her legs suggestively. "I'm going to need something in return for the information you want."

Catty growled.

"Really?" Lucien reached inside the jacket pocket and pulled out an envelope. Inside was ten thousand dollars Barrett had sent along with the direction.

He held it out to Ella.

"Money is something I don't need since I'm stuck inside this cemetery." She snorted and stepped up to him. "Now if there is something else you want to bargain with, then I'll talk." She ran her finger down the front of his chest.

He grabbed her hand and frowned. "How are you in human form if you're supposed to be dead?"

"Part of this damn curse. My body won't die and my soul

is bound to my body. I'm cursed, stuck inside this cemetery. What good is money to me here?"

"According to legend, you escaped. And burned the city." Lucien didn't trust this bitch as far as he could throw her.

"Well it was kind of a fluke, actually." She shrugged. "I knew I had to make a blood exchange. I had to sacrifice someone so I could escape. The innocent blood lowers the curse, therefore making it possible for me to escape. The first time, I escaped and set the town of Yazoo on fire for killing me. The second time, the time no one found out about, I made it all the way to New Orleans before being sucked back in this place."

"You have to kill a human?" Catty glared.

"I prefer someone with supernatural blood. Human blood is weak and it only lets me out for a little while before the curse brings me back here."

Catty propped her hands on her hips. "Who did you kill to be able to make it to New Orleans?"

Ella's smile grew predatory. "A werewolf. Like you."

Lucien's body tightened and a wave of protectiveness buzzed through his body. He stepped in front of Catty, blocking the witch's view. "But it doesn't release you forever."

"No. Nothing does. I know when the blood exchange begins to lose its power. I get dizzy and faint." Her smile slipped off her face. "When I open my eyes, I'm back in this shithole." She glared at her surroundings, her green eyes sparking with hatred.

Catty's cell phone rang. The ringtone, set to a Miranda Lambert song, broke the silence of the graveyard. She dug it out of her jeans pocket, looked at the screen, and then shoved it back in her pocket.

"What was that?" Ella craned her neck around Lucien, her eyes wide.

"It's a cell phone." Catty snorted.

"I know it's a cell phone, dummy. I meant the music." Her eyes glazed over.

"Country music. Haven't you ever heard her before?" He wasn't a fan, but it would be an improvement from the heinous seventies stuff she was making them listen to.

"I tell you what, I want that music." Her eyes lit up. "I'll take it in exchange for information you want."

He relented. "Fine. I'll buy you a CD."

"No. I want it now." She held out her hand to Catty. "Hand me your phone."

Catty frowned and met Lucien's gaze. He nodded.

Reluctantly Catty handed her phone over. Ella held the phone in the palm of her hand and closed her eyes. She spoke a few words in a language he didn't recognize and the phone began to levitate. Music drifted from the phone like wisps of pink smoke. Ella opened her mouth, letting the pink swirls and music into her mouth. When the last note left the phone, she closed her mouth and swallowed.

The phone drifted down into her palm.

She held out the phone to Catty, who stared at it like it was a coiled snake.

"Whatever music you downloaded to your phone is gone." Ella's sing-song tone grated on Lucien's nerves. If it grated his nerves, it had to be cutting Catty's last one.

Catty snatched her phone and tucked it in her pocket.

"It's your turn. Tell me who is taking the Guardians. Which other states have missing Guardians?" Lucien clenched his fists. He was done playing games with this witch and demanded answers.

Gone was the flirty curve of her mouth and the twinkle in her stare. Her gaze was empty and soulless, like a dead man's. She had funeral eyes.

Her eyes glazed over as she stared straight ahead, focusing on some unseen picture.

"Lucien, the only Guardians missing are the ones from Arkansas. If the other states know what's going on, they won't dare get their hands dirty by saying anything. The Pack Master of Mississippi took a chance by even sending you to me. He knows nothing of the plan."

"What plan?" He stepped forward. His gut twisted as impending doom pressed down on the back of his neck.

"The plan to wipe out all the Guardians. Arkansas is the beginning. With no Guardians in place, all hell will be loosened upon this earth."

"Who is behind this?" He grabbed her arm and tightened his hold.

She blinked her eyes back into focus. She frowned and snatched her arms out of his hold. "I can't see. All I know is you have to stop it. If any more Guardians get tortured and killed, then the other states won't have your back. They want Arkansas out of the way. They know to break Arkansas, they need to break the Guardians."

"What do you mean?" His heart thudded in his chest. This went further than he ever imagined.

"To break Arkansas, they know they have to eliminate your Pack Master, Barrett Middleton."

CHAPTER 17

"Who is behind this?" Lucien grabbed her by the shoulders and gave her a shake.

"If you don't stop grabbing me, I'm going to cast a spell to make your dick fall off." She snarled and snatched herself out of his hold.

"I can't see who's behind this. Whoever is doing this has blocked my ability. It's a veiling spell." She narrowed her eyes. "And the only bitch stronger than me is a witch in New Orleans. Emmalise." Hatred spilled from her eyes and settled into the hard press of her lips. She no longer looked like a twentysomething-year-old with a magic spell. She looked like the lethal, apocalyptic legend she was known for.

"She's the one who stuck me in here. She's the one who had me hunted, killed, and cursed inside this cemetery."

"Were you screwing her boyfriend too?" Catty arched her brow.

"It was her husband."

"Is there any way you can break the spell?" Lucien turned the conversation. He didn't give a shit who was screwing who. That wasn't why he was here.

"I'll need the right ingredients, but yes, I can break the spell." She looked up at him. "It won't be easy, though."

"Easy has never been my style. What do you need?" The quicker he got his info, the quicker he could report back to Barrett with hard evidence. Lucien dug in his leather jacket pocket and pulled out a pen and piece of paper.

She looked down as she scribbled on the paper. "You can only find the ingredients in the French Quarter. Once I break the spell, I'll be able to tell you everything you want to know."

"I don't trust her, Lucien." Catty slid close to his side.

"She's all we have." He didn't either.

Ella grinned and cut her eyes at Catty. She handed the paper and pen back to Lucien. He stuffed it in his pocket. "Don't worry, honey. I'm not going to take your lover. I've got my eye on another werewolf. Barrett Middleton."

Interesting. He'd have to warn his Pack Master never to go to Yazoo City.

The murmur of approaching voices and laughter had him tensing. He glanced around and spotted a group of teens in the distance.

"I think we have company." Ella's eyes blazed bright green as she glanced over her shoulder. "You two should go."

He studied the figures in the distance. A bunch of harmless teenagers out looking for some mischief.

"Don't hurt them." He shot her a warming glare.

"I never do," she said sweetly. As she turned toward the voices, he caught a glimpse of a fang elongating from her mouth.

"What exactly is she?" he murmured.

"Rumor is she is more than a witch. Right now, I don't want to find out. Come on. We need to go." Catty tugged his hand.

He hesitated for a second and then followed her lead.

They hurried to the entrance and she climbed on his back. Once again he scaled the fence effortlessly and landed on the other side.

He started the Harley and waited for her to climb on.

With the information he had gained he needed to get word back to Barrett ASAP. As soon as the stores opened tomorrow he would gather the ingredients for the spell. He had precious little time to wait.

Or it just might be the end of the Arkansas Guardians.

* * *

LUCIEN DROPPED Catty off at her place long after midnight. She'd been disappointed he hadn't stayed but she knew he was working. It hadn't taken long before she drifted off to sleep.

Waking long after the sun had risen, she had a cup of coffee before taking a shower. As the spray of the tepid water washed over her body, her mind kept drifting back to Lucien. Something wasn't adding up.

She couldn't shake the feeling that Lucien wasn't telling her everything.

Her gut told her he wasn't on the bad guys' side, but in the past she'd been a bad judge of character when it came to men, so she could be way off where he was concerned.

She turned off the water and stepped out of the shower. Grabbing a towel, she headed out of the bathroom and padded over to her dresser. She dropped the wet towel from around her body and opened the drawer. It was too hot for a bra, so she pulled out a thin T-shirt and some shorts to wear around the apartment.

"That's what I like about you, Catty. Not afraid to show off your body." Big Mike's voice cut through the silence of her apartment.

She screamed and clutched the clothes to her chest, an attempt to hide her nakedness. Her heart thundered against her chest.

"What the fuck are you doing in my apartment?" Her voice shook as she glared at her boss.

He smiled and stood from sitting on the bed. "I haven't seen you all day. I got worried about you so I popped over."

"I had the day off." She grabbed a blanket off the back of a chair and wrapped it around her body. Unease snaked up her spine and curled around the nape of her neck. Big Mike had never come over to her apartment. Something was off.

"I know. I was hoping to spend it with you. I came by earlier and you were gone." His assessing gaze held hers, as if he was studying her for a lie. She didn't look away, refusing to let him intimidate her.

"Are you keeping tabs on me now?" Her heart raced in her chest as her senses went on high alert. She wished she were a gun owner. The bullet wouldn't kill him, but it sure as hell would slow him down for her to get away if she needed.

"I like keeping an eye on all my girls. Make sure they're not into some kind of trouble doing something they shouldn't be doing." He narrowed his eyes. "Know what I mean?"

"If you're insinuating I'm doing drugs, I'll be happy to submit a urine test."

"That's not the trouble I was talking about." He stalked over to the window and looked down at the street. "I heard you went riding with some big fellow on a Harley. Heard he was a wolf."

Her heart tumbled in her chest. She quickly dressed while his back was turned. "I do have a personal life, you know. The club doesn't own me."

He slowly turned and leveled his gaze at her. "Is that

right? The club is good money and pays the bills. Sounds like you're thinking you're too good for your job."

"I didn't say that." Her throated tightened. She didn't need to rock the boat, not with him. When she got ready to leave for good, she planned on dropping off the face of the earth. She was going to be impossible to find.

"You're starting to act different, Catty. You're not as eager to please the customers as you used to be."

Rage boiled in her gut. She'd never done anything but dance at the club, despite what some the girls insinuated. She knew it stemmed from jealousy, so she shook it off.

"What does that mean?" She lifted her chin.

"I don't know. You tell me." He shrugged his big shoulders and took a step toward her. His buzz cut and goatee made him look intimidating. His dark eyes flashed with suspicion as he continued toward her. He was testing her, trying to see if she was lying.

"I can tell you I don't appreciate you breaking into my apartment while I'm in the shower."

His smirk disappeared and rage filled his eyes. He lunged and grabbed her by the throat. Squeezing, he lifted her off the floor.

"I own you. Don't you ever forget." His hot breath and snarled words shot through her like a bullet.

Panic filled her chest as her oxygen was cut off. She tried to suck in a breath but couldn't. She struggled against his hold and clawed at his ironclad grip, trying to escape. Her vision smeared and blurred and impending doom swamped her body.

This must be what death felt like.

He released his hold, and she crumpled to the floor.

His gaze roamed over her body before meeting her eyes. "I'll be needing you to come in tonight."

"But…" She coughed and sucked in deep breath and grimaced at the fire burning in her throat.

"No buts. We are shorthanded. Looks like another girl won't be making her shift. It's tourist season, and I need to fill the place." He glared at her. "And be sure you're real nice to the customers. You need to be incredibly accommodating. If you know what I mean."

His heavy boot steps tapped against the wood floor and he slammed the door behind him. Alone on the floor, she stared up at the ceiling. Desperation circled around her like a shark.

If she didn't get out of New Orleans soon, something bad was going to happen. And if Big Mike found out she'd been with Lucien, he would kill him.

She wouldn't let Big Mike hurt Lucien. She would protect him regardless of what happened to her.

* * *

"Fuck." Barrett stared at his cell phone after hanging up with Lucien.

"What?" Ryker asked. "Was that Lucien? Did he find out something?"

"Apparently this is targeted to our state."

Ryker was the only other Guardian besides Lucien who knew what was going on.

"It seems like I've pissed someone off." If they were targeting his Guardians, it meant they were targeting him.

Ryker gave him a thoughtful look. "They know how much your Guardians mean to you. They are trying to hurt you, and they know the best way to do that is to hurt your Guardians."

"If someone has a beef with me, they need to fucking man

up and take it out on me instead of acting like a pussy and going after my men."

Ryker nodded and then frowned. "Unless there is something more at stake."

Barrett let Ryker's words marinate for a while.

He stepped around from his desk and walked over to the wall. He pressed the camouflaged button in the wall. The wall slid back, revealing a secret chamber. It was loaded with weapons and ammo, along with a large digital map of the United States displayed on the wall.

He placed his hands on his hips and studied the map. His emotions were all over the fucking place. He wanted to find the fuckers who were doing this and rip out their spleen, then castrate them.

"I fucking hate this, Ryker." He turned and glared at the Guardian.

"I know, bro. This is getting way outta hand." Ryker ran his hair through his dark brown hair and looked at the floor.

"It's the not knowing that keeps me up at night. I don't fucking know if my men are alive and being tortured or dead somewhere in the woods."

"You'll get whoever is doing this, Barrett. You always do."

Barrett looked at him, his heart overflowing with outrage and heavy with helplessness. He was an atomic bomb waiting to explode. The fallout deadly.

"But how many of my Guardians do I have to lose before that happens?"

CHAPTER 18

"*W*hat the hell is wrong with me? I spend one night with Catty and now I can't sleep without her." Lucien shook his head and took another sip of the coffee he'd gotten from the nearby coffee shop. After tossing and turning last night, he needed the hit of caffeine.

He was already pussy whipped.

He'd already gone by Catty's apartment early that morning, but she wasn't there, so he decided to try to old lady's house. He didn't like her going there alone, but he doubted she would listen to anything he said. When he got to Mrs. Willis's house, he didn't pick up her scent. He knew right away she wasn't there, so he didn't even bother knocking.

After updating Barrett last night on the latest info, Barrett had asked him if he thought he needed backup. Lucien refused. He didn't want to lose another brother if whoever was targeting Guardians found a one in New Orleans.

He turned left and cut through Jackson Square, where a few people were milling about. It was early enough that the tarot card readers and the local artists were still setting up their stuff and settling in for the day. Soon curious tourists would be flocking around, eager to buy an original print from a local artist or get a glimpse into their future from a psychic. Half the fortune tellers were frauds, giving out false hope while sticking their hands deep into the pockets of the gullible. The other half were real. If people knew the truth, then they'd stay far away from them.

He glanced up at Andrew Jackson as he passed the gray statue. Nothing had changed since he'd left New Orleans years ago. It even had the same smells. Although he did prefer the morning smells of Café du Monde to the night smells of Bourbon Street.

A young couple strolled through the park. The mom sipped on a cup of hot coffee clutched between her hands while her husband bent down to lift their little girl on his shoulders. Watching something so simple sent an ache through his heart. He'd assumed he'd end up with a mate and a child or two. He'd assumed he would have a family, like his parents and their parents before them. He'd assumed he'd have a life full family meals, raising kids and making love late into the night with the mate of his heart.

He'd assumed wrong.

The loss hit him in the gut like a steel bat, surprising even himself that he still wanted such a life. He forced his gaze away and shoved down his emotions.

He didn't know why it mattered so much to him. He had a place with the Arkansas Pack, a place to lay his head at night, and he made damn good money being a Guardian. He had respect and prestige.

Somehow it didn't seem like enough. He'd always wanted more.

"Lucien, what are you doing here, sweetheart?" The sound of Granny's voice made him freeze in his tracks. The hair on the back of his neck stood up and he glanced around.

The blood drained from his face. He froze when he spotted Granny and Haley headed straight toward him.

It was too late to run.

"Granny, Haley. What are you two doing here?" He forced himself to take a sip of coffee.

"We're here getting stuff for Haley's wedding." Granny hiked her purse higher on her shoulder and smiled.

"You couldn't find that stuff in Arkansas?" Barrett should have given him a heads-up if he knew Granny was on her way down here. But then again, the old woman wasn't the kind to give people an update about her whereabouts or plans.

"Haley is from Louisiana, so we thought we'd get some cute little fleur-de-lis necklaces for the bridesmaids gifts." Granny cocked her head narrowed her gaze. "What are you doing here? I thought you were on a motorcycle trip?"

"I am. I just stopped here on my way back. I wanted to grab some beignets and coffee before making the next leg of the trip."

"Want to tag along with us? I've got another stop at this candy shop. I'm thinking of trying to expand my business. And I think I can make my own edible underwear versus going through the company." Granny pursed her lips and shook her head. "After the last fiasco, I can do a better job of making panties, and I guarantee you no one's toe is going to get bit off."

Haley snorted and fought a smile.

"That's... nice. But I am on a schedule and don't have time." The last thing he wanted to do was help Granny find a new flavor for her drawers.

"Too bad." She didn't hide the disappointment in her tone. "I suppose it's just us girls. Be careful driving back to Little Rock, Lucien," she said over her shoulder as they continued on to their destination.

Toe bitten off? He'd have to be sure and ask Jayden what that was about.

Once they were out of sight he glanced around, making sure no one had heard their conversation. Even in a town as busy as New Orleans, there were always eyes and ears everywhere. He walked in the direction of the apothecary, passing the tarot card readers and artists.

"There is a negative presence around you." The tarot card reader flicked the cards between her fingers while she spoke.

He stopped and turned around, the hair on his arms standing at attention.

The old woman with the dark wrinkled skin looked up and met his gaze.

"Are you talking to me?" His narrowed gaze swept the square, looking for someone tailing him. He saw nothing out of place.

"I know you are looking for trouble. And I know real reason you are here in New Orleans."

He took a step closer and stopped. The gentle breeze of the hot morning air ruffled her blood-red tablecloth. Unlike the other tarot card readers, she had no sign. Only a red tablecloth and a deck of cards decorated her table. An uneasy feeling stretched across his skin like old leather.

"Don't be afraid of me. I'm only the messenger," she said. "I only repeat what I see from the cards."

"I'm not afraid." He could handle one little old lady.

"Sit." She nodded at the chair.

"I don't have any money," he lied.

"I don't want your money. Consider it on the house."

He glanced around and hesitated.

He didn't believe in this mumbo jumbo. But something inside him told him to hear the old woman out.

Reluctantly, he sat.

She shuffled the cards, let him split them, and then shuffled again. Keeping her eyes on him, she laid out the cards in front of him.

"Something will happen between you and your lover. Death can't be stopped."

His gut twisted. *Catty.*

"You're wrong." He shook his head. "I don't have anyone special."

"Don't you?" The old woman snorted.

He growled and stood. The breeze lifted a card off the table and carried it into the street. She frowned and ran after it. When she sat back down, her eyes were wide with fear as she clutched the card between her trembling fingers.

"What is it?"

She pointed her gnarled finger at the black cat on the card. "You see this. There is something evil around you. Something hates you, wants to hurt you in the worst way." Her voice trembled as she spoke.

He didn't believe in this stuff, he reminded himself.

"You need to watch your step. Trust no one. Not even your instincts. Everything is veiled so you can't see who is bad and who is good."

"Wait." He placed his hand on the table and leaned in. "You said veiled. Why did you use that word?"

She eased back in the chair. "I only speak what I see. You watch yourself, hombre lobo."

Hombre lobo. The Spanish word for wolf man. She was clearly human. He could tell by her scent. How the hell did she know what he was?

"Relax. I've been around a long time. I've seen many things. I know too many things." She looked away as sadness washed over her expression. "I am no threat to you. Your secret is safe with me."

Lucien studied her weathered face for a lie. He saw none.

"Thank you," he whispered before walking away.

He quickened his steps down the sidewalk, his gaze assessing the people on the street. He knew he had to be careful not to run into Granny again. If she spotted him going into the apothecary, she'd want to know if something was wrong. She wouldn't stop until she was satisfied with an answer.

He came to a halt when he saw the worn sign for the apothecary hanging above the entrance. A *Closed* sign hung on the door. He checked the business hours, then glanced down at his phone.

He still had two more hours to wait.

Damn. He didn't have two hours.

He pressed his face to the glass and cupped his hand around his eyes. Wood shelves lined the wall, all filled with vials, bottles, and jars. The small space had a bookcase set up near the cash register, along with some candles of various shapes and sizes. Looked like any other shop in New Orleans.

The movement of a dark shadow near the corner of the room caught his eye. He squinted and made out the shape of a person setting some bottles on a shelf.

He rapped at the window.

The figure, a woman, stopped and turned to face him. She shook her head and motioned to her watch on her wrist.

He gritted his teeth and shook his head. "This is important," he called to her through the glass.

The woman stood, crossed her arms, and scowled.

"Please."

Shaking her head, she made her way to the door. She cracked the door a couple of inches and assessed him through the gap.

"We're not open yet." She scowled.

He inhaled her scent. Human. Her dark brown hair, which matched her dark eyes, was cut into a severe bob.

Wearing a dark blue skirt and matching top, she looked more like a principal than someone peddling spells and magic and potions.

"This is important," he insisted.

"It's always important." She snorted. "Let me guess, you need a love spell or something to heal a loved one?" She gave him a bored look.

"Not exactly. If you could look at this list and tell me if you even have the ingredients, I would appreciate it." He pulled out the list Ella had given him and shoved it through the crack in the door.

The owner took the list while keeping her gaze trained on him. She unfolded the crinkled paper and glanced down. Her eyes tracked down the page. She swallowed and raised her widened gaze back to him.

"Who gave you this list?" Her voice trembled, and she clutched the paper to her chest.

"Someone trying to help me find someone."

"Only a true witch would know the ingredients to a spell as powerful as this." She cut her gaze from side to side, looking over his shoulder before throwing opening the door and motioning him inside.

"Hurry up." She grabbed him by the arm and tugged him inside.

"Thanks for letting..."

"Shush. Keep your voice down and get away from the widow." She locked the door and took another glance outside before turning to face him. "The last thing I need is for someone to see you in my shop." She hurried toward the back of the shop.

"Why?" He followed her, frowning as the array of scents saturated the air.

She spun around on her heel. "Don't think I'm stupid.

These ingredients"— she waved his note in the air—"are for a specific spell."

She grabbed his arm and tugged him toward a small room near the back of the store. She motioned for him to step inside.

He scowled and shook his head.

"Look, you are going to get me into a whole lot of trouble if you don't get your big ass inside that room." She glanced back at the window.

"Fine." Grudgingly he stepped inside the room so no one passing by could see him.

"Who do you work for?" She narrowed her eyes. "I can tell you're not a witch. But you're not exactly human either."

"How did…" He fisted his hands.

"I can sense things." She shook her head. "And this… this list has trouble written all over it. It reeks of death."

His skin crawled at her words. It was going to mean death if he didn't get the ingredients.

"But somehow I sense you're not going to take no for an answer. Stay here and let me get all this together," she groused.

He stayed in the shadows of the small room and peered out, making sure she was doing what she promised.

She moved from shelf to shelf, sticking items in a small brown bag. She stopped in front of the candles and bit her lip. Hesitantly she reached for three red candles and popped them in the bag.

"Candles are not on the list." He'd carefully gone back over the list to make sure he wouldn't forget something.

"They are just in case."

"In case what?" He frowned.

"Look, wolf, accept help when its offered."

He bristled and growled. She knew what he was. Did he have a fucking sign on his forehead that said "werewolf"?

"Easy." She stepped inside the room with him and shoved the bag at his chest. "I've lived in New Orleans all my life. I've come to accept there is more supernatural shit that happens here than in any other place." She hesitated. "Well, except for Charleston."

"South Carolina?" He arched a brow.

She waved away his question and continued on. "I'm assuming the person you are delivering those ingredients to knows exactly how dangerous this spell is."

"Apparently." The real question was, how dangerous was Ella?

"Be careful with this spell. You probably should ask yourself whether this is really worth even attempting it." She licked her lips nervously.

"It is." He had no choice. He had to find out who was behind the torture of the Guardians.

She nodded once. The expression, one of knowing - something -bad -is- about -to -happen -and -wanting - nothing -to- do -with -it, spread across her face. "You need to go out the back way. I can't have anyone seeing you leave my place."

"Thank you." He followed her through another room to the exit, which led out into the alley.

She opened the door and poked her head out, looking both ways. Stepping back, she nodded for him to take his leave.

"Here, you didn't take my money." He shoved a wad of money at her.

She waved it away. "No. I'm not accepting money."

"But I can't…"

"I don't want anything traced back to me when you open that can of worms you are determined to open." She shot him a glare. "Just so you know, the spell can't be done tonight. It has to be done tomorrow."

"Why is that?"

"Because tomorrow is a full moon. You need the energy for the spell." She slammed the door behind him. The click of the lock settled into place.

He frowned and glanced down at the bag. Living in New Orleans, the shop owner probably knew a few witches and actual spells. But he hadn't missed the fear etched into her expression as she'd hurried to retrieve all the items he needed.

Whatever had her scared was bigger than he'd imagined. He couldn't help but wonder if it was the same person responsible for the missing Guardians.

CHAPTER 19

"*I*t's like a sauna out here." Catty stepped out of her apartment and into the steamy night. She sucked in a hot breath and hiked her bag higher on her shoulder as she made her way down the sidewalk. Darkness descended upon the city like a blanket, covering the sins and secrets of those it met in the shadows.

She plucked her sweaty shirt away from her sweaty body. Even in the dark, the humidity was still wicked.

After Big Mike's visit, she made an effort to stay away from Lucien. He'd come by her place, and when he'd knocked, she'd hidden in the bathroom. She didn't care what happened to her, but she wasn't going to let Lucien get hurt because of her.

She stayed in her apartment for the remainder of the day, not even going to visit Mrs. Willis.

Her chest tightened. She knew Mrs. Willis would be wondering where she was.

"Hey, sweetheart. What's your hurry?" a couple of guys hanging out at the corner called out to her. Her fingers tightened around the strap of her bag and she hurried her pace.

She'd been whistled at, yelled at, and even propositioned many times before. But tonight a sliver of fear skittered along her spine, like spider legs dancing on her back.

Something was different. Something was off.

She glanced around. There were plenty of people milling around the sidewalk, but they were all human. If she got into trouble she would need to shift to defend herself, but with the Pack Law, shifting in public was punishable by death.

Sometimes she hated humans. Not because she thought she was better but because they were so fucking entitled. If they knew how many times their lives had been saved from a rogue werewolf by Guardians, they would be shocked.

Not all humans were bad. Mrs. Willis was human and had a heart of gold.

Now her granddaughter, Shelly, was a different story. She didn't trust that chick as far as she could throw her skinny ass.

"Baby. What's your hurry?" The two men stepped up to flank her on both sides. One had a long untrimmed beard and dark eyes, while the other guy was clean shaven with snaggle-toothed smile.

They both reeked of whiskey and cigarettes. She cringed at the stench but kept walking. If she ignored them, maybe they would leave her alone.

"Hey, I'm talking to you. Do you think you're too good to talk to us?" The guy with the unkempt beard stepped closer. His arm brushed against her and she recoiled.

"I have to get to work," she murmured and kept her gaze straight ahead. Her heart clattered in her chest, and her lungs began to tighten and ache.

She was only a block from the club. Once inside she'd be safe. Only a few more feet.

"Yeah, we know where you work, angel." The other male

with the bad teeth ran his finger down her arm. "And we know what you look like under all those clothes."

Her stomach lurched. They knew she was a stripper.

"Say, how much money for a blow job?" the other guy sneered.

"I'm a dancer, not a hooker." She kept her voice businesslike and her gaze straight ahead despite the fear stomping up her spine.

"That's not what I heard. Hell, half those girls at the Triple X put out for the right amount." The dirty blond male leaned in close and sniffed.

She gritted her teeth and clenched her hands into fists. A tiny spark of anger ignited deep within her chest.

Panic that had crept up her spine was swiftly being drowned out by another emotion. Anger.

She was really getting tired of this shit. She was nothing but a pair of tits and a nice ass. They thought they could say whatever they wanted, do whatever they wanted, and she would be grateful for each time they grabbed her ass or told her she was hot.

She was done with this shit.

Stopping in her tracks, she stuck her finger in the bearded guy's chest. Her heart pounded as anger pulsed and surged through her body. "Let me tell you something. If you so much as try to touch me or put your hands on me again, I'm going to rip off your dick and stick it down your throat." Her voice grew louder with each word forced out of her mouth.

People stopped along the sidewalk to watch the interaction. The guy looked around and his face turned bright red. "Easy, girl."

"Stop touching me!" she screamed. The heat in her body raged as she fought back the impulse to shift and tear into these guys.

"This chick is crazy. She must be on something." The blond guy laughed and looked around at the crowd.

"Did you touch her?" A ball-headed biker with a substantial beer gut stepped up to the guy. He took off his shades and tucked them into the pocket of his leather vest.

"Look, we were having a little fun, ya know." The guy held up his hands and tried to laugh it off.

"Don't sound like fun to me." The biker whistled, and suddenly five other bikers stepped up behind him.

"Is there a problem?" A tall lanky guy with the same leather cut looked from his biker friend over to Catty.

"Yeah. These guys are harassing this young lady here."

She frowned. It had been a long time since anyone called her a young lady. Even longer since someone had stood up for her.

"Is that right?" The tall guy stepped up to the two guys harassing her and glared.

"Where do you need to go, ma'am?" The big biker asked.

"The Triple X." She dropped her shoulders a little. He'd probably leave after finding out what she did for a living.

He nodded and motioned for one of his friends, who stepped up beside him. "We'll walk you there."

She blinked, surprised by his offer. "Oh, that's okay. You don't have to."

"No, ma'am. My mama taught me not to let a woman walk alone if she feels unsafe. And after this, I reckon you don't feel safe right now. We'll escort you."

"Thank you." Her throat ached with emotion. While they looked like badass bikers, they certainly had their hearts in the right place.

They walked in silence down the sidewalk.

When they arrived at the front door of the Triple X, Catty turned and gave the burly man a smile. "Thank you. I appreciate what you did for me."

"Not a problem." He shrugged.

"There should be more gentlemen like you in this world. It would make for a better place."

The big guy ducked his head and his cheeks flamed red with embarrassment.

He wasn't used to getting a compliment, and she wasn't used to handing them out. She gave him another smile before walking inside.

She crinkled her nose at the smoke-filled room. Despite the depressing aura of the place, her heart felt a little lighter today at the kindness she'd been shown.

She hadn't expected respect from a total stranger when she needed it the most.

"What's gotten you smiling like a possum?" Celine groused, and she blew out a puff of smoke that enveloped Catty's head.

"Nothing." She shrugged and continued on her way toward the dressing room.

Celine walked beside her. "I guess you heard about Jill."

Catty stopped and turned. Unease settled in her gut. Surely she hadn't come back to the club. She had a plan and dreams and determination. "What are you talking about?"

"They found her body near the shipyard." Celine sniffed and stubbed out the butt of her cigarette into a nearby ashtray.

Catty's feet froze to the floor. She wrapped her trembling hands around her stomach in a futile attempt to stop the nausea snaking up her throat. "Oh my god. What happened to her? She was supposed to go back to school." Fear trembled in her throat with each word she spat up.

"It's a damn shame. That girl brought in a lot of customers." Celine looked point-blank at Catty. "If she'd stayed where she was supposed to, she'd probably still be alive."

"What?" She couldn't believe what she was hearing. Celine was a tough manager, but surely she didn't agree with keeping someone from living their lives.

"Her place was here, at the Triple X." She waved her fresh cigarette in the air. "You girls know what you are getting into here. And it's not like you aren't being well compensated. Hell, we even have dental. Do you know how many companies don't have dental?" Celine shook her head.

Catty's veins pumped cold blood through her body as she looked around the club. Suddenly the Triple X seemed to take on a whole new persona. A whole new bad vibe.

"All the other girls know about Jill. Best they use this as a learning experience."

"And what's the lesson in this?" Catty snapped.

Celine narrowed her eyes and pressed her thin lips into an invisible line. "She should have known her place in this world. Should've been grateful for her job and kept her ass where she belonged." She took a long drag and blew it out in Catty's face.

She cringed and held her breath. Anger bubbled in her veins and she wanted nothing more than to shift into wolf and escape this hell.

Hiking her bag higher on her shoulder, she headed for her seat at the makeup mirror.

And according to Celine, exactly where she belonged.

CHAPTER 20

*L*ucien weaved in and out of the crowd like a ghost dressed in black. The humid air clung to him. With the weight of his leather jacket, he was going to be soaked in a matter of minutes.

He rolled his shoulders and headed in the direction of the Bourbon Street. It was dark and hot, and he knew the city would only grow louder as the night drew on.

He shoved his hands in his pockets. He passed couples holding hands, families headed into restaurants to eat dinner, and single girls looking to celebrate and have a good time. People knew enough to keep their distance and step out of his way as he approached, but curious enough to stare.

He passed a group of bikers leaned up against their parked motorcycles. A couple of men looked up and gave him a nod by way of greeting. He returned the hello.

He had no destination in mind, but his feet did. When he ended up in front of the Triple X, he stopped.

He inhaled deep.

Catty was inside. He could smell her scent even though it was hours old.

He curled his fingers into fists and warred with himself about entering. He didn't like the idea of what she did. He understood why she did it, but it didn't mean he had to like it. The thought of other men looking at her and trying to touch her was enough to make him shift into a wolf on the spot.

None of it mattered. She wasn't his. She didn't belong to him. She never would.

He sucked in a deep breath and blew it out slow. He looked to the right at the bar next door. It would be better if he had a drink or two to take of the edge. Then he could think clearly. Then he could decide if he wanted to go inside or not.

* * *

CATTY SAT down at her dressing table and grabbed her bottle of water. Sweat glistened on her upper lip, and her eye liner was smeared from the heat in the club. She glanced down at the black leather corset and black G-string in her hand. She tugged her thin robe tight around her body. It was still see through it, but at least it was a barrier to her skin.

She snatched a tissue off the table and began the task of wiping her eyeliner off her sweaty skin.

"I can't believe that about Jill."

Her hand froze and she strained to listen to the other dancers mentioning Jill's name.

"I mean the way she died. It was so brutal," Muffy stated.

"No, it was personal," Meadow whispered and looked around.

"Meadow." Catty grabbed the girl by her arm and stood up. Muffy shot her a glare before walking away.

"What?" Meadow narrowed her eyes and snatched her arm out of Catty's hold.

"How did Jill die?"

Meadow looked around and leaned toward her. "They found her with her throat cut."

Nausea swamped up in her throat, and she grabbed her chair to keep her upright. Her hand went to her throat and brushed against the silver necklace. The necklace Jill gave her.

"Hey, are you okay?" Meadow arched her drawn-on eyebrow and gave her a curious look. "If you're getting sick, you should probably leave. You don't want the rest of us catching what you've got. Big Mike is low on dancers."

"Did they find out who did this?" Catty murmured. Her head swam with horrid images of Jill covered in blood as she lay gasping to breathe. As she'd drawn her last breath.

"Officially, no." Meadow lowered her voice.

"What does that mean?" Catty frowned.

"It means if you're smart, you'll drop all the questions." Meadow looked around to make sure no one was listening to their conversation. "Talking about this, especially here, is pretty stupid. You're asking for trouble. And I, for one, make it a point not to go looking for trouble." She gave her a pointed look before striding away on her black stilettos.

Catty slumped down in her chair. Meadow was insinuating that someone in the club had something to do with Jill's death.

But it didn't make sense. Jill had been gone from the club for almost a week. If they wanted retribution for her leaving the club, then they would have killed her the day she left. Not days later.

"Catty, you're on in ten minutes," Celine squawked out over the buzzing of the room.

She nodded and stood. Her legs wobbled, and she grabbed her chair to steady herself. She sucked in a deep breath.

She was leaving. On her own. Or in a pine box. Either way, she was leaving.

* * *

LUCIEN FINISHED off his fifth beer. With his werewolf metabolism, he didn't even have a buzz.

He glanced at the time. Almost midnight. It would be packed at the Triple X. Which meant more eyes on his Catty.

His Catty? He rubbed his hand through his hair and shook his head. He was living in a dream. They were never going to work. She deserved to be with a male who wasn't damaged. She deserved better than him. Not to mention how she would feel about him when she found out he'd lied about not being a Guardian. She'd never forgive him.

But it sure as hell felt right when he'd been inside her body. She felt like his.

He rolled his shoulder, where he'd been stabbed. The wound had long healed, and not even a scar remained.

He shoved away from the bar and stood. He tossed a couple of twenties on the counter for the bartender and made his way through the crowd to the front door. It was busier now than when he'd first arrived, and the noise of all the humans were grating on his nerves. There would be even more people at the Triple X.

He stifled a growl thinking about all the male eyes that would be on Catty. Possessiveness swamped his body until he was humming with anger. The urge to shift had never felt so strong in his life.

He forced his way through the crowd and out into the street. It was thick with people and he'd never felt so claustrophobic in his life. All he wanted was some fresh air.

He opened the front door of the Triple X and stepped inside. He cringed as the scent of cigarette and cigar smoke curled around him. The cool air was escaping out the front door, making the odor of sweat and body odor overwhelming.

"Hey sweetheart, you looking for a lap dance?" A tall brunette ran her hand across his bicep and up to his neck.

He grabbed her hand and scowled. "I'm not interested."

Irritation flashed across her eyes before she recovered and pasted on a sultry smile. "Well, there are other things I can do for you. For the right price, of course."

He took a step back. Was this something all the girls did? Was this part of the service? Had Catty done this?

He shook his head and walked away. The brunette called him a dick under her breath.

The music changed from an upbeat fast pop song to a slow seductive song. He scanned the crowd, looking at every blonde in skimpy clothes and trying to find the one stripper he needed to see. Some of the girls barely looked legal, while others looked like zombies with no life left in them at all.

Spying an empty seat next to the stage, he eased onto the bar stool and ordered a beer from a waitress. He glanced at the redhead dancing on the stage, but she didn't hold his attention for long.

His gaze scanned the crowd, but he didn't see Catty. Maybe she'd already left for the night.

The waitress appeared with his beer and he handed her some cash before turning his attention back to the stage.

His nostrils flared. Electricity seemed to skid across his skin.

Catty.

He could smell her, but he couldn't see her. He turned away from the stage, looking into the crowd for her familiar face.

"Want to stick something in?"

His body heated at the smooth sound of her voice behind him. He slowly turned back to the stage.

His mouth dropped.

Catty was on stage in front of him on her knees. Dressed in a red lacy bra and panties, she hooked her thumb in the side of her underwear and tugged. His body tightened and heated. Her scent washed over him and all he could think about was taking her right here, right now, on the stage.

She smiled as she watched him fumble with his cash. He gave up and stuck the whole damn wad in her thong.

"It's okay, Lucien. I'll give your money back after I get off work." She smirked and stood.

He might have been embarrassed, but he was too busy trying to keep his erection under control.

He couldn't tear his eyes away from her as she grabbed the pole and swung around. Wrapping her legs around the steel, she climbed up. Her toned legs corded under the movement, and when she was high enough she held on with her arms while stretching her legs out perpendicular to the floor.

The men applauded and whistled.

All he could think about was how her legs could feel around his back as he pounded himself inside her body, their bodies slick with sweat.

She let her gaze wander over to him as she maneuvered her body around the pole. She circled the pole in a graceful movement and slid down.

Keeping her eyes on him, she wandered over to an older man and offered her hip to him. He slipped a five-dollar bill inside and whispered something to her. She smiled but said nothing. Some younger guys called out to her, but she stayed away. As he watched her work, he noticed she didn't target the guys with a lot of money and attention. She usually danced for the quieter guys or older men.

Did she find them, in a way, safer than the younger men?

She knelt before him, careful not to touch him. He could see the desire in her eyes. He wanted to reach out and brush the hair out of her eyes. But he knew the rules and didn't want to get her in trouble at work. He certainly didn't want to get kicked out.

"What time do you get off?" he whispered.

"When we close."

"I'll wait for you and walk you home."

Her eyes widened for a fraction of a second. "Don't do that." Her music ended and the next girl was walking up on stage. She hurried and stepped out onto the floor.

He stood and made his way over to her. "Why not?"

She looked around, her face pale. "I'll get in trouble if I leave with a customer."

Somehow, after what he'd seen tonight, he truly doubted that. "Okay. I'll wait outside for you, then."

"No." She lowered her voice as an older woman with a clipboard and a cigarette hanging out of her mouth walked by.

"Catty, it's too dangerous to walk home by yourself at two in the morning."

"I've been doing it ever since I moved here." She arched her eyebrow.

"And I'm here now, so you don't have to anymore."

"And how long is that, Lucien? You're here on business. You don't plan on staying." She looked away.

"You're not either."

She glanced up at him and sadness flickered through her eyes.

"What is it?" He could smell the fear coming off her in waves, mixed with desperation.

"Nothing." She shook her head and glanced around the room, fear dancing in her eyes against the lights in the room.

"Are you in danger, Catty?" He touched her elbow. "Tell me. I can help you."

"Hey, no touching unless you are planning on paying for a lap dance." The older woman with a clipboard stepped up to them and pulled his hand away. He fought back a growl.

"I'm willing to pay," Lucien answered.

"Really?" The woman's eyebrows shot up. "Well, I'm afraid Catty doesn't usually do lap dances. So you might have to be generous, if you know what I mean, to even tempt her." The woman sneered.

"I'm willing to pay whatever."

"Catty?" The woman narrowed her eyes and waited for an answer.

"I'll do it." Catty held his gaze.

"Just so we're clear…" The woman stepped closer. The scent of cigarette smoke and bad breath made him hold his breath. "The Triple X allows lap dances in the special rooms. She can touch you all she wants, but you can't touch her. That's extra."

"Understood."

"Follow me," The woman led the way to the far side of the wall of the club. There were no stages or seating areas here. Only a line of rooms along the wall.

He glanced in the occupied rooms. The doors were clear glass and even though they were closed, he could still see a lot of what was going on inside.

A brunette dressed only in a G-string straddled her customer and was rubbing her tits in his face. In another room, a redhead was bent over at the waist and was shaking her butt in a bald guy's face while he grabbed her ass cheeks.

The older woman stepped into a room with a loveseat and a side table.

"I'll need the money. It's a hundred dollars for fifteen minutes." The woman held out her hand.

"But—" Catty protested, but the older woman sent her a glare and she didn't say any more.

"Fine." He dug in his wallet and pulled out two hundred dollars. "I want privacy. If you know what I mean."

"You got it." The woman smiled and stuck the cash in the pocket of her slacks before leaving them alone. He knew right then the owner of the club would never see a dime. The older woman was stealing from the club.

Catty rounded on him and crossed he arm. "You over-paid. A lap dance is only fifty dollars for fifteen minutes."

"I would have paid more."

She stared back at him and crossed her arms. The silence between them as heavy and deafening as new-fallen snow.

"Why are you doing this?" Her voice sounded small and unsure.

"I want to be with you. Alone."

CHAPTER 21

*H*er eyes softened. Her expression changed, shifted into desire and want and need. She stepped up to him and pressed her palm to his chest. His heart stumbled in his chest at the heat of her touch.

"Catty."

"Shush. Sit." She gave him a shove. He obeyed and eased down onto the couch.

She walked over to the wall to the built-in radio. She glanced at him and smiled before she pushed some buttons. A slow, sultry rock song spilled out from the speakers.

"Catty…"

She pressed her fingers to his lips. "No talking."

She stood and started to move and sway to the music. His body tightened as she moved with a fluidity he'd never seen. She knelt in front of him and spread his legs with the palms of her hands. She ran her hands up along the inside of his thighs and stopped inches from his crotch.

She trailed her hands down to his knees and slowly stood. Carefully, she straddled him and pressed her face to his neck.

"Be careful what you say. The walls have ears," she whispered near his ear.

He rested his hands on her ass as she pulled back to look into his eyes.

He nodded his understanding. He mouthed *Are you okay?*

For now. She answered back.

She pressed her palms to his chest and leaned her head back, undulating to the music.

"How many lap dances have you given?" he asked.

"You're my first."

Pride swelled in his chest.

"Good."

"You like what you see so far?" she purred as she looked at him.

"Yes."

Her hands trailed down his chest to his crotch.

"You can't come back in here, Lucien. Big Mike, the owner of the club, broke into my apartment and was questioning me about you. They know I've been with you. You don't want to mess with him. He's dangerous."

He cupped her cheek and held her gaze. Anger flared in his gut and spilled out into his chest. "Did he hurt you?"

She frowned and shook her head. "It's you I'm worried about," she whispered near his ear.

"Don't worry about me. I can take care of myself." He pressed his lips to the shell of her ear and inhaled her scent.

She moaned and tried to push away. "You are making it hard to concentrate on dancing."

"I was hard the second I saw you on that fucking stage." He pulled back to look at her. "What has you so scared?" he asked quietly.

She sighed. "One of the strippers who quit a week ago was found dead, out by the docks."

"Was it drugs?"

She leaned back and scowled.

He pulled her into his chest and held her tight. "I'm sorry. I didn't mean how it sounded."

"Her throat was cut."

His blood ran cold. He tightened his hold around her waist.

"Are you okay?"

"Shush." She leaned closer and continued to move her body to the music. Slowly she trailed her hands over his body, making his body respond with such a vengeance it shook him.

"Put your hands over your head," she murmured.

He frowned.

"Just do it." She leaned back and ground down on his crotch.

He hissed as he sucked in a breath in pleasure. If she kept this up, he was going to ruin his jeans.

He raised his hands and placed them behind his head.

She leaned in closer. "Be careful about what you say."

She held his gaze before sliding down his body. She stood and turned around, settling herself in his lap and spreading her legs. She laid her head on his shoulder and pressed her bottom into his lap.

"Why have you never given a lap dance before?" he whispered in her ear.

She looked into his eyes while moving her body slowly to the music.

"I've never wanted to be close to someone before."

"Until now?" His heart lurched in his chest.

"Until now," she admitted.

She grabbed his hands and dragged them down her breasts. His fingers itched to tug the lacy material away from her nipples and touch her, skin to skin. Slowly she guided her hands down her ribcage and across her smooth, flat stomach. She stopped when she reached the top of her G-string.

"I paid more so I can touch you, Catty." His voice was ragged as he sucked in a breath. His body was on fire with no relief in sight.

"Let me turn around," she moaned.

She stood and turned around and straddled him again. As she moved to the music, she slid her hand around to her back and unhooked her bra.

His body pulsed with lust.

Slowly she slid her bra off her shoulders. He reached for her. She leaned in to his touch, pressing her breasts into the palm of his hand.

"I want you," he whispered.

"Not here. It's too risky." She dropped her head to his neck and nipped him.

He groaned. He plucked her tight nipples between his fingers until she was breathing heavily and sliding up and down his lap. He could feel the heat of her core, and he knew she wanted him as much as he wanted her.

"Five minutes," the older woman called out as she passed by the door.

"Fuck," he cursed.

"Not this time, baby." She smiled as she bent to kiss his neck.

"When I get you alone, you're going to be naked for an incredibly long time. Don't plan on getting any sleep for hours." He cupped her head as he spoke.

"Sounds good to me." She flicked her tongue across her lips.

"I want you to be careful when you leave tonight. I'll wait for you outside."

"No. You can't. I'm sure they'll have people watching to see if I am taking anyone to my place."

"I'm not letting you walk home alone," he whispered in her ear.

"Meet me at my place. I've got another hour yet before I can leave."

"Fine." He didn't like it, nor was he going to let her walk home alone. He'd do what he did best. He'd keep to the shadows and watch her to make sure she was okay. She'd never know he was behind her.

* * *

"SOMETHING DOESN'T FEEL RIGHT." Granny sat up in her hotel room and glanced over at Haley. Her soon-to-be grand-daughter-in-law was still sleeping peacefully in the next bed after a long day of shopping for a wedding and seeing the sights of New Orleans. They were supposed to leave in the morning, but the thought of departing right now didn't sit right with her. Not after seeing Lucien.

She'd been surprised to run into him this morning and despite his attempts, she could sense he wasn't telling her everything about what he was doing in the Crescent City.

He was supposed to be riding the Pig Trail. Barrett never mentioned anything about Lucien coming all the way to New Orleans. Usually when the other Guardians crossed state lines, the other Guardians knew about it.

Unease settled in her gut.

She might be an old woman, but her instincts were never wrong. Lucien was in some trouble.

She reached for the brochure on the night stand and flipped through the pages. She needed a good reason to extend their visit. A reason Haley would agree to.

She smiled when her finger landed on the page of planta-tion home tours having a bridal expo. She ought to be able to talk Haley into going to get some ideas for her own wedding.

That would give her a reason to stay another day and give her a chance to do some investigating on her own.

Then she'd get to the bottom of whatever was going on.

* * *

"YOU SCARED ME TO DEATH." Catty pressed a hand to her fast-beating heart and sucked in a breath when she saw Lucien step out from the shadows of her apartment building.

"Sorry." A slow smile slid across his face.

Her anger was quickly forgotten when his eyes darkened. Her stomach warmed, and her heart flipped in her chest.

She was such a goner when it came to him.

He opened the door and she hurried inside. He pressed her against the dark corner, and his mouth descended on her in a fiery heat.

She moaned and opened her mouth under his assault. She clutched his shoulders and held him tight.

When he finally broke the kiss they were both breathless. "Let's get inside before I rip off your clothes."

They hurried to her door. She fumbled with the key, her trembling hands trying to force it in. When it slid in and she heard the click of the tumblers giving, she breathed out a sigh of frustrated relief.

They stepped inside and he kicked the door closed. Without wasting any time, he picked her up. She wrapped her legs around his lean waist and panted as she pressed herself against his thick erection.

He pressed her against the wall and grabbed the hem of her T-shirt. He tugged it over her head and tossed it to the floor.

"All of this has to go," he murmured as his mouth kissed her neck and his hands were busy getting rid of her bra.

Her nipples hardened as his hot tongue licked across the

sensitive flesh. He pulled her nipple into his mouth and sucked.

"Oh, god." She moaned and held his head to her breast. Her rhythm of her heart beat in her ears as her body pulsed with desire so thick she thought she would explode.

He walked over to her bed and laid her down. His fingers found the button on her jeans while his gaze stayed on hers. He pulled her jeans off and tossed them over his shoulder and then moved to her panties. Hooking his thumbs on either side, he tugged and tossed the lacy material to the ground.

His gaze moved over her nakedness, devouring her with his eyes. His chest heaved and his nostrils flared as he feasted upon her with his gaze.

She was used to men looking at her, but she wasn't used to feeling like this. No one had made her feel like this. No one but Lucien.

She rose up on her elbows and met his gaze.

"You're still dressed."

"I can fix that." In what seemed like two seconds, he'd peeled his clothes off his body. The street light spilled in through the window and illuminated his muscles like he was on display. A solid wall of strength and finely honed muscle stood before her. He was more beautiful than any male she'd ever seen before.

He climbed on top and lay between her legs. His eyes softened as he stared down at her.

The way he looked at her made her heart weep with joy.

He brushed the hair out of eyes with gentle fingers and then trailed then across her cheek. "You're so perfect, Catty."

"I'm far from perfect, Lucien," she whispered into the night.

"For me. You're perfect for me."

She fell for him in that one moment, heart and soul.

Before she could speak, he covered her mouth with his in a blistering kiss that had her arching up and rubbing her body to his.

His tongue tangled with hers, each tasting the other and reveling in the eroticism of the moment. His hand slid down and cupped her hip, and he ground his erection into her stomach. She tried to open her legs, but she was trapped under his weight.

"Not yet. I want to savor you for as long as I can."

His deep voice sent tremors across her skin like electricity. She was no virgin, but the way he spoke to her, looked at her, was different. The pull to claim him was strong, and it pained her to think of him with another female. It only meant one thing.

He was her perfect mate.

She squeezed her eyes shut to still the tears behind them.

Lucien would never mate her. He was too perfect. And what was she?

A stripper.

Her heart sunk to her stomach as his mouth nibbled along her neck.

Gritting her teeth, she forced her thoughts away and focused on now.

Now she was with him.

Now she was his.

Tonight she would give him everything and hold nothing back. Tonight she would make memories to sustain her a lifetime. Tonight she would pretend they were mated.

CHAPTER 22

*L*ucien's body ached with lust.

He dipped his head, skimming his tongue across her tender flesh, marking her with his own scent. By the time he finished, every wolf within a fifty-yard radius would know she belonged to another.

They would know she belonged to him.

His head swam with her sweet feminine scent and his chest tightened with an unrecognizable emotion.

His mouth captured a hardened peak of her nipple in his mouth, and she moaned low and deep.

It made him harder and more eager to please her.

He'd never envisioned himself with someone so beautiful who would accept him as he was.

But Catty did. His scars didn't scare her.

* * *

"Don't stop." She arched her wet heat against his erection. She needed him. All of him. Her body craved his next touch, his next kiss, the next lick of his tongue.

"I don't plan on it. I wasn't lying when I said you needed your energy for tonight." His mouth moved down to the flat of her stomach. He sucked the tender flesh around her navel. She bucked and threaded her fingers through his hair.

"Don't stop touching me. With your fingers, your body, your mouth." With him she found herself being emboldened, saying what she felt, telling him what she needed.

He poised his mouth between her legs and looked up into her eyes. Her heart twisted and pounded with the intimacy of the moment.

She cupped his cheek and spread her legs, offering herself to him. "Lucien."

He grinned and then licked the sweet sensitive flesh between her legs. She arched off the bed, her breath catching in the back of her throat.

He looked up and gave her a wicked grin.

He dipped his head between her legs and cupped her butt in his hands as he feasted. His tongue teased and taunted as he continued to use his mouth.

She was close. So close to finding her release.

She moaned as her heart beat against her ribcage. He captured her clit in his mouth and sucked. Her body tensed and she tightened her legs around his head as pleasure zipped through her body.

He opened his heavy-lidded eyes and watched as she threaded her fingers through his dark hair and held him close.

Her body tensed, and a moan spilled out from the back of her throat as her orgasm washed over her, sending her into ecstasy.

He continued to lick at her until she tumbled back down to earth, her body spent.

Panting, she looked down at him. He wiped the wetness

from his mouth with the back of his hand and crawled up her body.

"Your turn." She tried to roll him over onto his back, but it was like moving a freight train. Impossible.

"If you put your mouth on me right now I wouldn't last three seconds, baby." He grinned and pressed his erection to her wet entrance. "Right now I want to be inside you."

"Lucien," she whispered as he pushed inside, filling her with a pleasurable pain.

Seated deep inside her body, he looked down at her as his breath came out in heavy pants, his eyes dilated with a craving. A craving for her.

He said nothing, his gaze locked on hers. He didn't need to. She felt all the words in his touch, in their eyes, in their connection.

She ran her hands around to his back. He stilled but didn't flinch from her touch this time.

"All of you. I want all of you." She pulled him closer and licked his ear. Her fingers traced the puckered ridges of his back.

His mouth descended on hers. His hot scent was like a drug, lifting her higher and higher. She wanted more.

He slowly began to move inside her body, claiming her with every thrust, every stroke.

His body molded to hers in a perfect fit of flesh, muscle, and sweat.

"Catty," he groaned and reached between their bodies to the sensitive nub.

She inhaled as he began to tease her sensitive flesh while thrusting in and out of her body.

"Yes," she groaned out. Her body tensed as pleasure filled her body and then crested over with an orgasm so intense she cried out.

Trembling, she looked up at him and pulled his head down for a kiss.

He groaned into her mouth as he found his own orgasm, spilling his seed deep within her.

Exhausted, he collapsed on top of her. She wrapped her arms around him, holding him tight.

In the aftermath of their pleasure, he sighed as her fingers traced over his back.

"That was amazing." She smiled and kissed his shoulder.

"Give me five minutes and I'll really blow your mind."

"You already did." She laughed.

He rolled over and tugged her into his chest. He cradled her in the protective circle of his arms. The only sound in the dark room was the mingling of their breathing.

He glanced toward the window. "I used to love coming to New Orleans when I was a kid."

"You did?"

"My parents would bring us here Sundays for lunch. My mother always made sure we were properly dressed." He laughed. "That's one thing I don't miss. Dressing up to eat. Even at home, we had to dress for dinner."

"Sounds like your parents had money." Catty's parents were well-to-do, but they certainly weren't rolling in it.

"Yeah. They do. Or did. I haven't seen them in a while. Not since I moved to Arkansas." His voice sounded heavy, like he'd been carrying something for a long time, something he desperately needed to put down.

"They must live close." She pressed her lips together, waiting for him to answer.

"They do. It's a plantation home, not too far from here. My great-grandfather built it. It's not as old as the other plantations around here, but it still has a lot of history." He cupped her neck and rubbed his thumb across her bottom lip. "I once told my dad we should do tours of the house during holidays like Christmas and Valentine's Day." His lips turned up into a semblance of a smile. "He said no. Said he didn't want strangers in the house trying to case the place or steal the family silver."

She laughed. "Well, I can't blame him."

She settled back against his shoulder. "It must have been a great place to grow up. I remember my home. We lived in a subdivision, but the lots were big and our property backed up to a forest. Me and Skylar used to take my mom's sheets and make forts in the woods. We'd also take her spoons so we could dig in the ground and make a fairy city. She'd always find her spoons bent out of shape and ask if I knew what happened. I would always lie. Although I couldn't lie when Skylar was around. That girl had an honest streak a mile wide. She threw me under the bus one day when my mom asked if we'd seen her pearl necklace. I said no. Skylar spoke up and said I broke it while we were out in the forest working on our fairy house. We were going to use the pearls as a gate around the fairy house. I stretched it too far and the pearls went everywhere."

"Sounds like you had a good childhood."

"I did." She'd chosen a different path, far from the charmed life she once knew.

"It's weird when things you took for granted aren't there anymore." His wistful tone made her heart ache.

"Yes." She eased up on her elbow to look into his eyes. "Like Mom's meatloaf."

"Or digging up night crawlers to go fishing," he added.

She grinned. "Or irritating Zane."

"Oh, believe me he's still getting irritated by his Guardian brothers."

"How long have you known Zane?" She trailed her finger down the muscles in his chest.

"For a while." He shrugged. "We're not BFFs, if that's what you're asking."

"Do you like living in Arkansas?"

"I do. I miss things about Louisiana though. Like the food and my home." His voice trailed off.

"Why don't you go for a visit while you're here?" She lifted her eyes to his.

"Because I'm on business. Besides, I don't think they want to see me."

"That can't be true. They're still your parents. They love you no matter what."

A slow smirk grew across his gorgeous lips. "You should listen to your own advice, Catty."

"I'm different." She shook her head and fell back onto his shoulder. "I chose this path. I chose the consequences and the shame. My parents would be heartbroken if they knew what I've become."

He raised up on his elbow and lifted her chin with his finger. "What you've become is a beautiful, independent woman who looks after the interests of others. Like Mrs. Willis and your friend Jill. You have options and you are a survivor." His words trickled over her soul like a warm spring, filling her with hope. She'd never looked at herself in that light before.

"Well, maybe if you go see your parents, then I'll go see mine." She arched her brow. She couldn't imagine going home, but she would encourage Lucien to.

"We'll see." He laughed and fell back on the bed. "Right now, I've got other plans for you." He wrapped his arms around her waist and pulled her on top of him.

"I made a promise you were not getting any sleep tonight. And I never break my promises."

* * *

CATTY STOOD at the foot of her bed and watched Lucien sleep. A sheet wound around his waist, the white material hiding his nakedness from her gaze.

Dark hair brushed his forehead, while his face looked almost angelic as he slept. His large muscled body made her ache for him once again.

She shook her head. She needed to snap out of it. She was acting like a nympho. They'd had sex five times last night. She'd been amazed at how much pleasure he could pull from her body with ease.

Before they'd drifted off to sleep, he'd told her he had to go back to see the witch tonight.

No way was she going to let him go alone.

She'd set her alarm, woken early, and grabbed a shower without disturbing him.

She glanced at the time. She had time to drop by and see Mrs. Willis before they left.

She placed the note telling him where she was by the side of the bed. Sighing, she picked up her backpack and headed out the door.

She stepped out of her building and glanced around. The morning still had a heavy gray look before the sun made its appearance. The air was heavy and thick, making each breath an effort.

She hiked her bag higher on her shoulder and began the trek toward Mrs. Willis's house.

She ducked into a small coffee shop and was greeted with the delicious aroma of coffee beans and freshly baked pastries.

The shop was relatively empty except for one older man at a table and two people in line. She stepped in behind an older woman and glanced up at the menu.

"I don't know, Haley. Get me whatever you think I'd like."

The gray-haired woman turned and smiled at Catty. "Good morning."

"Good morning." Catty returned the smile. "The chocolate croissants are really good." She nodded at the display case.

"That sounds good." The woman turned away from the pretty blonde she was talking to and looked at her. The woman leaned in and gave Catty a strange look.

"You look like you didn't get much sleep, dear." The older woman lowered her voice.

Her face heated. She was thrown off guard from the woman's blunt comment.

"Granny, that's not nice." The young girl turned and gave Catty an apologetic smile.

"What?" Granny gave the girl an innocent look. "What I wouldn't give for a night where some hot man kept me up and had me glowing."

"Granny!" The young woman shook her head.

"It's okay. I didn't get much sleep last night." She pressed her lips and suppressed a smile.

"A guy, right?" Granny asked.

She nodded.

"I figured."

Haley coughed as she tried to hide her embarrassment.

"I may be old, but I can tell when a girl has the attentions of a man." She leaned in close and lowered her voice. "Or should I say male, since we're not exactly fully human. Are we, dear?"

Her eyes went wide and she inhaled. The woman was a wolf. How had she not noticed?

"It's okay, dear. You are among friends." She patted Catty on the arm and smiled.

"I'm Granny and this is Haley." The old woman nodded

toward the pretty blonde who was holding two cups of coffee and a bag of pastries.

"Nice to meet you. I'm Catty." She'd been too busy thinking of Lucien and what they'd spent the better part of the night doing to realize the two women were werewolves.

"We're visiting New Orleans to get some stuff for my wedding." Haley's eyes twinkled when she spoke. The girl was practically glowing.

"Wedding." Catty arched her eyebrow. Wolves mated. It was the same thing as a wedding. The mated bond was stronger than any human ceremony.

"Yes. He said he wanted to be double-bonded." Haley lowered her voice.

"Well, congratulations. He's certainly a lucky guy." Jealously stung her in the gut, reminding her of her failures. She wouldn't be mated. The only one she could imagine binding her life to was Lucien. And he was too fine a male for her and completely out of her reach.

"No." Haley shook her head. "I'm the lucky one. I gained a family when I found Jayden."

"They are both lucky to have found each other." Granny turned back to Catty. "Like you and your guy."

She forced a smile. Her good mood had evaporated.

"Well, we better get going. Lots to do today." Granny smiled before heading for the door with Haley.

She watched after them with a small heaviness in her heart.

"Ma'am, what will it be?" the barista asked.

Forcing her thoughts to the back of her mind, she turned back to the counter and quickly ordered a coffee and some croissants for Mrs. Willis. She was going to grab something to eat herself, but she suddenly didn't have much of an appetite anymore.

CHAPTER 23

"*I* should have more information by tonight." Barrett leaned back in his chair and stared at Ryker over his desk. Ryker had been there way before the sun began to peek over the horizon.

Barrett hadn't left his office since this whole shit storm had started. Ryker stayed close to the compound in case the situation changed.

There was a loud knock on the door. Both males turned and scowled.

"Who is it?" Barrett's hard tone echoed in the room.

"Jaxon."

"Fuck." Barrett sent Ryker a warning look before getting up from his desk. Opening the door, he scowled at his Guardian.

"Do you need something, Jaxon?"

"I need to know what's going on with Lucien." He pushed past Barrett and into the office.

"Jaxon…" Barrett narrowed his eyes on his Guardian and curled his fists into hands.

"Look boss, I know. I'm interrupting. But I can't let this

180

go anymore." The blond werewolf turned his astute blue eyes on him. Jaxon was much like Jayden in appearance, but they were starkly different in personality. Jayden had grown more serious, more intense, while Jaxon was left to revel in his bachelorhood and easygoing manner.

His easygoing manner was not on display today.

"Barrett, please." Jaxon held out his hands to his sides. "My gut is telling me something is wrong, very, very wrong. I want to help."

Ryker spoke up. "I think it's time we start letting everyone know what's going on."

Barrett shot him a glare. Fucking Ryker and his big mouth. Ryker shrugged his shoulders and popped a piece of gum in his mouth.

Barrett looked back at Jaxon. His gut told him not to say anything. To wait. He didn't need his Guardians to go all vigilante and go off halfcocked.

"Barrett, you have to give me something."

"I don't have to give you anything, Jaxon. Not now." He narrowed his eyes at the Guardian. "I'm your Pack Master. You seem to forget. And my patience for your lack of respect is quickly running out."

Jaxon looked at the floor, took a deep breath, and then looked back at Barrett. Conflicting emotions flashed through his blue eyes as he seemed to struggle with what to say next.

"I understand you are worried about your friend." Barrett kept his voice calm but stern. He needed his men to see he was still in charge. Once Guardians lost respect for their leader the whole Pack would fall.

He couldn't— no, he wouldn't— let that happen.

"He's more than a friend. He's a brother to me." Jaxon looked away and cringed. "Although I'm sure he doesn't feel that way himself. He's always kept to himself, kept himself apart from us." He looked back at Barrett. "But family is family. No matter what."

"Good. That's what I wanted when I accepted the position of Pack Master here in Arkansas. I wanted my Guardians to be a brotherhood, to be willing to lay down their life for each other." He nodded, something hard settling in his chest.

"I know you aren't going to tell me much, if anything. I just came in here hoping to let you know, I realize Lucien is in some kind of trouble."

"Why would you say that?" Barrett narrowed his eyes. Had Lucien contacted him? Had Ryker opened his big mouth?

Jaxon shook his head and scrubbed his hand down his face. "I know it sounds crazy. But since he left, I keep getting this bad feeling. That's he's in some trouble." He looked up at Barrett. "He's not on a riding trip, is he?"

"He's not." It was the only information he could give him.

"Barrett…" Ryker pleaded.

"I'll tell you what. When there is something to report on Lucien, I'll let you know." Barrett walked over to his door and opened it wide. "For now, I need you to remember my position. We clear, Jaxon?"

"Yeah, we are." Jaxon stiffened and stormed out of the office.

Barrett locked the door behind him.

"Barrett…"

"I don't want to hear it, Ryker. The less he knows, the better." He walked around the desk and sat, shooting the werewolf a glare that spoke volumes.

"I agree. But there comes a point when you are going to have to let the others know what's going on." Ryker shoved his hands in his pocket.

"I'm not putting any more Guardians in danger. Lucien has this under control. Tonight he'll be able to find out who's behind all this. Until then, we wait." He'd been putting out feelers to any and all contacts to see if anything came up. So far, nothing.

"I need you to go follow Jaxon."

"Why?" Ryker frowned.

"Because he's about to do something stupid and try to find out where Lucien is."

"How do you know that?"

"Call it instinct." He shook his head. He needed a few more hours until Lucien could get the information from the witch. Everything hinged on that meeting.

Right now, Lucien was their only hope.

* * *

"I THINK they are all so lovely. It's hard to pick a favorite." Haley looked up from the table filled with bridal bouquets ranging from pastel to vibrant colors. She should be excited about shopping, but today she couldn't get in the mood. A twinge of guilt stung her gut as she dug in her purse and checked the time. "I'm worried about staying another day. I did promise Jayden I'd be on my way home today." She looked at the older woman who was more a mother to her than her own biological one.

After she'd been kidnapped by rogue wolves, Haley's parents thought she'd been raped and therefore ruined in their eyes. They'd transferred her from LSU to the University of Arkansas. It was there she'd met Jayden when he was protecting her from a stalker.

"I know, dear, but you know what they say. Absence makes the heart grow fonder." Granny picked up a white bouquet with lilies and baby's breath and sniffed. She wrinkled her nose and set the bouquet down. "Besides, you want to have as much stuff done while we're here as possible so once you get back home you can concentrate on Jayden."

It sounded good to her.

"So, when you talked to Jayden, did you mention we saw Lucien?" There was a different tone in Granny's voice. One that seemed cheerful enough but held an edge of barely concealed curiosity.

"I did." She looked at Granny under her eyelashes. "He sounded surprised. He thought he was riding the Pig Trail. I guess he decided to make his trip longer and come visit New Orleans."

"Oh." Granny's tone almost sounded normal. Granny never sounded normal.

She picked up a pink bouquet and frowned. Her gut told her the old woman had another reason for staying another day in New Orleans. Something she wasn't telling her.

Something that had nothing to do with the wedding.

* * *

Jaxon headed for his room in the barracks. He knew better than to expect Barrett to reveal anything to him. Barrett would take a secret to the grave.

He ducked in his room and locked the door. He opened the closet and pulled out a saddlebag and slung it on the bed. He tossed in some T-shirts, a pair of jeans, and some underwear before opening the drawer of his nightstand.

He reached for his .9 mm, loaded a full mag, and slid the action back, throwing a silver bullet into the chamber. While a normal bullet wouldn't hurt another werewolf, a silver bullet would send a werewolf into a world of hurt before he finally died.

He tucked the gun in the back of his jeans and pulled his

T-shirt over to conceal the weapon. He tossed in two more full magazines into the saddlebag for good measure.

His moto was *Always come prepared.*

Barrett was wound tighter than Dick's hatband. His Pack Master never got himself worked up over anything. He ran a tight group, enforced the law, and was more than fair.

Now, Barrett was on the edge. Completely unlike the ruler he'd come to respect.

Barrett was hiding something. And it involved Lucien.

* * *

LUCIEN WALKED up the uneven path to the old yellow house of Mrs. Willis and glanced around the neighborhood. The house next door had graffiti painted along the side, and its shutters were hanging on by sheer desperation. A beat-up car was up on blocks in the front yard like a lawn decoration, and a couch was perched on the front porch. He cringed as he imagined the numerous bugs and rats that had made their nests in the furniture.

He looked back at the front door of Mrs. Willis's house. Despite its age, the home had a cozy feel to it. It stood out among the rest of the run-down houses on the street. Mrs. Willis's house seemed to emit hope among the otherwise desperate neighborhood.

He'd discovered a note on the side table from Catty when he woke up. He didn't want to leave for Mississippi before talking to her. Not after last night.

An image of their bodies moving together as they made love throughout the night flashed in his mind. His body tightened as he remembered how she had called out his name, lost in her pleasure, locked in his arms.

He'd hoped to have her again that morning, but she'd been gone when he woke up.

He frowned and stepped up to the door and knocked.

A staccato of taps on the floor followed the door opening. Mrs. Willis stood there, eyes unfocused and wearing a green muumuu.

"Catty, is that you?" Mrs. Willis called out.

"No, ma'am, I'm Lucien. I'm a friend of Catty's." He glanced over the old woman's shoulder into the house. "She said she was coming over here this morning. I wanted to talk to her before I went out of town. But I see she's not made it here."

"Oh! It's so nice to meet one of Catty's friends." She reached out and patted his arm. "I worry she doesn't have anyone to look after her. She doesn't have family here, you see."

"Yes, ma'am. I know."

"Well, look at my manners. Come on in, honey. Any friend of Catty's is welcome in this house. I'm sure she's on her way." She smiled and opened the door wide to allow him access.

"Thank you." He stepped inside. The house was old with tall ceilings and hardwood floors. The antique furniture was well worn, and photos covered the wall. It was like he'd stepped back in time.

"Would you like some tea? Or coffee perhaps?"

"Coffee would be nice." He hadn't gotten his caffeine infusion for the day. He'd gotten dressed and headed over here as soon as he read Catty's note.

"Who's this?" A slender young brunette sauntered into the living room. She wore black shorts that had her ass hanging out and a T-shirt with a plunging neckline. Even with her makeup on, she looked barely legal.

"Hi, I'm Lucien. I'm a friend of Catty's." He held out his hand. She took his hand in hers and held on a second too long as her lips curled up into a slow smile.

"Catty's lucky. I wish I had friends like you." She stepped into his personal space. Her breast brushed against his arm.

"This is my granddaughter, Shelly. Shelly, can you bring us some coffee?" Mrs. Willis cleared her throat, clearly not impressed with her granddaughter's flirty tone.

The old woman might be blind, but she could still see.

"Sure." Shelly's tone was less than eager, and she took her time walking out of the room.

"Please sit, Lucien. Sometimes Catty stops and picks me up some sweet treats at the coffee shop." Mrs. Willis made her way to the rocking chair and sat.

He waited until she was seated before he took a seat on the couch.

"So tell me, how well do you know Catty?" She rested the handle of her cane on the arm of her rocking chair and laced her fingers together and placed them in her lap.

He knew her pretty damn well, he wanted to say. But Mrs. Willis probably wouldn't appreciate his language.

"I actually met her this week. I know her brother, Zane."

"Ah, and what does her brother think about your interest in his sister?" The corners of Mrs. Willis's mouth tipped up.

He cleared his throat and shifted in his seat. Mrs. Willis let out a laugh.

"Don't worry, Lucien. I'm glad she has you. I may not see a person's appearance, but I can see their heart. You don't need eyes for that."

"I guess you don't." He smiled at the old woman. "Catty speaks very highly of you, Mrs. Willis. Thank you for being so kind to her while she's been in New Orleans. I know it's meant a lot."

"That girl has helped me more than I could ever thank her for." Her face lit up with emotion. The maternal affection she felt for Catty made him homesick for his own mother.

"Catty is like that. Incredibly generous."

"Yes, that's what worries me." Mrs. Willis thanked her granddaughter as Shelly handed her a mug of hot coffee.

"Thank you," Lucien murmured as Shelly passed him a cup. She smiled and sat next to him on the small couch.

"Shelly, dear, are there any tea cakes left in the pantry? I'm sure Lucien would love some with his coffee."

"I don't know. I didn't see any." Shelly kept her gaze fixed on him and continued to ignore her grandmother.

"I'll go check." Mrs. Willis stood up.

"No, Mrs. Willis, don't bother yourself. The coffee is perfect. I don't eat anything sweet first thing in the morning."

"I bet I have something sweet you would love to eat." Shelly murmured and leaned into him.

He glared at the girl's sexual innuendo.

She leaned in closer and rested her hand on his thigh.

He grabbed her hand and looked into her eyes.

"No, thank you. I've already had my appetite satisfied." He shot her a glare.

She arched her brow, knowing what he was insinuating.

"Mrs. Willis, when do you expect Catty? I hate to impose on your hospitality." Even though the woman couldn't see him, he turned and gave her his full attention and ignored Shelly. Maybe she would get the hint he was not interested.

"It's no imposition at all, Lucien." A smiled brightened her features. "It's been a while since this house has had a man grace its presence."

"How long has it been since your husband passed?" he asked quietly.

Shelly sighed and got up, already bored with the topic of conversation. She sashayed into the kitchen.

"About twenty years. We moved into this house right after we were married." She tapped her cane gently on the floor. "She's a grand old house. Or used to be, anyway."

"Still is."

"You're sweet, Lucien. I can see why Catty likes you." She shook her head slowly. "With losing my eyesight, I can't keep her up like I used to. Maybe it was God's way of not letting me see the state the neighborhood has fallen into." She rested her cane at her knee and felt for the side table before resting her cup on the surface. "Catty is a sweet girl. Always coming by and checking on me. She even brings flowers to hang on my front porch. I can't see them, but I can smell them when I step outside. She's always thinking of others."

"She's a regular Mother Teresa," Shelly muttered as leaned against the doorway leading into the living room.

Lucien's irritation flared.

"Shelly, I'm sure I don't understand your meaning." Mrs. Willis frowned.

"Oh, I'm sure Shelly was complimenting me." Catty appeared in the doorway holding two Styrofoam cups of coffee, a bag of sweet treats, and a face full of irritation.

CHAPTER 24

"Catty, I didn't hear you come in. Look who's here. Your friend Lucien." Mrs. Willis's cheerful tone should have eased the tension in the room.

"Lucien, what are you doing here?" A slow blush crossed Catty's face.

"I thought I would surprise you." He stood and walked over to her.

The tension in the room was heavy, and all he wanted was to rip her clothes off and have her once more.

"Ah, now I see." Shelly flashed a bitchy smile. "Catty, I have to say I didn't think you'd hook up with someone so hot. Seems a bit out of your league."

Catty flinched as if she'd been hit.

Lucien shot Shelly a glare.

"Shelly!" Mrs. Willis's sharp tone echoed in the room. "That's uncalled for. And you owe Catty an apology."

"I'm pretty lucky that Catty even gives me the time of day. I place a lot of value on our relationship." He kept his gaze on the woman who'd bared her soul and her body to him last night.

"Is that so?" Shelly narrowed her eyes at him. Clearly the girl was jealous of Catty.

Catty shifted her weight and cleared her throat.

"I brought some chocolate croissants. I know how much you like them." She looked at Mrs. Willis.

"You're such a sweet girl." Mrs. Willis smiled. "Come sit down and we'll share some good coffee and some good conversation. Shelly, can you bring Catty a cup of coffee?"

Shelly narrowed her eyes.

"I brought my own." She headed over and set the bag of treats down on the coffee table.

"Come sit, dear. I was just having a nice conversation with Lucien." Mrs. Willis accepted the croissant Catty handed her. She placed the pastry on a small napkin Catty produced from the bag.

Catty turned to Lucien. "What were you guys talking about?"

"Ah, just about how close you too are." Mrs. Willis pipped in before taking a bite of the croissant.

Lucien lifted his brow and looked at the older woman. Not exactly the conversation he remembered.

"Really?" Catty blushed.

"Yes, Lucien is quite the... catch." Shelly slid up to him and raised up on her tiptoes to place a kiss on his cheek. "I've gotta run. See you around, Lucien." Shelly strutted to the front door.

Catty shot daggers at him with her eyes.

"You know, Mrs. Willis. I forgot about an appointment I had made this morning." She stood and gathered her bag off the floor. "I've got to run before I'm late."

"Oh, I was looking forward to talking more with your friend Lucien."

"Oh, he can stay. I'm sure he has no place to be." She gave him a death stare before hurrying to the door.

"I'll see you in a few days, Mrs. Willis." Catty called out over her shoulder before the door slammed shut.

Shit. He was clearly in trouble.

"Well, Lucien. Don't just stand there. Go after your girl." Mrs. Willis smiled before taking a bite out of her croissant.

He mumbled a quick goodbye and hurried out of the house.

Catty was more than pissed. She was hurt.

Standing on the sidewalk, he scanned the area. No sign of her. He closed his eyes and inhaled.

Her scent.

He hurried after her.

His footsteps pounded against the concrete sidewalk. Sweat broke out under his leather jacket and seeped into his T-shirt.

He turned and headed down an alley. When he reached the end, he stepped out onto the next street. He caught sight of Catty in jeans, boots, and a thin T-shirt heading toward her apartment.

He took off at a run.

"Stop, Catty." He grabbed her elbow, but she snatched out of her grip.

"Leave me alone, Lucien." She kept walking, her hands jammed in the pockets of her jeans.

"Caty, Shelly was just being a bitch."

She stopped in her tracks and turned on her heel. "That may be, but the fact is she's right. You deserve to be with someone who's your equal. Not a stripper." Pain flashed through her eyes as she continued walking.

"What the hell are you talking about?" He hurried beside her, matching her pace.

She stopped again and met his gaze. "Look, this thing between us needs to stop."

"Why?" His heart froze in his chest. He figured once it

started beating again it would fracture into a thousand pieces.

"I can't keep living in this daydream. That we will somehow be together when next week comes." She gave him a sad smile. "I live in the real world. And in my world, the best I can hope for is to leave this place and start over where no one knows me or my past." Her smile faltered and she glanced away.

He grabbed her by the arms and forced her to look at him. "Listen to me. I can't promise you next week, hell, I can't promise you tomorrow. In the line of work I'm in, I have no guarantees."

"It sounds dangerous. What line of work are you in exactly, Lucien?" Her gaze narrowed on him and she lowered her voice.

"Doesn't matter. What does matter is I care for you, Catty. And I'm not ready to walk away from this, from us." His heart beat rapidly in his chest. He felt open and vulnerable, yet he couldn't stop the words from spilling out from his mouth. "And I don't think you're ready to walk away either."

"Look at me. Tell me the truth. Do you regret what we did, do you regret what has happened between us?" His chest squeezed as he waited for her answer.

She smiled. Her fingertips trailed down his jaw.

"No. I think what happened between us will keep me going for years to come. You've given me more in a few days than I can ever get in a lifetime. For that I'm grateful."

His heart shattered in his chest for her. He wanted to grab her and take her back to his place and make love to her until she was consumed with him. Like he was for her.

"You don't give yourself enough credit." His heart tugged in his chest, and he kept his gaze on hers. "You don't see what a wonderful person you really are. It goes beyond your beauty, which is pretty damn hot."

She let out a reluctant laugh.

"I'm serious. You are more woman than I ever thought I would find." God, he wanted to tell her more, tell her how much he wanted to spend the rest of his life with her. But he couldn't.

If this mission went south and he didn't live, he didn't want her to feel like he'd abandoned her in his death.

Suddenly the idea of being done with this mission and going home rushed into his chest. He'd lived his job for years, but now with Catty he longed for something different. He longed for someone to come home to at night.

"What are you saying?" She looked up at him, hope shining in her eyes like stars.

"I'm saying right now, today is all we are guaranteed. I want to live each day like it's my last."

"You say that like it's a possibility." Her brows furrowed.

He shrugged. "I want to be here, present in this moment with you. And once I'm finished with New Orleans, I ..."

"You what?"

He swallowed. "I want you to come home with me. Back to Arkansas."

There. The words were out. There was no going back now.

"You do?" Her voice waivered, like she didn't dare to believe what he was saying to her.

"Yes, I do." He meant it.

The busyness of the morning moved around them. The hum of cars passing slowly on the street, coupled with the scent of breakfast in the nearby diner, seemed dull in the space between them.

"I need to hurry up and be done with this business for the Guardians. It's important I get this done first. You understand, don't you, Catty?" Suddenly, finding his brother didn't seem so important. Not anymore.

"Of course I do." She stepped closer and rested her palms against his chest.

He wanted to take her in his arms and kiss her senseless, but he knew too many people could be watching them. He wouldn't jeopardize her safety for his selfishness.

"Good." He didn't know what the future held for him, but he sure hoped she was part of it.

"I was worried when I woke up and you were gone. I wanted to tell you goodbye before I left for Yazoo City." He reached for her hand and intertwined his fingers with hers.

"The reason I left before you woke up was to check on Mrs. Willis. Besides, you're not going to Yazoo City without me." She cocked her head.

"I don't think you need to be going. I don't trust that witch."

"Why do you think I'm going? After seeing how Shelly was all over you? Forget it, Lucien. I'm going."

* * *

LUCIEN TRIED to persuade her not to go, but Catty wasn't having it. She definitely wasn't going to let him be alone with the witch. It wasn't that she didn't trust Lucien. She did. Somehow she felt this draw, this compulsion, to trust him.

It was the witch she didn't trust.

As soon as they made it back to his motorcycle, they took off.

She laid her head on his back as he tore down the highway on his Harley. She tightened her arms around his lean waist. She loved how he felt against her, like he was the missing piece of her body.

When he reached down and held his hand over hers in an affectionate touch, it nearly melted her heart. He could be so intense in bed and so gentle out of it.

She closed her eyes, letting herself envision a life with Lucien. A home, lazy nights making love, and, maybe a few years down the line, a child or two.

Tightening her arms around his waist, she settled into the trip, holding on to her fantasies and her love for him, which was growing with each mile.

CHAPTER 25

*T*he sun dipped low over the horizon by the time they hit the city limits of Yazoo City. He lowered his speed and pulled into a crowded gas station.

She climbed off the bike and he followed.

"I'm getting gas so once we meet with this chick we can haul ass out of here." He glanced around as people passed him by. "I don't like staying longer than I have to."

"Me either." She dug in her jeans pocket and pulled out a couple of bills. "I'm going to grab a water. Do you want something?"

He stared at her for a beat, and a seductive smile spread across his handsome face. "Yeah. There is something I want." He pulled her into his arms. She smiled before he dipped his head and kissed her lips. When he pulled back, his eyes were dark with lust. "I want you."

"After we get what we need from this witch, you can have me," she whispered near his ear. "I promise."

He groaned and let her go.

She couldn't stop smiling as she walked into the convince store.

When she came out, he was waiting by the door.

Her stomach warmed at the sight of him on the Harley. Dark hair and leather jacket made him look like something off a biker magazine.

She opened the bottle of water and took a drink, then handed it to him.

She watched as the condensed water dripped from his hand onto his shirt. A couple of girls passed by, and both gawked at him. She turned her glare on them and growled.

Lucien laughed and pulled her into his chest. "Easy, baby." He nuzzled her ear. "I don't need you shifting in front of everyone."

She kept her gaze on the two girls as they hurried inside the store. "I don't need to shift in order to rip their throats out. I can do that now."

"I have no doubt." He pulled her down for a heated kiss. Between the heat of the day and the heat of the kiss, she was going to burst into flames.

She climbed on behind him and held on tight as he maneuvered out of the gas station and back on the street.

They drove down the residential area of town toward the cemetery. Kids were playing in their front yards while parents talked to neighbors. The scent of freshly mowed grass made Catty long for her home and the days of her childhood when she'd felt safe and loved and cherished.

She swallowed the knot in her throat as she thought of her mom and dad and most of all Zane. He was one person she'd always wanted to make proud.

Now she never would.

Purple streaks stretched across the sky as the day faded. Soon it would be dark. The heat wound about her like a heavy wool blanket, threatening to drown her in the humidity.

Lucien took a right.

When he turned down Main Street, she knew they were not even close to their destination.

He slowed his speed along the street flanked by rows and rows of tall buildings that had been there for a while. The buildings were each painted a different pastel color, and it reminded her of a picture she'd once seen of Rainbow Row, the famous street in Charleston, South Carolina.

He pulled into an empty parking space and killed the engine.

She slid off the bike and waited for him.

"What are we doing here?" She looked around at the quaint shops and stores.

"Getting something to eat." He nodded at a restaurant named Tom's and lowered his voice. "The witch can't perform the spell until midnight. A full moon at midnight is the best time for the spell, or so I've been told. We have hours. Figured we could grab a bite first, since nothing will be open after midnight."

"Good idea."

He placed his hand on the small of her back and guided her inside the restaurant.

It was already full of people in line from the dinner crowd and there were only a few tables available.

"How many, sir?" The young red-haired hostess reached for some menus.

"Two."

"Right this way. You guys got the last table." The hostess laid the menus on the table as they sat in the chairs.

"Is it always this busy?" Catty looked around the room at all the people.

"It is. We just opened and so we get a lot of business right now." The hostess smiled. "Your waitress will be right with you."

"Are you hungry?" Lucien picked up his menu.

"Starving." She hadn't eaten lunch and had missed break-fast. But she didn't dare say anything. She didn't want him to regret letting her go with him.

"Think I'll get the burger." He laid his menu down and let his gaze shift through the crowd.

The aroma of grilled chicken, burgers, and French fries had her tummy rumbling. She pressed her hand to her stomach.

"Sounds good. Order me the same." She pushed back her chair to stand. Lucien rose with her. "I'll be right back." She headed for the bathroom.

She stood at the sink washing her hands and glanced up in the mirror.

Lucien was so different from any other male she'd encoun-tered. He was kind and gentle and he had manners. He also had a deadly edge about him. From the way he dressed to the way he could shoot holes through someone with just one glare.

She dried her hands and sucked in a deep breath. She needed to be focused on what they had to do tonight. She needed to focus on helping Lucien get the information he needed so he could complete his mission.

The sooner he was finished with his business, the sooner they could be together.

She walked out of the restroom and made a beeline for their table. Their drinks had arrived and Lucien was giving the waitress their order.

His gaze met hers, and he stood as she approached. Her heart nearly stopped in her throat as he pulled out her chair for her. Such a gentleman.

She looked around the room and was met with jealous looks from more than a few females. She didn't blame them. She'd be jealous too.

"Thank you." It had been a while since she'd been around

someone like him. Her father and Zane had set the bar high when it came to the male species. She'd given up hope of finding a guy with those qualities. Until Lucien.

"So what's the plan?" She took a sip of her beer. She pressed the cold bottle against the inside of her wrist to help cool her down.

"We get to the cemetery before midnight. I'll give the witch the ingredients she needs and she'll make the spell. Tonight she'll tell me everything I need to know."

"How can you be so sure she will cooperate? Or if she is even telling you the truth?"

"I'll know."

"You that sure of yourself?" She smirked.

"I am." He leaned across the table and took her hand in his. "And once this is over, we can talk about us."

She bit the corner of her lip.

"What's wrong?" His brows furrowed and he leaned closer and lowered his voice. "I know there is something on your mind."

"Just thinking about tonight."

"You're a terrible liar."

"I am not." She pulled away and crossed her arms over her chest.

He laughed. "Yes, you are."

"Remind me never to play poker with you." She snorted.

"Believe me. Honesty is sexy in a woman. Every male wants that. Complete honesty with their female."

Her heart leaped in her chest. Their female? Was Lucien claiming her as his? She didn't want to press the issue right now, not with everything at stake, so she locked it away for a later date.

"I think this is our order." He sat back. The waitress approached and set their plates in front of them.

JODI VAUGHN

"Dig in. You're going to need your strength for tonight." He settled his gaze on her before picking up his burger.

"Think I'm going to get into it with the witch?" She arched her brow.

"Nope. I think you're going to need your strength for what I have planned after. And it involves you naked in my bed."

* * *

AFTER DINNER, he led her to the bar down the street to kill some time. The cigarette smoke and loud music was too much to handle so Catty talked him into driving to the library near the center of town.

It was closed but that wasn't why she wanted to go. She wanted to sit underneath the large oak trees and stare up at the sky. They spent their time talking and laughing and kissing.

It had been a perfect simple moment. Just them together while the world ceased to exist.

He wished he could stay in that time forever.

But the urgency of his mission called to him.

At eleven thirty they'd headed for the cemetery, ready to meet the witch.

He slowed his speed as he approached the road that led into the cemetery. He pulled up to the locked gates and parked. He waited for her to get off first before he followed.

The little town had gone to sleep hours before as the traffic dwindled off and the house lights went dark. The security light at the entrance of the cemetery cast a yellow glow on the ground and shrubbery and the drone of frogs echoed in the darkness.

Lucien grabbed her hand and tugged her toward the fence, away from the lights. Hidden by the shadows, he waited for her to climb on his shoulders so he could climb the fence.

"I got this, Lucien." She laughed as she grabbed the fence.

Before he could speak, she was scaling the wrought-iron fence. She slung her leg over the side, barely avoiding getting caught on the iron spike. She shifted her weight and jumped to the ground.

Landing on her feet, she gave him a wide smile.

"You could have been hurt." With his heart in his throat, he scaled the fence and landed on the other side.

"But I wasn't. I know what I'm doing. I've been climbing poles for years now." She snorted.

"Not funny." He grabbed her hand. "Come on. Stay close. I'm not sure what Ella has in mind."

He led her deeper into the cemetery and stayed off the path and away from the security lights. Habit of being a Guardian. Always staying out of sight while doing the job.

He threaded his fingers between hers and kept scanning the area for any movement.

The closer they got to the witch's grave, the quieter it became.

"Well, well, well. You came back. Hope you're not empty-handed."

He turned and nudged Catty behind him.

Dressed in a black flowing dress, Ella looked more like a witch tonight than the last time he'd seen her.

He pulled a white bag out of his jacket pocket. "Everything is here. Just like you asked."

Her eyes widened for a brief second before she recovered. She took the bag out of his hand.

"You seem surprised." He arched a brow.

"I didn't think anyone would help you. They risk a lot in doing so." She held his gaze in an unapologetic way.

"The shop owner wasn't all that ecstatic."

"No doubt." Ella turned. "Come with me. I need to do this over my grave." She glanced up at the sky. "Perfect. No clouds. The light of the full moon will give energy to the spell."

They followed behind her. He noticed she picked up the hem of her dress and stepped over each grave instead of walking on it. She stumbled once and touched a headstone to steady herself. She hissed and snatched her hand away.

"Why did you do that?" Catty asked.

"Do what?" She continued to walk.

"Did it hurt when you touched that headstone?" Lucien asked.

"I'm not supposed to touch them. When they sealed me in here, they decided I can't touch the stones or they shock me."

"That's weird." Catty looked at him.

"Just one more punishment they tacked on. Not only can I not leave, I can't touch the stones. They did it so I wouldn't ruin them with my 'wickedness.'" She made air quotes and snorted. "Not like I can ruin someone that's already dead."

"Can you not step on the graves either?" Catty asked.

"I don't step on the graves because it's good manners." She turned and glared at Catty. "How would you like it if people jumped up and down on your grave after you've died?"

"That's very thoughtful of you." Something in Catty's tone softened, and Lucien knew she felt bad for the witch.

"Where do you go when you disappear?" Catty ventured.

"I'm still here. You just can't see me."

"So you're invisible."

"Not exactly." She turned and looked at Catty. "I go into the world between the living and the dead. It's like being trapped in a mirror. You can see what everyone is doing but you can't interact."

"How long will the spell take?" He steered the conversation back on track.

"Shouldn't take long since you brought me the right ingredients." She cocked her head and stared at him. "Are you sure you want to know? Once you start down this path, it will put you and all you love in danger." Her gaze flitted to Catty.

"He wants to know. Don't worry about me. I can take care of myself." Catty propped her hands on her hips.

"I bet you can. I bet you are stronger than anyone gives you credit for, little wolf." Ella nodded her approval. "That's good. You'll need that in this life."

Ella turned her attention back to her grave. The large rusted chains that circled the grave had a few chinks missing. Lucien had read up and knew the legend had stated that on the night Yazoo City burned, the witch's grave had been broken, unleashing her from her grave.

She didn't seem like a vindictive woman. She seemed lost.

"Do you need us to do anything?"

"Are you offering?" The witch gave him a sultry smile.

"No. He's not." Catty growled.

Ella looked at Catty and gave her a sympathetic look. "Word of advice. No man is worth losing yourself over. No man."

"Easy." He pulled Catty back into his chest and wrapped his arms around her waist and glared at Ella.

"Fine, fine. You guys are no fun at all." Ella sighed and knelt down on her grave. She poured the contents out of the bag onto the ground.

She sat back on her knees and took a deep breath as she looked up at the sky.

She mixed the ingredients into a pile, crushing the leaves and herbs into a heap. She reached into her pocket and pulled out a lighter. She held the orange flame to the ingredients.

It caught fire and sparked to life. The orange flame

suddenly turned a brilliant blue as wisps of blue smoke circled around the witch.

Lucien and Catty stepped back.

Ella looked up at the sky and fixed her gaze on the moon. She lifted her hands out to her side.

"Deeds and intents, words and thoughts,
Look forever into the valley of the lost.
Hidden will and treachery abound,
Life's taken and secrets buried underground.
Let that which was hidden, now be made known,
And reveal the lives that now are gone.
Oh moon illuminate what the wolf seeks to know
And reveal the enemies and its secrets that grow.
For what was once lost let once be found,
Reveal to me so the evil can be brought down."

The fire jumped toward the sky, twisting and turning and growling tall like a tornado. The fire enveloped Ella, yet she didn't move.

He reached for the Ella to drag her out of the fire, but Catty held him tight.

"Don't," she whispered near his ear. "Look. The fire isn't burning her."

Though she was engulfed in flames, she wasn't burning.

Suddenly the blue fire turned white and began to drift back to the ground. Ella looked straight ahead her eyes blank and entranced.

Suddenly her head dropped forward and the fire died out.

"Stay here," he ordered before he rushed forward.

He knelt down and took Ella by the shoulders and gave her a gentle shake.

"Hey, are you okay?"

"Get me off this grave," she pleaded weakly.

He picked her up and carried her to a nearby tree.

Catty knelt beside her. "What happened?"

"I'm weak. That kind of spell always takes my energy." Ella pushed herself up on her elbows and rested back against the large oak tree behind her. Her face was deathly pale.

"Did you see something?"

"Yes." She lifted her gaze to his.

"I saw a werewolf being held captive underground in New Orleans. I watched as his flesh was cut away from his back." She squeezed her eyes tight and grimaced.

Lucien's gut tightened. She was spot on.

"Oh, my god," Catty's hand went to her mouth as she looked at Lucien.

"What else?" He needed to know.

Ella sucked in a deep breath.

"Ella, I need to know where I can find them and who's doing this." His rough tone cut through the silence of the night.

"So this is true?" Catty's horrified gaze landed on him.

"That's why I was sent here. To find out who is doing this and stop it."

CHAPTER 26

"*E*lla, I need to know where I can find them. I need to know if they are still alive."

"He's gone. Forever lost." All the seriousness had gone out of Ella's tone. He knew then she was telling him the truth.

"Dead?" Fuck. He'd held out hope Mitchell was still alive. "Where?"

"Under the ground of New Orleans. Look near the shipyard." She glanced over at Catty and glared. "You won't have to look too hard. Isn't that right, Catty?"

"What the hell are you insinuating? You think I knew about this?" Catty's voice grew louder.

Lucien's blood ran cold. He looked from Catty back to Ella.

"Tell me! Did you see me in your vision?" Catty asked.

"I saw something called the Triple X and the man who owns it. He knows about it. I saw the wolves being tortured. I saw your face, looking on." Ella sneered and looked away.

"That's bullshit." Catty stood and crossed her arms over her chest. "I don't even know anything about this. The first I heard of Guardians being in trouble was when Lucien found me. I had no idea this was going on." She looked to him to gauge his reaction.

"It's true. Catty doesn't know anything about this." He knew when someone was lying to him and he knew without a doubt she was telling the truth.

"I see what I see." Ella glared and stood. She lost her balance and grabbed for the tree for balance.

"Are you all right?" Lucien placed his hands on her shoulders to support her, but she waved him away.

"Doing that spell drained the energy out of me. I would love some water if you have it." She gave him a weak smile.

He cut his eyes at Catty.

"I'd go, but I'd have to jump over the fence, and I know how much you hate that." Catty shrugged.

"Fine." He held Catty's gaze before heading back to the bike.

He jogged toward the gate. He could grab the extra water bottle out of his saddlebag and be back in less than a minute.

When he reached the wrought-iron gate, he wrapped his hands around the metal and scaled the fence. He landed on his feet on the other side.

He opened the saddlebag and felt around for the water bottle. His fingers brushed against the cool plastic.

He stuck the bottle into the pocket of his leather jacket and headed back to the fence.

A scream rang out through the night, sending chills up his back.

Catty.

He leaped for the fence, cleared it, and landed on the other side. He ran toward the witch's grave with his heart jumping in his throat.

"Catty," he growled.

"Lucien, help me!" The sheer agony in her voice had his heart beating out of his chest.

Frantic, he turned toward a copse of trees near the back of the cemetery and raced toward her.

She was leaning against the tree, her face twisted in agony.

"Catty, what's..." His voiced died off when he reached her. A large sword stuck out of her shoulder, impaling her to the large oak tree. Blood streamed down her chest, and she struggled to take a breath.

"Fuck." He shouldn't have left her.

"Just get me down." Tears streamed down her face.

He cupped her face between his hands. "This is going to hurt, sweetheart."

"I don't care. Do it."

Nausea washed over him as he griped the handle of the sword in his sweaty palm. With his other hand, he pressed his palm in the middle of her chest to hold her still. "Catty..."

"Just do it," she begged.

When he found that fucking witch, he was going to gut her.

Gritting his teeth, he pulled the sword from her body. She screamed as the blade passed through her flesh, and then she crumpled.

He dropped the sword and caught her. Gently he laid her on the ground to better assess her wounds. Grabbing her T-shirt, he ripped the material away. A large wound near her shoulder gushed blood with every beat of her heart.

He took his jacket off and pulled off his T-shirt. He made a bandage out of her ripped shirt and held it to her wound.

"Hold this, sweetheart." He held her hand over the bandage. He made quick work of tying his T-shirt over the bandage to secure the dressing.

"She escaped." Catty looked up at him. "After she stabbed me, she said something about my blood being her key to getting out of here. I don't know where she went, Lucien." Her face pale from the blood loss.

"I don't give a fuck about that bitch. You are my concern right now. Right now I need to get you out of here." He looked up and fixed his gaze on the fence in the distance. There was no way he could scale the fence with her. She didn't have the strength to hold on.

"I'm sorry," she whispered.

"For what?" He brushed the sweaty hair out of her face.

"For letting her go. For messing this up."

"Baby, you didn't mess anything up." His voice cracked as emotion filled his chest. He had to get her out of here.

"I need to go get my bike, okay? Do you think you can ride?"

"I can hold on with one hand." She nodded weakly.

He pressed her hand harder on the dressing, and she flinched. "Keep pressure on this, okay? I'll be right back."

He raced across the cemetery, the adrenaline pumping through his heart and into his limbs. When he reached the fence, he jumped, clearing it with one leap. Landing on his feet, he looked at the lock on the gate.

He grabbed the lock and pulled. The metal twisted and groaned in his hand until it fell free to the ground. He swung open the gate and ran back for his Harley. He started the engine and the bike roared to life. Gunning it, he headed inside.

He stopped a few feet away from Catty. Kneeling beside her, he noticed her breathing had turned to a pant and her fingers clutching the bandage were covered in blood.

"I won't die from this. The sword wasn't silver." She gave him a small smile.

Werewolves didn't die from most wounds.

But she was still in agony.

She didn't deserve that.

"I'm going to pick you up. You are going to have sit in front of me facing backwards. That's the safest way I can hold you on the bike, okay?"

She gave him a painful smile. "Like something in a movie."

"Yeah, something like that." She stifled a moan as he gathered her in his arms and carried her to the bike. He eased on and settled himself with her sitting in his lap facing the back of the bike. She wrapped her legs around his waist.

"This is going to be a long trip back to NOLA." She moaned as he shifted her closer.

"We're not going to New Orleans." He needed to take her somewhere isolated, somewhere they wouldn't draw the attention of humans.

It was a place he'd visited in the summer as a child. It was a place he never thought he would return to.

But for her... he was willing to risk anything.

CHAPTER 27

Catty tried to tighten her hold on Lucien as he tore down the highway, but her strength was slowly leaving her. The pain was unbearable and all she wanted to do was sleep.If she ever found Ella again, she was going to rip her spleen out through her mouth.

After Lucien went back to the bike, Ella had fallen to the ground. She'd bent down to help Ella up. The second she was on her feet, the witch had said a few words and Catty found herself flying backwards into a tree. As she struggled to catch her breath, the witch was suddenly in front of her with a sword.

Ella leaned in close and she actually looked a little sad. "I'm sorry, Catty. It won't kill you— it's not silver. It'll hurt like a bitch. But I need your blood to be able to leave this hell I'm stuck in."

Like lightning, Ella drove the sword through her shoulder and pinned her to the tree like a bug.

White-hot pain tore through her shoulder as she screamed. It had seemed like an eternity before Lucien was there, standing in front of her looking scared to death. She

JODI VAUGHN

didn't think it would have hurt any worse to pull the sword out, but she'd been wrong.

"Stupid bitch."

"What?" Lucien leaned his head closer as he drove down the dark highway.

"I'm going to kill that witch if I ever see her again."

"You won't have to. I'll beat you to it." He growled and lowered his speed. He made a turn onto a dirt road.

"We can't be in New Orleans yet."

"No, we are going somewhere else so you can rest."

She shook her head against his chest as tears fell down her cheeks. "We don't have time. We have to get back to New Orleans to stop whoever is doing this horrible thing."

"We will. We'll stop it. We will just take another day to do it." He cradled her close with one arm as he slowed his speed.

"Where are we going?"

"Someplace special. Someplace I've never taken a woman."

"Home to Mommy?" She tried to laugh, but it hurt too damn much.

"Actually..."

He hit a rut in the dirt road and pain seared through her body. Nausea welled up inside her stomach. Her head began to swim, and she tried to stay conscious. But it was no use.

Blackness descended upon her and sucked her into delicious oblivion, away from the reality, away from the hurt, away from the pain.

* * *

"Catty?" Lucien felt her go limp in his arms and he tightened his hold. Her heart beat against his in a slow and steady beat.

The large house in the distance loomed ahead, in all its

grandeur. Although it wasn't his childhood home, it was pretty damn close.

It was his grandparents' home. After his grandfather retired, he'd built his own mansion. Only this one was hidden on acres and acres of land. His grandfather had prided himself on privacy and made sure to keep his family protected from the prying eyes of humans.

The house was illuminated as he pulled into the paved driveway. He hadn't expected anyone to be here.

His grandparents had died when he was a teenager, and the house had passed to his parents. As far as he knew, they didn't come much. But that was years ago and times could have changed.

Time had certainly changed him.

He killed the engine and set the kickstand. Holding Catty tight against his chest, he got off the bike. She stirred but didn't awaken.

The tall live oaks seem to whisper to each other as the breeze rustled the leaves and settled across the yard. He hurried toward the front door.

Music from the living room drifted outside. He could see through the large windows numerous couples laughing and talking. There weren't any cars in the driveway, which meant the cars had been valeted around to the back near the six-car garage.

He took the steps two at a time, and before he could reach for the doorbell, the large ornate doors swung open.

The woman he'd known all his life stood there dressed to the nines and holding a glass of white wine. Despite the fine lines around her eyes, she was still a gorgeous woman.

Her gaze met his, her mouth dropped open, and she went white at the sight of him.

"Lucien?" Her voice trembled.

He felt like a specter returning to where it had once lived but was no longer wanted.

"Mother."

Her eyes darted to Catty and then back to him. He opened his mouth and uttered the five words he swore he'd never say to her again.

"Mother, I need your help."

* * *

HE SAT on the edge of the bed he'd slept in as a child. The glow of the bedside lamp cast a soft light on Catty's face as she slept.

She hadn't woken since he laid her down.

The door creaked open and his mother hurried in with a plastic first aid box.

"Was she shot?" She frowned and sat on the other side of the bed and opened the first aid box. She dug out some gauze and tape.

"No. She was stabbed."

She jerked her head up. "Was it silver?"

"Thankfully, no. But I'm sure it still hurts like a bitch."

"Lucien, language." His mother pressed her lips together and gave him her best stern look.

It still worked. A twinge of guilt hit his stomach. He shifted under the weight of her stare but continued to look at Catty.

"I need to see the wound. You should leave so I can take her shirt off."

He gave his mother a look of incredulity and shook his head. "I'm not leaving."

"I'm guessing you two are more than friends." His mother's voice was tight.

No way was he going to have a sex talk with his mother. No way.

"I care for her. If she wakes up, she won't know where she is and I don't want her to be afraid. So I'm sorry to disappoint you, Mother, but I'm not leaving."

His mother's silence weighed down the room.

"Are you mated?" She finally asked.

"No." As much as he wanted to be bound to Catty in this life, he wouldn't give himself permission to dream. After he'd put her in danger of that witch, she probably never wanted to see him again.

Who could blame her?

His mother cut her gaze to him. "What's her name?"

"Catty." His stomach twisted in agony. He hated to see her like this, hurt because of him.

"Catty," his mother spoke softly, "I'm going to remove your shirt so I can tend to your wound."

She didn't make a sound. The only visible movement was the rise and fall of her chest as she panted while she slept.

"She can't hear you, Mother."

"You don't know that. Besides, on the off chance she can, I want to reassure her of what I'm doing so she isn't afraid." She reached for the scissors out of the kit and began cutting away at her shirt.

His mother's thoughtfulness tugged something deep within his chest.

"There we go." She set the scissors down and removed what was left of her shirt. She quickly reached for the sheet and covered up Catty's naked breast.

He'd forgotten to warn her about Catty not wearing a bra.

He rubbed the back of his neck.

"It was really hot and…"

"Well I suppose if my breasts were that perky, I'd go around free as a goose too."

His eyes widened.

She chuckled at his embarrassment. "Lucien, I'm kidding."

"I know, I just never heard you talk like that. Growing up you were so…" He shook his head as a grin grew on his lips.

"Hard? Unloving? Tough?" She stopped what she was doing and looked up at him. The faint lines around her eyes and mouth made her look frail. She didn't look like the same woman with a backbone of steel who'd raised him.

"I was going to say 'proper.'"

She frowned and nodded before attending to the wound.

"Being proper isn't wrong, Mother."

"I should have been more loving with you and your brother." She shook her head as she placed the gauze over the wound and taped it down. The bleeding had stopped, and soon it would heal. "Maybe if I had, then our family wouldn't be fractured."

She gently tucked Catty's arms under the sheet and pulled the coverlet up to her chin.

"I should have been more patient with you both."

He laughed. "I don't think it would have helped. We were both hell on wheels. It's amazing we made it through high school. If you only knew half the shit we used to do."

"Language." His mother scowled.

"Sorry." He stood and walked over to the window. Laughter and loud voices drifted up to him from the yard where couples were getting into the vehicles the butler had valeted from around the back.

"Don't you need to go say goodbye to your guests?" He looked over his shoulder at her.

"No." She smiled. "I already told James to tell them I had a migraine and to make my excuses."

"Is James still alive?" Lucien arched his brow at the mention of their butler who had been with them since he was a child. Unlike them, he was human.

"Don't be rude, Lucien." His mother stood and straightened her shoulders.

"Sorry." He ducked his head and looked back at the cars pulling out of the driveway.

"Is Father home?"

"He's away in Charleston on business."

"Some things never change." He turned away from the window. "I would have figured since you two didn't have kids at home, you'd be traveling the world together."

"I don't think we could still be married if we were forced into each other's company every day, Lucien." She shook her head.

He looked at Catty. "I think being with someone every moment would be heaven."

Silence hung between them.

"Come on." She opened the door and waved for him to follow.

"I'm not leaving her."

"Relax, honey. She's not going anywhere. Come downstairs with me. It's been a while since we've talked."

He looked back at Catty and then at his mother.

"Come on, dear. Let her rest." She waited patiently by the door. "Besides, I think there might be some homemade sugar cookies left over from the party. As I remember, they were your favorite when you were a boy."

A small smile tugged at his lips. Nostalgia washed over him and he took a step toward the door.

Looking back at Catty, he nodded. "Okay, but leave the door open in case she needs me."

His mother nodded. "I will, sweetheart. I will."

CHAPTER 28

*L*ucien bit into his fourth cookie and let his gaze scan the kitchen.

"Looks like you redecorated. Again." The cabinets were new and glazed a soft cream color. The hardwood floors were the same, but the granite countertops had been replaced with white and gray quartz. New colorful window treatments decorated every window and gave the room a cozy French vibe.

"Yes. Well. With no children at home anymore, I get bored." She held the crystal glass at the stem and took a sip of her expensive wine. "It's either drink all day or decorate. So I decided to do both."

He laughed. His mother had always had a dry sense of humor, but now he realized how much he had missed her.

"It looks good on you." She nodded.

"What?" He glanced down at himself.

"The smile. I'm guessing she's the reason for your happiness." She looked at him from under her lashes.

He fidgeted. "Would that be so hard to imagine? A female wanting to be with me?"

She sucked in a breath at his words. Setting her wine glass down, she went over to him and put her hands on either side of his face. "Lucien, that's not what I meant. Any female would be lucky to have your love."

Guilt stung his gut. He dropped the cookie on the platter and met her gaze.

"Forget about it. It's not important."

"It is important." Her voice cracked with unshed tears. "You're my son and I love you. I never wanted to make you feel unloved."

"Don't waste your breath, Mother. Lucien is being whiny, aren't you, brother?"

Lucien's blood ran cold and every muscle in his body tensed at the sound of his brother's voice. His heart rate sped up as he eased off the barstool and stood.

He'd known this moment would one day come. He'd expected to be better prepared to have a showdown with one of the three Assassins of Louisiana.

"Lorcan." He turned and faced his brother. He wore black leathers over his black jeans. His biker boots and his black leather jacket both were covered in studs.

"Lucien. I'm surprised to see you here." Lorcan narrowed his eyes and curled his hands into fists. He had the same dark hair and blue eyes as Lucien. But that was where the similarities ended.

"Just dropping by for a visit," he lied.

"You never have before." He cocked his head. "Why start now?" Lorcan took a step forward.

"I asked him to come visit." His mother spoke up.

Lucien blinked but said nothing at the blatant lie.

She stepped between them and placed a palm on both their chests. "Stop it, you two. This is the first time in years you're both home at the same time, and I won't allow any fighting in this house, do you hear me?"

"You shouldn't have come back, Lucien." Lorcan curled his fingers into fists and lasered his gaze on Lucien. The hatred in his eyes matched the tone of his voice.

"Why?" Lucien's heart pounded and his hands ached to punch Lorcan in his pretty face before sinking his teeth into his flesh. The pain he intended for his brother would be slow and long.

"You forget, brother, who I am." Lorcan lifted his chin.

"You are a hired killer. No one has forgotten." Lucien sneered.

"You think what you do is more honorable?" Lorcan walked toward him. "Working for a Pack Master who tells you what to do and where to go? How's being a servant working out for you?"

"I serve and protect the Pack of Arkansas."

"And here you are, back in Louisiana, in a state no longer your home." Lorcan picked up a cookie and popped it in his mouth. He chewed thoughtfully before he spoke. "Tell me, brother, what is it exactly you do for Barrett Middleton? You can't be a Guardian, because I saw to that years ago."

White-hot rage shot through Lucien's body at volcanic speed. He lunged and grabbed Lorcan around the neck. He pinned him against the wall as he felt his body began to shift into wolf.

"Stop it!" His mother shouted.

Lorcan grinned and lifted his feet. He kicked Lucien in the chest. Lucien fell back onto the ground, his head smacking into the hardwood floor.

Lorcan landed on top of him, knocking the breath out of his lungs. He twisted his body and grabbed Lucien in a choke hold.

Years of combat training, natural instinct, and long-awaited revenge kicked in.

Lucien slammed his elbow into Lorcan's nose. The sick

sound of cartilage and bone breaking echoed in the room. His mother screamed. Their butler, James, ran into the kitchen.

"Master Lucien, Master Lorcan. Stop this right now," the butler demanded.

Lucien growled and readied for another blow to his brother's face.

"Stop it!" their mother called out. "You're brothers. You need to remember that."

They both froze. Lorcan's grip loosened around his neck and he rolled off.

Lucien stood.

Lorcan got to his feet and glared at him. A stream of blood dripped from his now broken nose. He wiped at the wetness with the back of his hand but didn't take his eyes off Lucien.

"Not changed a bit, I see." James shook his gray head and looked at the floor in disappointment. He still had his black and white butler attire on from the party.

"I'm sorry, Mother," Lucien admitted.

"You should have better control over your emotions by now, brother." Lorcan taunted.

"You shouldn't aggravate him, Lorcan," James said as he handed him some paper towels for his nose.

Lorcan scowled at the old man.

"Lorcan, what are you doing here, anyway? It's been months since you last visited." His mother wet a dishtowel and dabbed at Lorcan's face in an attempt to wash the blood away.

He ducked his head. "I got back from an assignment and thought I'd spend the night here."

Lucien's heart sped up. If Lorcan stayed, he'd find Catty. No way in hell was he letting his brother get near her. He'd kill him first.

"You mean you killed someone," Lucien shot back.

Lorcan smiled and met his gaze. "I prefer 'assassinated.' Since I am an Assassin."

"Oh, Lorcan." His mother's tone dripped with disappointment.

"It's an honor to be the mother of an Assassin, Mother." Lorcan cut his gaze up at her.

"It's an honor to be the mother of a Guardian," Lucien added.

Lorcan's face clouded with rage. "And tell me, Lucien, how is it you're a Guardian and yet you don't hold the Guardian tattoo?" Lorcan grinned evilly. "Did Barrett make you a Guardian out of pity?"

Lucien growled and lunged, but his mother stepped in between them.

"Enough. I won't have this in my house." She glared at both of them.

"I think I've changed my mind about spending the night." Lorcan stalked toward the back door. He stopped and leaned into Lucien's personal space.

"I don't know what your business is in Louisiana, but you need to make sure you don't come back. You might find yourself in more danger than you can handle. Leave and don't ever come back."

"Is that a threat, brother?" Lucien growled.

"No. It's a fact." Lorcan passed him and went out the back door. He slammed the door behind him, rattling the windows.

Lucien turned his attention to his mother. "You should have told me he was coming tonight."

"I had no idea. Lorcan usually arrives late at night and leaves early, before I get up. The only way I know he's been here is finding his unmade bed." She shook her head. "I don't like that he's an Assassin. That's not him. It's turning him into a monster."

Bitterness seeped into his soul. Once again, she was making excuses for her son. He should have known better than to think she'd take his side for once.

Lucien took a long, hard look at his mother. "Mother, Lorcan was a monster long before he joined the Assassins."

* * *

CATTY COULDN'T TEAR her gaze away from Lucien as he slept. It was becoming a hard habit to break.

The pain in her chest had woken her up early in the morning. She found Lucien sleeping next to her, still fully clothed. His dark lashes rested on his cheek and his lips were slightly parted. She watched the rise and fall of his chest as he slept, mesmerized by his handsome features.

Her heart melted. He'd not left her side since they'd arrived.

She looked around the elaborate room. The crown molding and ceiling height hinted that the house had been built years ago. But the décor suggested it had been updated recently.

The light blue walls and crisp molding complemented the earthy color of the comforter and drapes. The floors were original hardwood and the furniture was large and ornate and expensive. A small sitting area near the window was complete with a chair and tufted ottoman.

"Good morning."

His deep voice melted her heart. She turned her head in his direction. He pushed up on his elbow and edged closer to her, his eyes studying her face for any signs of pain.

"Good morning." She smiled.

"How are you feeling?" His brows creased and his fingers

found the top of the sheet and he tugged it down. He ran his fingertips across the bandage and looked up at her.

"Better. Still hurts but not anywhere as bad as last night." Her heart pounded against his fingertips and her body heated.

"I'm going to take this off and get a better look, okay?"

She nodded, and he went to work removing the tape around the bandage. Slowly he pulled back the gauze. She looked down. The wound was beginning to close up. Soon there would be no sign of an injury.

"You don't need this anymore." He placed the bandage on the bedside table.

"Is this your home?" She cleared her throat and looked around. It was hard to imagine a badass biker growing up in opulence.

"It was my grandparents' home. My father inherited it after they died. I spent the better part of my youth here." The corners of his lips tugged upward as he brushed a strand of blonde hair off her forehead.

"Whose room is this?"

"Mine."

"How did you know it was empty?" Her stomach warmed at the way he was staring at her.

"I didn't. And it wasn't."

She pushed up on her elbows and cringed.

"Wait, let me help." Cradling her in his arms, he helped her up in a sitting position. He grabbed a pillow and placed it under her back to support her.

"I'll go get you something to eat." He turned to get off the bed, but she placed her hand on his arm.

"Thank you," she said softly. God, he was beautiful. Not just in appearance, but he had a beautiful soul. "For taking care of me."

"I didn't do much." He shrugged. "My mom bandaged

your wound."

His mother. Holy shit.

Lucien's mother was here. Her heart sped up as her eyes widened. She wasn't ready to meet his mother.

She cleared her throat. "I'll have to thank her then." Maybe he would say his mother had already left, or maybe they could leave before she woke up.

"You're welcome, dear."

Catty froze at the sound of the feminine voice. Holding her breath, she turned her head.

A beautiful older woman with dark hair and familiar blue eyes stood in the doorway, dressed in a white silk robe. Her hair was pulled up in a messy but chic bun, and she had an air of natural elegance, like she rolled out of bed looking beautiful without trying.

"I hope you're hungry." She mother held up the tray. "I wasn't sure what you liked, so I made a little of everything."

"You made breakfast, Mother?" Lucien arched his brow and took the tray out of her hands.

She narrowed her eyes at her son. "James made it." She looked back at Catty. "James is the butler. But I told him what to prepare."

Lucien grinned and set the tray in front of her. It was full and held blueberries, bacon, eggs, and yogurt and pancakes. She almost sighed with delight when she spotted the silver coffeepot with wisps of steam coming out of the spout.

She laughed. "If I eat all this, I won't be able to fit into any of my clothes." She looked up at his mother. "Thank you. For this, for everything."

His mother pursed her lips and gave a brief nod.

"Lucien, there's more for you in the kitchen. Go on down and fix yourself something to eat."

"I'll wait until after Catty's finished."

"No, go." Catty nodded. "I'll be fine."

"I'll stay with her." His mother smiled.

Lucien stilled.

She didn't want to be left alone with his mother, but she didn't want Lucien waiting for her to finish before getting something to eat. Besides, she could handle herself.

"Yes, Lucien. Go. I'm fine." She shooed him away with her hand. She picked up the tiny silver pitcher of creamer and poured a generous amount into her black coffee. Picking up a spoon, she stirred until the liquid turned a pretty caramel color.

"I'll hurry." He bent and pressed a warm kiss to her forehead.

She blushed at the show of intimacy in front of his mother. Her stomach clutched. His mother must think she was some Jezebel trying to steal her son.

She took a sip of coffee and steeled herself for Mrs. Sauvage.

CHAPTER 29

"*I*'m afraid Lucien has forgotten his manners." The woman stepped closer to the bed and smiled.

Catty looked up from her coffee.

"He's forgotten to properly introduce us." She held out her hand. "My name is Marie Sauvage."

Catty shook the woman's hand. "Nice to meet you, Mrs. Sauvage. I'm Catty Steele."

"No, dear, call me Marie."

"All right." She nodded and reached for her fork. She cut into her pancake and looked up at the woman. "I want to thank you again for letting me stay here last night and for taking care of me."

"Oh, I didn't really do anything. Just bandaged you up." Marie walked over to the chair near the window and pulled it closer to the bed and took a seat. "It was Lucien who took care of you. He refused to leave your side." She cocked her head and studied her. "It's been a while since I've seen my son. And ironically, last night both of them showed up."

Catty swallowed her food and cut her gaze at the woman.

"Lucien saw his brother? How did it go? I can't imagine it went well."

"So you know about Lucien's back." A knowing looked passed through the older woman's eyes.

Catty blushed.

Marie looked away and sighed. "Their reunion didn't go well. Not at all like I imagined."

"Did he hurt Lucien?" Catty stilled.

"Actually, they hurt each other. But Lorcan was the one with a broken nose."

"Good," Catty said.

Marie's eyes widened.

"I'm sorry. I know they are both your sons, but what he did to Lucien is unforgivable."

Marie took a deep breath and slowly blew it out. "Sibling rivalry goes back to the Bible, you know. The ones closest to us are the ones who hurt us more deeply than anyone else."

"Not like that." Her appetite was gone and she leaned back against the pillow. "I'm sorry. It's none of my business."

"I think you made it your business when you got involved with my son," Marie murmured.

Catty jerked her head toward the woman as irritation flared in her chest.

"What do you want with Lucien, Catty?"

"No offense, but I don't think it is any of your business."

"Well, I make it my business when I see he's falling for someone who has the capacity to hurt him. I don't want to see him get hurt. He's been through enough as it is." Marie held her gaze.

Nausea rose up in Catty's stomach at the woman's harsh words. Was she planning on sticking around for Lucien? She wanted to. She very much wanted to.

"I would never hurt Lucien. Ever."

"Good." Marie smiled and stood from the chair. "Then I

hope you and Lucien can stay for a few days. I'd like to get caught up with my son. And I would like to get to know you better."

Catty frowned. She wanted to get to know her?

"You'll have to ask Lucien. I think he has business back in New Orleans." She eyed the woman. "But maybe later. After his business is done."

Marie smiled. The joy reached her eyes. "I would love that." She headed for the door and then turned. "And Catty, it was a pleasure to meet you."

* * *

LUCIEN STOPPED his mother as she came out of Catty's room. He leveled a stare at her.

"What was that about, Mother?" He'd heard part of the conversation. He'd been tempted to interrupt but had been curious to hear Catty's answers to his mother's interrogation.

She patted his arm and smiled. "That was a mother testing the girl my son loves. And I'm glad to say she passed the test. I like her, Lucien. I like her a whole lot."

Lucien opened his mouth and sighed. His mother kept up appearances. It was how she was raised and what she'd instilled in her sons. "Would you like her even if you knew her history? Would you be so accepting then?"

His mother stared at him for a long time before she answered. "Everyone has history, son. It's what you do with the history that determines your future. The greatest of men have walked through the fires of hell." She nodded at the bedroom. "That girl of yours is a survivor. My advice to you is don't let her go."

He watched her walk down the stairs toward the kitchen.

He didn't hide the smile that settled on his lips. A new

respect grew and blossomed in his heart for the woman who gave birth to him.

He walked over to the room and peered inside. Catty popped a piece of pancake into her mouth and sighed. She needed all the nutrition she could get to help her heal.

He quietly stepped back and walked the opposite way down the long hallway, letting her have some peace and quiet while she ate. He stopped at a door and opened it. The small sitting area with a French country desk and overstuffed chairs faced the gardens in the back yard. The room was a favorite of his mother's, and she often came here to have some quiet time to herself when he was younger.

He pulled out his phone and punched in Barrett's number. This was one phone call he dreaded making.

"Hello?" Barrett's voice echoed on the other end of the line.

"It's me."

"I know. Why the fuck are you just now calling me? You were supposed to call last night after you met with the witch. Did she not tell you anything?"

"She came through. She said the Guardians were being held underground near the shipyard of New Orleans. She said the owner of the Triple X is behind this."

"And you're just now telling me, Lucien?" The hard tone in Barrett's voice made his gut twist. He'd let Barrett down.

"Something happened last night. I had to take care of a situation and couldn't call."

"What situation? And don't you think about lying to me." Barrett growled and he could swear the phone vibrated in his hand.

"Catty Steele got stabbed by the witch. I was busy trying to take care of her and get her somewhere safe."

"Shit. Is she okay? Was it silver?"

"It wasn't silver, thank God. She's okay. She's sitting up in bed and eating right now. She's going to be fine."

"I'm not even going to ask why she was with you." Barrett's tone revealed he suspected he knew how close Lucien had gotten to her. "I'm going to let Zane handle that when he sees you."

Fuck.

"Why did the witch stab Catty?"

Lucien cleared his throat. "She needed her blood."

"What the fuck for?"

"So she could escape the cemetery." He grimaced and waited for the wrath of Barrett to come through the phone.

"Please tell me you are shitting me," Barrett thundered.

"I wish I were."

Lucien stayed quiet while Barrett hurled a string of curses. Lucien barely flinched.

"Well, I guess it means I've got to make a phone call to Jack Welbourn. I'm sure he's not going to be pleased his witch has escaped and is running willy-nilly through the fucking state."

"Barrett, I'm sorry. I truly am. But at least we got the information."

He sighed. "Yeah, there is that."

"What do you want me to do now?"

"I want you to stay wherever you are. I'm sending some Guardians down there tonight. I want to get this taken care of ASAP."

"I can meet you guys there. You're not going to know where the club is…"

"I can find it. You've done your job, Lucien. Take a few days off. You've earned it. I'll see you back in Little Rock." Barrett hung up.

"Damnit!" He slammed his hand on the desk. After all this, he was now told to wait.

He turned and strode out of the room. When he reached Catty's room, he stopped and took a deep breath to get his anger under control.

He took a step inside the room. Catty looked up from sipping on her cup of coffee.

"Hey." She smiled and set her cup down.

"Hey yourself." He walked over and sat on the edge of the bed. "How are you feeling? Did you get enough to eat?" His gaze landed on her half-eaten tray of food.

"I'm beyond full." She sighed and then touched her fingertips to her chest. "The wound is healing pretty quick now. It should be completely healed in a few more hours."

He nodded. "That's good."

"What's wrong?" Her gaze narrowed. "Is it your brother?"

"What?" His eyes widened slightly.

"Your mom told me he dropped by last night."

"What else did my mother tell you?"

"Not much." She smirked. "Just that you two got into a fight. And you broke his nose." She threaded her fingers through his. "Good for you."

"She shouldn't have told you about that."

"I'm glad she did." She held his gaze and touched his arm. "Really, Lucien, what is it? I know something is bothering you."

"Barrett wants me to wait here while he sends some Guardians to New Orleans." He looked away. This did not sit well with him at all. He wasn't sure why. Barrett was giving him time off, time where he could go looking for Lorcan and finish what they'd started last night.

But now, with his Guardian brothers headed toward danger, he had an overwhelming urge to go with them, fight alongside them, even if it meant death.

"But they won't know where to look." The urgency in her

tone made his heart tumble in his chest. She was concerned for them as well.

"That's what I tried to tell him, but he wouldn't listen."

"Then we need to leave now." She pulled back the covers and held a pillow over her naked breasts. She swung her legs over the side of the bed. "Where are my clothes?"

"Wait, you're not going anywhere." He placed his hand on her arm to keep her from standing.

"Lucien, I need to go back. After what happened last night, I decided I'm leaving New Orleans." She lifted her chin. "I'm not going to wait any longer until I have enough money to start over. As soon as we get back, I'm packing my stuff and leaving."

His heart raced and his throat thickened. He leaned forward, needing to touch her, to make sure she was real and he wasn't dreaming. Gathering her in his arms, he nuzzled the crook of her neck.

"Good."

She pulled away and looked him in the eyes. "I'm not sure where this thing with us is going. But I'm willing to try if you are. Even if it means facing everyone back in Arkansas."

He grinned like an idiot. It was too good to believe. She was coming home. With him.

Picking her up, he placed her on his lap. Cupping her cheek, he gently placed a kiss on her lips. She sighed and leaned in.

"I take it you two are getting ready to leave," his mother called from the doorway.

Catty squeaked and covered her breasts with her hands. Lucien scowled and wrapped his arms around her to hide her nakedness.

"We are."

"Catty, you're going to need a shirt since I cut yours off

last night. I don't have any T-shirts, but I have something that will work." She headed off in the direction of her room.

"Oh my god. Your mom must think…"

"My mom must think I'm the luckiest guy in the world to have a female like you." He looked down at her and smiled.

She pulled him in for a kiss. "So let's go finish this thing so we can start living."

CHAPTER 30

"*I*s everyone here?" Barrett looked around his office at all his Guardians.

"Yes, except Braxton. He's back in Eureka Springs," Damon said and he leaned against the wall next to Jayden.

"That's fine. You guys are the ones I need to talk to."

"Is this about Lucien being in New Orleans?" Jayden blurted out.

"Lucien is in New Orleans? How the hell do you know that?" Jaxon glared.

"Because Haley and Granny saw him while they were there shopping for wedding stuff." Jayden shrugged and looked back at Barrett. "Is that what this is about?"

Barrett closed his eyes and counted to ten.

Granny.

She was going to be the end of him. She had a bigger mouth than Jaws and was more crafty than any private investigator he'd ever seen. Maybe he should offer her a position.

"I need to tell you something. I've got some news you all need to know about." He looked around the room at Damon,

Jayden, Jaxon, Ryker and Zane. He'd never betrayed one of his men before. They were, after all, his brothers. But now was no time to keep secrets.

"I sent Lucien on a mission to New Orleans. Something has been going on with the Arkansas Guardians and I needed him to go alone and see if he could find something out."

"Like what? Like Guardians going rogue?" Zane cocked his head.

"Like Guardians going missing." He kept the emotion out of his voice. He had a lot to tell them and he didn't need emotions getting in the way.

The room grew silent.

"Maybe they can't contact you, Barrett. I know I've been working a case where either I don't have reception or calling would put me in danger." Damon shrugged.

"There's more."

He stood from his desk. "I got a package in the mail with no return address. When I opened it, it was Heimy's Guardian tattoo. They'd skinned him."

"Are you fucking serious?" Damon pushed off the wall and fisted his hands. The other Guardians let out low growls and curses under their breath. He could feel their anger rolling off them in waves.

"DNA tests confirmed it was Heimy's. And then a few days later I got his middle finger mailed to me."

"Why the hell didn't you tell us sooner?" Jaxon narrowed his eyes.

"Because I knew if I did you all would go off halfcocked and get yourselves killed." He glared at Jaxon. "Just like I knew you were back in your room packing to go find Lucien. That's why I sent Ryker to stall you.

"I wasn't even sure who was behind this or where it was taking place," Barrett continued. "The only thing I had to go on was that Heimy guarded the lower part of the state and he was from Louisiana. So that's where I sent Lucien."

"He needed backup. Why would you send him alone?" Jaxon thundered.

"I couldn't send any of you with him because if they caught you realized you were a Guardian, you'd end up like Heimy."

"Dude, and what do you think they'll do if they catch Lucien?" Zane frowned.

"Lucien is different." He looked at the ceiling and then back at his men. "If they caught Lucien, they wouldn't find the identifying Guardian tattoo on him."

"I don't understand." Damon shoved off the wall. "He's one of us, he's got the tatt like the rest of us."

"No he doesn't." Barrett stated.

Silence filled the room.

"Why not?" Jaxon asked.

"I've already told you too much. It's Lucien's secret to keep. Let's just say the ink won't take on his back."

"So you sent the only one of us who couldn't be traced back as an Arkansas Guardian." Zane nodded. "I can understand that."

"I heard from Lucien. He's found out the location where the Guardians are being held."

"Damn, it's more than Heimy?"

"Mitchell is missing too. Heimy, I believe to be dead." His throat hurt as he spat the words out.

"I can't imagine him to be alive after being skinned and cutting off his finger," Jayden snarled.

"Are any of the other states missing Guardians?" Jayden asked.

"No. I've asked the other surrounding states. Even met with Mississippi's Pack Master. He seemed shocked to hear about such a thing."

"And you trust him?" Damon asked.

"I could tell he wasn't lying."

"So what's the plan?" Zane flexed his fingers as he waited orders.

"The info Lucien gathered indicates the Guardians are underground near the shipyard. We believe the owner of the Triple X strip club is involved. It makes me think the Pack Master of Louisiana knows about it. Maybe turning a blind eye."

"What the fuck?" Jayden spat on the floor. "I knew that motherfucker was nothing but a punk ass, shit face…"

"Easy, brother." Damon placed his hand in the middle of Jayden's chest. "We need to concentrate on what Barrett needs us to do first."

Barrett applauded Damon's restraint. He knew the werewolf wanted to avenge his fellow Guardians as much as the rest, but he also had developed the patience to know how the order of things worked. Damon was becoming a better leader with each passing day.

"Right now I want you all ready to ride. We're headed to New Orleans and I want you all weaponed up. Let me make myself clear. It is my belief we are going into a hostile territory. Keep your weapons on you at all times and keep your tattoo covered. Once we are inside where the Guardians are being held, you can shift. Don't fucking hold back." He walked around to the map on the wall of the United States. "I don't know how this is going to play out. All I know is I believe the Guardians are being targeted because of me and what went down with the Louisiana Assassins."

"That's bullshit, Barrett," Zane growled. "Boudier was the one who broke the law by sending the Assassins into this state without letting you know what was going on."

"Boudier holds a grudge. That's for sure," Barrett agreed.

"We've got this Barrett. Whatever we need to do, we're ready." Damon stepped up. "Isn't that right, boys?"

"Hell, yeah." A chorus of curses and shouts went up in the room.

Barrett nodded. "We all leave in half an hour."

As the last Guardian left out of the room, Barrett was left alone with his thoughts.

Had he brought this on his own men? Was he the one to blame for Heimy's— and possibly Mitchell's— death?

He'd find out soon enough.

CHAPTER 31

*T*hey pulled into New Orleans around nine p.m. It was dark and the streets were getting crowded with tourists.

Lucien pulled into a parking lot and killed the engine. He let Catty get off first before he climbed off.

"How are you feeling?" He brushed her blond hair out of her face.

"Good. I'm completely healed." She rubbed the area on her chest where she'd been stabbed. She spread her arms and looked down at the shirt his mom had given her to wear. It was sleeveless and white and billowed when the wind caressed it. "Doesn't really go with my biker boots, does it?"

He grinned and pulled her close. "You look great in anything."

She burrowed her face in his chest and chuckled. "I can't believe your mom gave me a bra to wear. That's so embarrassing."

He'd overheard his mother tell Catty she needed to wear a bra with her shirt because it was see through. Thankfully his mother had bought some personal items for the women's shelter. She happened to have a bra in Catty's size.

"She really likes you," he murmured against her hair.

She pulled back and looked at him, uncertainty in her eyes. "You think so?"

"I know so. You impressed her. That's hard to do."

She smiled and reached up on her toes to place a kiss on his lips. "So what's the plan?"

"According to the witch, the Guardians are underground. The Triple X is close. So I'm wondering if there isn't a tunnel running from the club to the shipyard. I remember when I first got here I was talking to a waitress who said bad stuff happens at the Triple X. She was a wolf and she was trying to warn me about even going to the club."

He looked at her and frowned. "Do you know of any rooms in the club that have an underground compartment or some way to get underground?"

"No." She shook her head. "Wait. The rooms near the back of the club where they do lap dances. There's a room in the back that's always locked. None of the girls are allowed to go in there. They said it's where the supplies are kept." She looked at him. "Or so they've told us."

"It's worth checking out. In the meantime, go back to your place and get your stuff packed. I don't know how long this is going to take, but once this is over I'll come get you. So pack light." He grinned.

"I will. There's not a lot I want to bring with me." Her eyes lit up.

"Want me to walk you back to your place?"

"Nah. I've got it." She kissed him long and hard. "Lucien, please be careful."

"I always am."

He watched her walk in the direction of her apartment until she disappeared around the corner. He fished his cell phone out of his jacket pocket and pulled up Barrett's number. He sent a quick text regarding the possibility of an underground tunnel leading from the Triple X toward the shipyard. It was his only lead on where they would be holding the Guardians.

He pressed send, turned his phone on silent and tucked it away in his pocket.

He needed to get to the club before his Guardians did to see if Catty's hunch panned out.

He grabbed his .9 mm out of his saddlebag and tucked it in the back of his jeans. The club owner might have humans guarding the tunnel and if so he couldn't shift in front of them. But he sure as hell could shoot.

* * *

CATTY DUMPED the contents of her backpack out on her bed and glanced around the room. She would need something bigger if she wanted to cram as much stuff in as she could.

She knelt by the bed and pulled out a duffle bag. It was bigger and could be attached to the back of her seat on the Harley.

Excitement pounded in her chest as she packed her laptop and then opened the drawers on the small dresser. She couldn't take all her clothes so she decided on the essentials: underwear, bra, three pair of jeans and some shirts. She glanced down at her feet. She would wear her biker boots and could pack her tennis shoes.

She opened her closet and rifled through the numerous jackets. Her fingers landed on the soft black leather of her favorite jacket, and she quickly tugged it off the hanger and tossed it in the bag. She pulled a chair over to the window and stood on it. She pulled the curtain rod down and stepped off the chair. She unscrewed the finial on the end. She smiled at the roll of hundred-dollar bills stuffed inside.

She'd saved as much money as she could for months now. She didn't understand her compulsion at the time, but now it made perfect sense. Long before she accepted the fact she was leaving, she was making her escape.

She laughed as she dug out the roll. She quickly counted the money on the floor. When she was done it was close to three thousand dollars.

Not much. But more than enough to get her through until she found another job. A respectable job.

Hope swelled in her chest and crested. She was on her path to a new life. She was getting her do-over. She was getting it with Lucien.

She grabbed the money, wrapped it in a rubber band and tossed it in her bag.

She glanced at the time.

Mrs. Willis.

She needed to go see Mrs. Willis before she left. She didn't want the old woman to think she'd abandoned her.

Setting her duffle by the door, she grabbed her keys and checked the time. She'd make a quick trip to say goodbye to Mrs. Willis and then come back and wait for Lucien.

Then she was going to start living.

She hurried out the door and made her way downstairs. As she stepped outside she inhaled deep. A sense of hope for the future settle around her. Smiling she took off in the direction of Mrs. Willis's house.

As she got closer, Catty kept to the shadows so she wouldn't draw attention to herself. It was after ten and people were hanging out on the street and front porches.

Mrs. Willis's house came into view. She waited until the men on the porch next door finished their cigarette and headed inside before running over to Mrs. Willis's house.

Her heart banged in her chest as she knocked on the front door.

After a few moments, Mrs. Willis called out. "Who is it?"

"It's Catty, Mrs. Willis. Can I come inside?" She pressed her hand to the door as she spoke. One of the men next door had come back outside and was watching her with interest.

"Catty?" Mrs. Willis fiddled with the locks before throwing the door open. "Dear, is everything okay?"

"Yes ma'am." She stepped inside and shut the door behind her.

"It's late. You shouldn't be over here this late at night." Mrs. Willis chided.

"I know, but this couldn't wait until morning."

"Well, come on into the living room." She led the way, tapping her cane against the hardwood floors.

"I don't have much time. I just wanted …" Catty's voice trailed off when her gaze landed on Shelly sitting on the couch. The girl looked up and shot her a glare.

"Shelly dropped by for a visit as well." Mrs. Willis smiled.

"I see." Catty forced herself to smile at the girl. "Hello, Shelly."

Shelly arched her brow as she silently studied Catty.

"Shelly brought a friend over. He must have gone to the bathroom." Mrs. Willis smiled. "Would you like some coffee, dear?"

"No, I'm fine. Listen, I just wanted to come over and tell you I'm leaving." The hurried words came out in a rush of excitement.

"You are?" Mrs. Willis seemed taken aback. "But what about your job?"

"Yeah, Catty. What about your job?" Big Mike walked out of the kitchen and into the living room. Shelly stood up and wrapped her arms around his waist as she nuzzled him close.

Catty's heart nearly stopped in her chest. Big Mike.

"What are you doing here?" She murmured. He'd heard everything. She wrapped her arms around herself to keep Big Mike from seeing her tremble.

"Catty, this is Shelly's friend, Michael." Mrs. Willis's smiled faded. "Now tell me more about you leaving, Catty."

"Mrs. Willis, I had no idea you knew my friend Catty," Big Mike said. He kept his focus on her, searing her with a glare. "Why, me and Catty go way back."

"Is that so? It's a small world." Mrs. Willis eased into her chair. "Tell me, Catty, where are you moving to?"

"Probably to some little town no one's ever heard of," Shelly murmured.

"I don't..." Her heart thundered in her chest as Big Mike lifted his shirt revealing a large gun on his side. Her mouth went dry and she couldn't find the words to speak.

"I think this calls for a celebration. I'm gonna take Catty out for her last meal... here in New Orleans." He looked down at Shelly. "Shelley go ahead and start the car. We'll be out in a minute."

Shelly shot Catty a glare. It was clear she didn't want her anywhere near Mike.

Stupid girl. He'd brainwashed the college student into thinking she was the only woman in his life. He was probably trying to coax her into stripping at his club.

"Fine." Shelly took the keys and slammed the door behind her.

"I don't know. It's really late. Don't you think you should just go on home?" Mrs. Willis frowned as she worried the top of the cane with her finger.

Big Mike pulled out his gun and aimed it at the old woman's head.

"No."

Big Mike smiled.

"I mean, no, I don't think it's too late for dinner. I've not eaten so it's… fine." She wasn't sure how she got the words out or exactly what she said. She just didn't want Big Mike to hurt her friend.

"Good." Big Mike holstered his gun and held out his hand. "Let's get going then."

"Bye, Mrs. Willis." Catty gave the old woman a hug and a tear ran down her face. She scrubbed it away with the back of her hand and walked over to Big Mike.

She trembled under the evil of his smile. He placed his hand around her shoulder and walked out the door.

"If you try to run, I will shoot you. Then I'll drag you back to the club and show you what happens to girls who go against me," he whispered near her ear.

"I'm not a slave. I can come and go all I want. You don't control me." She hissed.

He grabbed her by the arm and shoved her inside the car. Shelly turned around and shot her glare. "Why is she here? You said you wanted to meet my family, Mike. That didn't include her."

Big Mike followed her in the back seat and slammed the door. He looked at Shelly and forced a smile. "Sweetheart, I need you to drive back to the Triple X."

"But…"

"Shelly, if you don't put your fucking foot on the pedal I'm going to crawl up in the front seat and show you pain you've never felt before." He growled.

Shelly blinked and then pulled out into the street.

"Shelly, I don't know what he's told you, but he's not what he seems. He's a monster." Catty blurted out.

"Ha. I can't believe you, Catty. You are such a whore. I know your type. You aren't satisfied with the man you got, you want more. You and what's his name, Lucien? He's plenty of man for any girl but now you want Big Mike too."

She glared at her through the rear view mirror. "Well you know what? He's mine."

"He doesn't care for you, Shelly. He doesn't care for anyone but himself."

Big Mike brought his hand down across her cheek. Stars splintered before her eyes as she screamed in pain.

Shelly looked over her shoulder, fear creeping across her face. "What are you doing?" Her voice trembled and her wide-eyed stare looked at them.

"Shut up or you're next." He glared.

Shelly turned around and put the car in drive.

"You see, I've had someone following you for weeks now, Catty. I knew all about your friend Mrs. Willis. I didn't have a problem with that old bat. But when I got wind of you hanging out with a large biker guy, I knew something was up. It was a stroke of luck when Shelly came into the Triple X wanting a job."

"Shelly, why would you want to work in a strip club? You're already in college." Catty glared at her in the mirror.

"I'm not doing well in my classes." Shelly looked at her in the rear view mirror. "I'm going to lose my scholarship for next semester. I heard how much money strippers make and hoped to make enough to pay for my tuition."

"You've been taking things from your grandmother, haven't you. Like the silver tray."

Shelly's face heated and she looked away. It was all the confirmation Catty needed.

"He's never going to let you go back to college if you start stripping for him." She met Shelley's gaze. "He won't ever let you leave the club once you start working there."

"Shut the hell up." Big Mike slapped her across her cheek. Stars burst behind her eyes and she buried her face in her arms.

"Anyway, after talking to Shelly, I realized she was Mrs.

Willis's granddaughter. I told her to keep an eye on you for me. She told me all about your friend Lucien and how he made a visit to Mrs. Willis's house."

Catty's heart sank to her toes. Fear pounded in her heart and she tried the door handle. It didn't budge.

He bent near her ear and whispered. "Would you like to know that the Pack Master of Louisiana doesn't like Arkansas werewolves, especially Guardians in his state, nosing around?"

She looked at Shelly. The girl hadn't heard Big Mike say werewolves.

"Anyway, you two have been followed from here to, let's say Mississippi." He grinned. "And it seemed like you are in a whole world of trouble, Catty."

Shelly stopped in a parking lot behind the Triple X. She turned in her seat. "We're here."

"Good. Go on in and grab a seat at the bar. Tell them I said you can have anything you want, on the house." He gave her a charming smile.

She nodded and then cast a worried look at Catty. She hurried out of the car and into the club.

"You're such an asshole." She shot him a glare.

"And you, my dear, are so dead."

CHAPTER 32

Lucien entered the Triple X and shoved his way past the crowd of people to the bar. He scanned the crowd for a stripper but they were all occupied. The female manager, he believed her name to be Celine, passed by him with her cigarette and clipboard.

He grabbed her arm.

"Hey, don't touch me," she spat out.

"Sorry. Look, I want a lap dance. But I don't see any girls available."

"Yeah. It's crowded tonight." She cocked her head. "Aren't you the guy that got the dance from Catty?"

"Yeah, that's me."

Her eyes lit up. She must have remembered how much he paid.

She looked down at her clipboard and then back at him. "Come on, I'll get you a room and send a girl in. Any preferences?"

"Blonde." He placed a wad of money on her clipboard.

"You got it." She grinned. "Come on."

She led the way to the back of the building to the private rooms.

"I want privacy, if you know what I mean." He gave her a look.

"Sure do, buddy." She took him to the next to the last room of the hall and opened the door. She waved him in. "No one will bother you here. Give me about five minutes and I'll send Bambi in. You'll be more than satisfied with her." She grinned and headed back down the hallway.

Lucien poked his head out in the hallway.

Empty.

He quietly made his way to the last door. He studied the padlock. The music in the club was loud enough to cover the sound of him breaking the door. He glanced over his shoulder and made sure no one was in the hallway. Turning back to the locked door he rammed his shoulder into the wood. The door broke free from the lock and swung open.

A quick look inside told him no one was there. He stepped in and closed the door behind him. He had to move quick before Celine discovered him missing and the door open.

His eyes quickly adjusted to the dark and he scanned the room.

It was small and had a floor to ceiling shelf filled with toilet paper, boxes of liquor and cocktail napkins. There was a large picture of angels floating around in the sky on the other side of the wall. He looked down to see if maybe there was an opening in the floor that led down.

Nothing. Not even a grate. He ran his hand through his hair and gritted his teeth.

Frustrated he punched the wall where the picture hung. A hollow sound reverberated in the small room.

He stilled. The wall shouldn't be hollow.

He grabbed the picture frame and pulled.

The picture swung free, opening up a stairwell behind the painting.

"Son of a bitch." He dug out his phone and sent a quick text to Barrett with the exact location. Barrett would be angry at his disobedience, but he would deal with that later.

Right now he had to save Mitchell if he was still alive.

He made his way carefully down the steps. The musty scent of damp walls and mold seemed to seep into his bones.

Pain shot through his head and light flashed behind his eyes. He turned in time to see two large men hit him again with a metal baseball bat. The last thing he heard was menacing laughter.

* * *

"THAT'S FAR ENOUGH." Big Mike led her inside the club to the storage room. He moved a painting, revealing secret opening into the wall He led them down underground to a room lit by portable lights run by generators.

She gagged as the smell of blood and excrement overwhelmed her. She pressed her hand to her mouth and tried to slow her breathing down.

It smelled like horror and death.

A moan on the far side of the room drew her attention as her heart beat like a drum.

"I've got someone I want you to meet, Catty." Big Mike stepped over to the unlit wall. Something moved in the shadows but she couldn't make it out.

He grabbed a floor lamp and angled it to shed light on the wall.

She gasped.

A man beaten and bloody was chained face first to the wall. His clothes had been stripped from his body and his back had been whipped until blood pooled on the floor. He panted as he struggled to catch his breath.

From his scent she knew he was a wolf.

Big Mike grabbed the male's hair and forced him to look at her. "Recognize him, Catty?"

She shook her head. "No."

"Hmmm. So you don't know Mitchell. That's interesting." He released the guys hair and walked to the other side of room. "I just figured since you knew one Guardian, you knew them all."

"What are you talking about? I don't know any Guardians." Did Big Mike know about Zane? Could he have found out Zane was her brother?

"Let's try this again. Here's a familiar face you might recognize." Big Mike grinned and turned the spot light on the wall.

Nausea rolled up into her throat. Horror settled in her gut as she looked at the man on the wall.

All he wore was jeans. His bare feet didn't even touch the floor as the chains that bound his wrists lifted him up into a crucifixion position. His head lolled down and he struggled to speak. He lifted his head and blood ran down his face from a deep cut near his eye. His face was almost unrecognizable from the beating he'd received. But she would know those eyes anywhere.

Lucien.

* * *

"Fuck!" Barrett growled and glared at his cell phone.

"What is it?" Damon looked over at him as the rest of the Guardians got off their bikes and gathered around the parking lot off Bourbon Street.

"Fucking Lucien. That asshole went against my orders

and went to find the missing Guardians on his own." He held up his phone so Damon could read the message.

"So there's a tunnel under the Triple X." Zane cocked his head. "Why does New Orleans have old tunnels?"

"Because years ago they were going to use it as a way of transportation. That's before the highway and trains took over. And plus, there was the flooding issue." Jayden shrugged.

"So what's the plan?" Damon looked at Barrett.

"The plan is to go in and get all my Guardians out." Barrett looked at all his men. "I don't care what the condition the body or bodies are in. I want them back. All of them."

"You got it, boss." Jayden nodded and flexed his fingers.

"The other part of the plan is to survive." He met each of their gazes. "Do whatever it takes to survive."

They nodded at the meaning of his words. He turned and tucked his phone away and hurried toward the club with his men right behind him.

CHAPTER 33

"*D*on't hurt him," Catty cried out. She tried to go to Lucien but two of Big Mike's men came from out of the shadows and restrained her arms. She kicked and screamed but she couldn't get away.

"Aww. Isn't that sweet." Big Mike slapped Lucien's face. "I think she likes you, man. You know, I remember a time when she couldn't wait to crawl on top of me and ride me like a horse. Catty's quite the professional in the sack, wouldn't you say?"

Lucien growled and tried to lunge, but the iron restraints held him back.

"You see, Catty, it's important that Lucien see you for what you really are. Just a stripper who will take her clothes off for anyone. Guys like him don't mate with females who are dripping with sin. And that, my girl, is what you are."

"And you are the devil himself," she spat out.

"Yes, I am." He stepped closer. "If I had known that Jill had started putting ideas in your head, I would have killed that girl sooner."

"You killed Jill? Why? She didn't do anything to you!"

"Jill got too nosy for her own good. She came in to get her last paycheck and she followed one of my men down here. She hid until after he left when she saw old Mitchell strung up like a Christmas goose. Stupid girl. She was trying to free him when I found her down here." He shrugged. "I had to kill her. Didn't have time to bury the body. I'm a busy man and got shit to do. So I told my men to dump her in the shipyard. Let the birds feed on her pretty face."

"You bastard."

"Now, now. That's no way to talk to your old friend." Big Mike looked from her to Lucien. "If you thought you had a chance with Lucien then he was lying to you the whole time. He's a Guardian, you know."

"No he's not." She looked from Big Mike to Lucien. He didn't have the tattoo. Guardians always had the tattoo. Big Mike was lying.

Big Mike barked out a laugh. "Wait a minute. He didn't tell you he was a Guardian, did he?" Laughter rolled out of him. "That's fucking priceless."

"Leave her alone." Lucien growled.

"Lucien? Tell him it's not true." Unease snaked down her spine and she knew when she met his gaze, he'd lied to her.

Why didn't he tell her? If he hadn't been honest about that, what else had he been lying about?

"I guess he was using you until he moved on to his next piece of ass." Big Mike shook his head.

"Why are you doing this?" She glared at him under her lashes.

"Torturing Guardians?" Bike Mike looked at her and cocked his head. "Well, because number one, I hate how they are always in my fucking business. Damn Guardians were always in my club causing problems. They want my girls pampered, no sex and no drugs in the club. They don't understand I have a business to run. So I had a chat with

Edward Boudier, our own Pack Master. Told him I didn't appreciate his Guardians making trouble for me. He actually agreed. Said he was going to get rid of his own Guardians." He glared as he stalked over to a table where numerous knives and operating items were laid out.

"Number two, when your Pack Master of your home state gives you an order and a hefty salary to hunt down Guardians, you don't question him."

"How did you capture them?" She had to keep him talking. As long as he was talking he couldn't hurt Lucien.

"Well, after I got a list of the Arkansas Guardians, I got one of the girls to call Heimy. She said that his mama had been in a car accident and he needed to come on back to New Orleans. He was so worried, he didn't even tell Barrett what had happened. Just rode on down to New Orleans."

"When he captured him, he was in the parking lot of the hospital. Managed to knock him out long enough to get him down here." He smiled. "Heimy was one tough fucker. Even after we skinned his back and cut off his hand, that asshole held on for hours. Refused to die." Big Mike shrugged. "So I finally cut his head off and had them dump him in the swamp."

"Mitchell, that's him." He pointed at the figure on the wall. "Well, we just got lucky with him. He was on the border of Arkansas and Louisiana and one of my hired werewolves followed him into a bar. Injected him with silver, which weakened him, and then carted him back here. For me to play with."

"Oh, my god." She couldn't stop the tremble that ran through her entire body. She was going to die. Lucien was going to die. In a tunnel filled with blood and waste and hatred.

"How is Edward Boudier's Guardians going to feel about him allowing the Arkansas Guardians to be killed?"

"Edward don't give two shits what the Louisiana Guardians think. Why do you think he's firing them right and left? He wants to rule the state himself, without having to answer to anyone."

"You don't have to do this." She pleaded.He picked up a horrific instrument "Know what this is? This is a rib spreader, like they use for open heart surgeries. Have you ever seen the inside of a man's chest before, Catty? Do you know how exciting it is to crack open the rib cage and see his heart beating inside his chest? Or hear him scream when you pull his heart out?"

"You can't kill Lucien. He doesn't have the Guardian tattoo on his back." Her heart jackhammered in her chest. He was going to kill Lucien, but first he was going to torture him. She had to somehow stop him.

"Well Arkansas seems to have to have some lax rules concerning their Guardians. Not all of them have a tattoo. I would have missed him. He wasn't on my list. Good thing I've got some intel of my own in Arkansas." He glared at Lucien. "Enough of all this jabbering. Let's get down to business."

He looked at her over his shoulder. "I'm going to skin your wolf alive and you're going to watch."

* * *

"DON'T YOU FUCKING TOUCH HER." Lucien ground out. The pain from being beaten over the head with a baseball bat was nothing compared to the anger he felt at what Big Mike was going to do with Catty. He wanted to shift but the silver cuffs on his arm prevented him.

If he could just get down...

"I tell you what, Guardian. If you make a sound while I'm peeling the flesh from your bones, I'm going to stop and I'm going to let Catty take your place." His manic eyes flashed with glee. "I've never seen a female without her skin. Think she will look so pretty after I do that?" He laughed.

"You're one sick fuck." His body pulsed with anger.

Big Mike stopped laughing and grabbed Lucien's face. "Don't call me that. I'm not sick. I'm the only one around here in my right mind." He sneered. "I know what you're doing. You're stalling, wolf. Well, it's not going to work. Let's get started, shall we?"

Lucien gritted his teeth as Mike brought the knife down across his chest in a slow, agonizing cut. The white hot pain bore down on him like he was being burned alive.

Catty screamed.

Lucien gritted his teeth and slammed his eyes closed.

No matter what, he wouldn't make a sound.

* * *

THEY'D MADE their way inside the Triple X without any trouble, but when they'd tried to gain entrance to the back rooms, security had stopped them. Barrett, Jayden and Damon and quickly knocked them out while the other Guardians looked for the room."I heard a female scream." Zane looked over at Barrett.

"Son of a bitch." Barrett rounded on Zane and pressed his hand in the middle of his chest. "Zane I want you to stay back and guard the entrance."

"Why me?"

"Because I fucking said so. Are we clear?" Barrett growled. The last thing he needed was Zane seeing his sister tortured.

"Yeah, sure." Zane scowled but stayed at the bottom of the stairwell while the rest of them rushed into the tunnel.

Barrett handed Zane his .45. "Take this." He looked at

Damon, Jayden and Jaxon. "the rest of you shift. I want to get in that room and find Lucien and the rest of the Guardians."

Barrett didn't wait for a confirmation from his men before he began shifting into wolf. The familiar pain and pleasure of his bones lengthening and cartilage shifting shot through his entire body. He could smell Lucien and he could smell blood.

Lifting his head back he growled, shaking the tunnel with his voice. He looked over his shoulder at his men, all in wolf form, except for Zane.

He nodded once and took off down the tunnel.

The tunnel shook around him as his skin was being cut. Lucien trembled as he held in his screams.

He kept his eyes squeezed tight, refusing to look at Catty's face. He couldn't see her like that.

At least Barrett knew where to come look for his body. If Barrett got here in time, there would be a chance to save Catty. His death would be the only casualty of this mission.

That's all he wanted. That's all he asked for.

As he sucked in a breath to take the next cut into his skin, a monstrous howl echoed in the tunnel, stinging his ears and rattling his brain. Using all the energy he had left he lifted his head expecting to see the devil himself ascending into this horrific hell.

What he didn't expect was the enormous wolf that was his Pack Master.

CHAPTER 34

*B*arrett burst in the room with his Guardians right behind him. He spotted Mitchell hanging on the wall barely alive. He searched for and found Lucien being flayed alive.

He rushed for Lucien's captor and slammed him to the ground. He knocked the knife out of his hand and the blade tinged along the concrete floor.

Barrett saw a flash of fear in the male's eyes before he lunged for his throat. Bone and cartilage cracked under his teeth as he bit down. He pulled back, ripping the male's throat out of his neck. Blood spurted as the man's eyes grew wide with panic and fear. He opened his mouth but Barrett slammed his paw over it.

Barrett wanted blood and vengeance for what was done to his Pack and he was damn well going to get it today.

A female scream had him looking over his shoulder.

Catty Steele.

He spat out the man's bloodied throat as he watched Damon and Jayden head for the two men who were restraining Catty.

Her fingers found the silver necklace and she tugged it off. She stabbed one of her captures in the eye. He cried out and dropped to his knees as Damon and Jayden descended on them in wolf form. She looked scared as hell but otherwise was unharmed.

Jaxon was already by Lucien, paws on his chest and licking his face to make sure he was alive.

Barrett shifted back into human and looked at Catty.

She met his gaze, unflinching.

"You're Catty, right?"

"Yes," she whispered.

"You've got about ten seconds before your brother comes running in here. So get it together and assure him you're okay." He looked at Lucien. "I need to take care of Lucien."

Catty beat him first and ran over to Lucien. She brushed his bloodied hair away from his forehead. "Lucien, please open your eyes. Please don't be dead."

Barrett reached for the chains that bound Lucien's hands. "He's not dead. Not yet." He pulled the chains apart and Lucien slumped to one side. "Move back. I've got to get him down."

"Jaxon, shift back," Barrett ordered over his shoulder. He knew he shouldn't be walking around in front of Zane's sister buck ass naked but he had bigger concerns than worrying about offending her.

Jaxon shifted back and wrapped his arms around Lucien's waist to take his weight while Barrett cut his other wrist loose.

Lucien slumped and blood spurted from his chest wounds. Barrett eased him on the ground.

He looked over at Jaxon. "Go cut Mitchell down and check on him. And then go tell Zane we need transportation out of the city. Something that will carry us and our bikes."

Damon and Jayden killed the two guards and shifted back

into human form. Covered in their enemies' blood, they stood over Lucien with worried expressions.

"We need to get out of here as soon as possible."

Barrett looked back at his Guardian and silently cursed. "Lucien, you hold on. You hear me." He looked up at Catty. He knew then she meant something to him. "Tell him, Catty. Tell him he better not fucking die."

She buried her face against Lucien's, and whispered to him.

He looked around and grabbed some dirty sheets laying on the floor. He quickly made a bandage. Before he placed them over Lucien's gaping chest, Barrett stopped. He looked around on the floor and found the knife. Picking it up, he slashed his hand and made a fist.

"What are you doing?" Catty whispered.

"He'll thank me for this later." He squeezed his hand over his wound. Blood dripped from his hand into Lucien's wound. He reached for the makeshift bandage and tied it around Lucien's chest.

"I can't get any transportation out of New Orleans. It's going to be hours before someone gets here." Zane ran in yelling.

Zane stopped and glanced around the bloody carnage. He looked at Barrett and then at Lucien lying on the floor. Catty lifted her head and met his eyes.

"Katy?" Zane's voice cracked. "Oh my god, are you okay?" He knelt beside her and pulled her into his chest. "Did you get hurt? What are you doing here?"

"I'm fine, Zane." She wiped her tears and looked back at Lucien. "Lucien's not."

Zane frowned and looked at the Guardian.

"Will he make it?" Zane looked at Barrett.

"Stop talking about me like I'm not here," Lucien managed to say.

Everyone in the room came over and knelt beside him.

"It's just a fucking scratch," he murmured.

Catty buried her face in the crook of his neck and sobbed.

"It's more than a scratch, dude." Jaxon's tone was low and serious.

"I'll be all right." He gave a weak smile.

"So how the fuck are we going to get out of here?" Jayden asked.

"We're going to walk out of here."

Everyone turned toward the unfamiliar voice on the other end of the room. Barrett jumped up, ready to shift. His Guardians flanked him, making a protective wall between the danger and Lucien.

"Easy. I don't want a fight. Least of all with the Arkansas Pack Master." The figure stepped forward into the light. He was covered in signature head-to-toe black leather and he held his hands up.

"Lorcan." Barrett cocked his head. "What the fuck do you want? Come to gloat over your brother's body?"

"Brother?" Jayden looked from Lucien to Lorcan. "Holy shit, Lorcan is Lucien's brother? Did you guys know this?" He looked around the room and the other Guardians shook their heads.

"Don't everyone sound so pleased," Lorcan said. He frowned when his gaze landed on Lucien. "Why the hell is Lucien here? I told him not to come back to Louisiana. It was too dangerous."

"Well, he didn't listen. Lucien was on a mission to find my Guardians." Barrett nodded over his shoulder. "We've gotten Mitchell, but Heimy is still missing."

Lorcan's eyes darkened. "Not missing. Dead. If I know Boudier, he probably fed his body to the alligators in the swamp."

"You fucker," Zane lunged but Barrett caught the were-wolf before he could make contact with him.

"What are you doing here, Lorcan? Are the Louisiana Assassins now hunting Guardians? Is that what your Pack Master has assigned you to do?" Rage boiled in Barrett's veins until he was consumed with hatred.

"You won't believe me if I told you." Lorcan looked away and then back at Barrett. "Right now you've got to get out of here." Lorcan pulled out his phone and punched in a text. A few seconds later it dinged with a message.

"Fuck." He slammed his hand into the wall of the tunnel. Concrete fell to the floor from the hole he left. "I thought I had an ambulance that could carry your men out of here. But it's stuck in traffic five blocks away."

"Why are you doing this? Why are you helping?" Barrett didn't trust Assassins.

"Because I don't like the ruler of our state. Because tyrants like him will always find a way to make others suffer. I believe in judgement and justice, that's why I became an Assassin. Boudier is neither of those things. He rules his state with fear. I want out."

"I don't believe you."

"Then don't. My focus is to get Lucien out of here." He looked at his brother. "I owe him that much."

"You owe him more than that."

The trill sound of a cell phone echoed in the cavernous space.

"It's not mine." Lorcan held his hands out.

Everyone looked around before looking at Jayden.

Jayden frowned and picked his phone out of his pocket. "Hello?"

Everyone watched as he listened intently to the unknown caller.

He hung up.

"We have our ride. Right outside the door of the club."

Jayden shook his head and snorted.

"Who was that?" Barrett asked.

"Granny."

CHAPTER 35

The Guardians marched right out of the Triple X, carrying Lucien and Mitchell.

Barrett had seen some strange things in his lifetime but the fact they were walking out bare ass naked into the public was one thing he'd never forget. They'd ripped their clothes during shifting so the only one who was covered was Zane and Catty.

Lorcan walked beside them, holding back anyone who dared to get close.

Thankfully Catty had the presence of mind to grab some tablecloths off the tables on their way out and cover Mitchell and Lucien up.

Waiting right in front like she promised was Granny in the driver's seat and Haley in the passenger's seat of an old RV.

They all climbed in and slammed the door before Granny pulled away from the curb.

"Good lord, none of you have any clothes on." She pressed her lips together. "I swear I have never seen so many moons in all my life."

"Granny, I never thought I'd say it but I'm damn glad to see you." Barrett admitted.

Her face brightened as she turned off the street onto the main highway. "Does that mean you can put me on staff?"

"No!" they all answered in unison.

She scowled.

"Hey, sweetheart." Jayden grabbed Haley and kissed her hard.

"Hey yourself." She giggled.

"How did you know where we were?" Jayden quickly tied a towel he'd found in the bathroom around his waist.

"I knew something was up when I saw Lucien. So I got Haley to stay a little longer. While we were here, I met that young lady there." She motioned to Catty. "At the coffee shop. I could smell Lucien's scent on her and knew they were together. I knew Barrett had a tracer on all his Guardian's phones. So I hacked in and found out where Lucien was. And I saw that you were all headed this direction. So I stayed. I kind of figured you boys might need some help getting out of trouble."

"You hacked my system?" Barrett could feel another migraine coming on.

"Not me, I had help."

"Who?"

"I can't tell you." Granny waved her hand in the air. "Anyway we saw you all roll into town and we followed you to the Triple X. When you guys didn't come out, I knew you were in trouble and I knew you needed help. So I commandeered this RV to come get you."

"Commandeered? You mean you stole it." Jayden's mouth dropped open.

Haley shook her head. "She said she would go out with this old man if he let her borrow his RV."

"Well, I lied. I don't like bald men. Plus he had bad breath. I'll have someone drive it back to him later." She shrugged.

"What about our bikes?" Damon asked.

"I've got it covered." Lorcan pulled out his phone. He dialed and number and after a quick conversation hung up. "I've got Brutus and Killan on it. They are going to load them up and drive them back to Arkansas." He glanced at Barrett. "That is, if it's okay if we cross into your state."

Barrett glared. "There better not be one fucking scratch on any of those bikes."

"Understood." Lorcan nodded.

"So now what?" Damon came and stood by Barrett. Some of the Guardians gathered around Lucien on the bed while the rest crowded around Mitchell on the couch.

"Now we get home and we bring this before the other Pack Masters." Barrett looked at Lorcan. "Do you know if any of the other states are involved?"

He shook his head. "I don't think so. If they were, Boudier would have bragged about it."

"What do you want in return for your help, Lorcan?" Everyone wanted something. It was the way of the world.

He walked over to Lucien and lowered his voice as he addressed Barrett. "I want my brother's forgiveness."

"You did something that most find unforgiveable, Lorcan." Barrett stated. "When you scarred his back. He could never take the Guardian tattoo."

"That's exactly why I did it." He looked up, his eyes filled with pain. "When I found out what Boudier was and how cruel he was to his own Guardians, I didn't accept the position. I lied and told my parents I didn't get in. I had no idea Lucien was going to apply. We got in a fight and I wanted to stop him. I accidently pushed him in to the fire. When I pulled him out and saw the state of his back I knew Boudier wouldn't accept anyone less than perfect. So I poured salt in the wound to keep it from healing. He felt that pain for months but I felt it every day of my life since."

"I thought he was at least safe from Boudier if he wasn't a Guardian." He cut his eyes up at Barrett "I didn't count on a Pack Master accepting him into his Pack."

"I don't look on the outside. I prefer looking at a man's soul." Barrett stated.

"The only thing I want in return in my brother's forgiveness. It's one thing that has always eluded me."

"It's the only thing you never asked for," Lucien whispered. Everyone turned and looked at him.

The room grew silent. Lucien opened his swollen eyes and gazed up at his brother.

"I forgive you, brother." Lucien closed his eyes and drifted off to sleep.

* * *

CATTY CHECKED on Lucien in the infirmary one last time before gathering her meager things. Barrett had allowed her to stay at Lucien's bedside with strict orders that her family leave her alone. He knew she wasn't ready to see her parents and she appreciated the time with Lucien.

Lucien had healed quickly over the last few days and she wondered if it had something to do with Barrett's blood.

She glanced at the time and grabbed her bag.

She couldn't put it off any longer. She had other business she had to tend to. Business which included her parents and Zane.

She walked out of the building into the sunshine and squinted. She'd not been outside since they arrived in Little Rock and she wished she had some sunglasses to protect her from the glare of the sun. She had come here with nothing but the clothes on her back. Everything else had been left behind in New Orleans. Even her money.

She walked along the sideway toward the pub where she knew her parents and Zane would be waiting, where they'd be asking her a ton of questions. She'd gotten Barrett to arrange this meeting so she could talk to them all at once. She wanted to get this over with and move on with her life.

When she reached the front door she took a deep breath and opened the door. She stepped inside. Immediately she spotted her mother looking around for her and froze. When her mother met her gaze and she hurried toward her. Her father was right behind.

"Katy." Her mother enveloped her in a tight hug and wouldn't let go. Tears streamed down Catty's face and emotion welled up in her throat.

When she pulled away her father cradled her in his arms. "Hey, sweetheart, I've missed you."

Zane was next. He hugged her so tight she thought she'd suffocate. When he let go Skylar grabbed her and cried along with her.

When the hugs were all done she looked at each of them and took a deep breath. "There's a lot I need to talk to you about. Where I've been and what I've been doing."

"Honey we don't care. As long as you're home."

Catty shook her head. "No. It's something I have to get off my chest. I need to tell you. You all need to know the truth."

Skylar smiled and reached for her hand. She squeezed it and nodded. "Let's sit down. We need to listen to what you have to tell us. Just remember, it doesn't matter. We still love you."

Catty blinked back the tears and followed them to the quiet table in the corner. She waited for all of them to sit before she started.

"I should say this and get it out. Then I can get through

the how and why." Everyone was giving her their attention. She told herself this was like pulling off a Band-Aid. Just hurry up and say it.

"First of all, I changed my name to Catty. I did it for my job, but now, I'm used to it." She loved the way it sounded on Lucien's lips. She'd made the decision after they escaped she would keep her name. She was a different person than when she left Arkansas. She was now Catty.

"Okay, I like Catty. It suits you." Her father nodded and smiled.

"There's more. While I was in New Orleans, I worked as a stripper." The words fell out into a bottomless bucket. She held her breath waiting for the disappointment from all her family members including her best friend, Skylar. When no one said anything she frowned.

"Did you hear what I said?"

"Yes, dear." Her mother nodded. "And Barrett told us if we didn't listen to everything you said and give you a chance to speak, then there was going to be hell to pay." She leaned in and whispered. "Frankly dear, Barrett might be good looking but he's quite scary."

Catty didn't know whether to laugh or cry.

So she did the only thing she could. She told her story.

* * *

LUCIEN HAD BEEN WAITING for Catty to get back from visiting with her parents. He'd been worried since she left and he hadn't stop watching the clock.

The door opened and he lifted his gaze. A smile broke out across his face as Catty hurried over to his side and pressed a kiss to his lips.

"Hey sweetheart." He kissed her back. "I missed you."

"I was only gone half an hour." She giggled and climbed in bed with him.

"How did it go?"

"Pretty good. No one was angry and everyone said they still loved me. I think the only one upset was Zane."

"Really?" He'd have to set her brother straight when he got out of this bed.

"He said he didn't appreciate you touching his little sister." She giggled.

He laughed. "Well he better get used to it. I'm going to touch you a lot from now on." He pulled her close for another kiss.

"I guess you were right. My past doesn't define my future. So now I can focus on what I want to do." She looked up at him and blushed. "I told my dad about that online test. Lucien, I think I want to research what it takes for law school."

"I think that's a great idea."

"You think so? You think I could do it?"

"I know you can."

He entwined his fingers with hers and looked into her eyes. "I know this is soon and I know you've wanted to be on your own and find yourself. But I have to tell you something."

"What?"

"I love you. I loved you since the first day you yelled at me. I know you need time to find what you were meant to do and I'll support you. I'll support whatever you want to do. I just want a chance to date you, to take you out and love you like the lady you are. Catty, will you give me a chance?"

She blinked and then threw herself into his arms. He winced.

"Oh, sorry." She pulled back and looked at his wound. "Did I hurt you?"

"The only way you will hurt me is if you say you don't want to be with me."

"I want to be with you, Lucien. I love you."

His heart thumped wildly out of control with love for the woman in front of him and the future he saw ahead of him. This time, he was getting everything he wanted. And he wasn't going to take it for granted.

* * *

"I JUST GOT off the phone with Jack Welbourn." Barrett glared at Ryker across his desk.

"And?"

"And he's not surprised about Edward Boudier. Says he's been unhinged for years. He said the other Pack Masters try to steer clear of him, and try not to rock the boat."

"Are you shitting me? So what the hell are you going to do? Surely this has to go before the council or an investigation into his Pack?" Ryker stood and paced the room.

"I'm calling for an investigation. But Jack said don't hold my breath. He said the only one who could accuse Edward is Big Mike and apparently since I ripped his throat out, there's no living witness."

"But Catty heard Big Mike confess. She's a witness."

Barrett shook his head. His thoughts were going a mile a minute. "In order for an accusation to be made against a Pack Master his accuser has to do it in person. Catty heard it second hand and it won't ever stick. Plus I wouldn't want to put her in that position. Boudier is evil enough to come after her. I'm not putting her life in danger."

"So now what? You call for an investigation? An investigation you know won't turn up anything?"

"For the time being." He looked at Ryker. "Boudier is

thinking I'm going to follow the rules like always. He's not expecting me to do otherwise."

Ryker's eyes lit up. "I'm listening."

"So while the investigation is going on, I'm going to do a little investigation on my own,"

"You gonna tell me? Or make me wait?"

"I'm going to make you wait." Barrett grinned.

"You're such a hardass, Barrett." Ryker scowled.

"Well here's something to cheer you up. Welbourn is pretty pissed about his witch escaping from Yazoo. He wants her back so she won't cause any more trouble."

"I thought she could only escape for a little while. Should she be back in the cemetery by now?"

"She should but she's not. So we need to send a few Guardians out to find her."

"Don't send me. Heard she's like a black widow. Will fuck her mate to death."

"I'll send Jaxon." Barrett grinned. "He always did like a challenge."

* * *

LUCIEN PULLED up to the worksite of Skylar's House on his Harley. He'd spent half the night making love to Catty so he slept in today.

"Dude, you're late." Jaxon teased as he picked up a stack of two-by-fours.

"Yeah, I am." Lucien pulled of his leather jacket and draped it on the seat of his bike.

He was hot as shit and he wasn't going to keep wearing his jacket to hide what he was. They'd all seen his back when they got him out of the underground tunnel. They knew what he looked like. No point hiding now.

"What's up?" Damon walked over and pounded his fists. "Ready to get to work?"

"Hell, yeah." Lucien headed to the truck. He piled up some lumber and grabbed a hammer.

"Hey man." Jaxon eased up beside him. "Glad to see you here today."

"Me too. The alternative is pretty fucking bad." He laughed.

"No shit." Jaxon agreed. He tugged his shirt off and tossed it on the back of the truck. "I swear it's like a hundred and fifty degrees and not even noon." He picked up his wood and walked back to the site.

Lucien set his lumber down and looked around at his brothers. They were all shirtless and still sweating like pigs.

"Fuck it." He tugged his shirt up and over his head. Picking up his wood he headed toward the work site.

He held his breath and walked over to the rest of the Guardians. His back was to Damon and Jayden and Jaxon was beside him.

When no one said anything he stood up and sighed. "I was burned in a fire. That's why my back looks like this."

"I know dude. We all heard Lorcan cop to it in the RV." Jayden said.

"I was going to rip his throat out for you but he said he felt like shit. So I didn't," Damon stated.

Lucien frowned. "You all heard?" He'd gone in and out of consciousness on the ride back home. The only thing he did remember was Lorcan's apology.

"Well yeah. It's not much space for all these large asses in an RV. Plus I was trying to get to the back so I wouldn't hear Granny talk about some old fart propositioning her for a booty call." Jayden cringed.

"Yeah it's the stuff nightmares are made of." Damon snorted.

"That's not funny, man." Jayden stood and shoved Damon in the chest.

"Don't wanna go there with me, Jayden." Damon growled.

"Don't talk about my Granny." Jayden bowed up.

"You're the dickhead who brought it up." Damon countered.

"For fuck's sake, can you two ladies stop with your cat fighting? We are supposed to be listening to Lucien." Jaxon groused.

"Actually," he held up his hands and shook his head. "I'm good. Continue with whatever you were doing." He looked at Jaxon as Jayden and Damon continued to bitch at each other.

"You could have told me, you know." Jaxon arched his brow.

Lucien ducked his head. "I should have. I'm sorry, man."

Jaxon grinned. "It's okay, dude. But I do have to say something. You really should put your shirt back on." He narrowed his eyes. "Your abs are better than mine. I don't need the competition. Understand?"

Lucien laughed.

Yes, they were a dysfunctional family. But they were a family nonetheless.

AUTHOR BIO

Jodi is an USA TODAY bestselling author and a National Readers Choice Award finalist for best paranormal. She is the author of the Werewolf Guardian Romance series and writes paranormal romance as well as contemporary romance.

Born and raised in Mississippi, her deep Southern roots and love of the paranormal led her to write Southern Paranormal novels. When she is not conversing with characters in her head, she can be found at her home in Northeast Arkansas with her handsome husband, brilliant son, a temperamental swan, and yellow lab that is fond of retrieving turtles when duck season is over.

Find her on Facebook, Jodi Vaughn, author.
Follow her on Twitter and Periscope @JodiVaughn1
Sign up for her newsletter and check out her website
http://jodivaughn.com/

Find her on Instagram at VaughnJodi

COPYRIGHT

Please Note

Werewolf Guardian Romance Series
    Her Werewolf Bodyguard (book 1)
    Her Werewolf Protector (book 2)
    Her Werewolf Defender (book 3)
    Her Werewolf Champion (book 4)
    Her Werewolf Hero (book 5)

The Vampire Housewife Series
    Lipstick and Lies and Deadly Goodbyes (book 1)
    Merlot and Divorce and Deadly Remorse (book 2)
    Bullets and Booze and Dead Suede Shoes (book 3)
    Aces and Eights and Dead Werewolf Dates (book 4)

Veiled Series
    Veiled Secrets
    Veiled Enchantment

ALSO BY

Somewhere Texas
    Saddle Up
    Trouble in Texas
    Bad Medicine
    Somewhere in Paradise